Diana Appleyard is a writer, broadcaster and freelance journalist for a number of national newspapers and magazines. Until two years ago she was the BBC's Education Correspondent in the Midlands, before deciding to give up her full-time job and work from home. She has two children, eleven-year-old Beth and five-year-old Charlotte, and lives with husband Ross in an Oxfordshire farmhouse with four dogs, two cats, three ponies and a great deal of mud. This is her first novel.

HOMING INSTINCT

Diana Appleyard

BLACK SWAN

HOMING INSTINCT
A BLACK SWAN BOOK : 0 552 99821 4

First publication in Great Britain

Black Swan edition published 1999

1 3 5 7 9 10 8 6 4 2

Set in 11/13pt Melior by
County Typesetters, Margate, Kent

Black Swan Books are published by Transworld Publishers Ltd,
61–63 Uxbridge Road, London W5 5SA,
in Australia by Transworld Publishers, c/o Random House
Australia Pty Ltd, 20 Alfred Street, Milsons Point, NSW 2061,
in New Zealand by Transworld Publishers, c/o Random House
New Zealand, 18 Poland Road, Glenfield, Auckland and in
South Africa by Transworld Publishers, c/o Random House (Pty) Ltd,
Endulini, 5a Jubilee Road, Parktown 2193.

Reproduced, printed and bound in Great Britain by
Cox & Wyman Ltd, Reading, Berks.

To Ross, Beth and Charlotte

1

JANUARY

Monday 5 January

Why is it that men can spend so much time inert, like a gas? Ever since Christmas and New Year – which, combined, left the house looking like it had played host to a convention of poltergeists – I have desperately been trying to pull things together and achieve at least a semblance of order in our lives. Mike, on the other hand, has lain like a sea slug on the sofa, exhausted by over-indulgence and the inescapable presence of two children under seven. How thankfully he slunk back to his office this morning, clutching his mobile phone and brushing off the last of Tom's early-morning milk-puke from his pin-striped shoulder. How thankful *I* was this morning to witness the arrival of the Angel Claire. Hugely embarrassed at the state of the house, I spent a feverish hour kicking toys under beds and hurling knickers and underpants into the wash basket before she arrived. I do not want her to think she has been employed by a slut. That can become clear in its own good time.

The Angel Claire is a Sloaney-type with a velvet hairband over very neat long dark hair, who, when she came for interview last month, made me feel that the curse of middle age has definitely struck. She seems so *young* – hardly more than a child herself. I sat there with the children twining round me, and asked stagey questions like: 'What are your views on smacking?' and 'What would you do if one of the children choked?' in a voice remarkably similar to the Queen's. She answered with confident aplomb in a surprisingly well-spoken voice (why does she want to be a nanny? Is she thick?) and turned out to be the only girl I interviewed who seemed to have half a brain and didn't actually look like an axe murderer. Halfway through our 'little chat' Tom began straining towards her, and she picked him up quite unselfconsciously. She's clearly used to children. He sat on her knee like a big fat contented teddy bear, purring loudly. The turncoat. I hope he's not going to forget me so easily. Rebecca was more wary, and circled Claire like a suspicious fox. She is currently going around with the martyred expression of a six-year-old due back at school at the end of the week whose mother has still not found her ballet clothes. They're definitely here somewhere. Perhaps the fridge? I *must* get organized before next week. Lists are going to be the answer.

Thursday 8 January
Had a quick glance through my wardrobe this morning. What exactly am I going to wear for my grand return? All I've been dressed in for the past six months are over-sized leggings and vast T-shirts, like one of the Diddymen. My work suits look suspiciously small. Was I ever really such a tiny size? I sneaked up on one of my skirts while it wasn't looking and heaved it up over my thighs – but the waistband exacted revenge by garrotting me in the middle. It gave me not so much an hourglass figure – more a figure of eight. I shall have to go into work bent double, and refuse all food.

Meanwhile Claire, my lovely perfect nanny, was downstairs playing with Rebecca and Tom. They're actually painting – well, Rebecca is painting and Tom is sticking his fat little hands into a tray of paint to make hand-prints. I'm all for the *idea* of painting, but the reality of the event often falls far short of the expectation. Some of our painting sessions have been known to end with both children sitting whimpering in their bedrooms while I thrash about with a mop and bucket swearing loudly, wondering how the hell we managed to get paint *inside* the breadbin. The same often happens with baking. I'm quite happy to make cakes with both of them, as long as Tom is in his high chair where I can see him and Rebecca stands by the door. But Claire seems to go in for the full-blown painting-with-easels job and, most miraculously, the kitchen was tidy afterwards. If Mike could be persuaded to have sex with her (and I'm sure he wouldn't be too reluctant on *that* front), I could move out completely and no-one would ever notice.

Friday 9 January
Last night Mike had an extended, and I suspect heart-felt, if-not-somewhere-else-felt, moan about how little sex we have been having since Tom was born. But how can I feel sexy when my tits still look like vast blue-veined Gorgonzola cheeses and my stomach ripples and flutters in the wind? At one of the handful of ante-natal classes I attended prior to Tom's birth (been there, done that – kuh! What can you tell *me* about having babies? With the first baby you're so desperate to gather every teeny-weeny bit of information you can, you hang onto the ante-natal teacher's every word as if she's the Dalai Lama, whereas with the second you *know* how bloody awful it all is so

9

the less you have to think about it, the better) they handed out a questionnaire for us to fill in about the things we'd most like to know about after the birth. Over half of these mad women put sex! Still, most of them were first-time mothers. We old-timers laughed hollowly and rejoiced in the private thought that if their husbands came near them as much as three months after the birth they'd attack them with a pitch-fork.

I remember in the immediate days after Rebecca's birth, when I was lying in bed like a stunned mullet breastfeeding her, which I did more or less continually until I went back to work, the midwife came round to see how we were all getting on. We chatted about cracked nipples and bathing routines, while Mike sat on the end of the bed with an increasingly red face. Eventually, he came out with it. 'How long,' he said, oh-so-casually, 'is it normally before we can have – erm – *make love*?'

The midwife looked at him with a pitying air, while I looked at him in horror, my thighs involuntarily squeezing themselves together. 'Six weeks would be the very earliest,' she said.

'*Six weeks!*' he exploded.

Anyway, there we were, lying together on the bed like two exhausted kippers, and he began stroking my back (always a preamble to much more). I instinctively stiffened and he said, 'But it's been over two weeks.'

'I know, I know,' I said, turning towards him and pushing my hand into his thick, blond hair. It isn't that I don't fancy him – how could I not, with his tall, lean frame and eyes of Sinatra blue – it's much more the case that I can't conceivably see how he could fancy me at the moment, post-Tom. How true it is that women need to feel good to want sex, whilst men want to have sex to feel good. 'I'm just so knackered, and I'm really worried about going back to work. How will Rebecca cope?'

'The children are the last thing on my mind,' he said, turning over in a huff. 'You seem to forget that *I'm* here too.' What he really means is that his little needs are just as important as those of two small demanding children. He then made a point of reading his book in a very loud and sexually frustrated way, with lots of crackly page-turnings and humphing about. (Don't I realize that sex is vital to release the only hormone in men's brains which allows them to sleep deeply and peacefully?) The problem is that I do feel *so* unattractive, and when we do (very occasionally) make love, I have to stop myself peering down obsessively at my vast spreading thighs and surreptitiously pinching the spongy cushion of flesh between waist and hip, instead of concentrating on the matter in hand. So to speak.

Monday 12 January
What a novelty. I took Rebecca back to school this morning. In the past, I've tried to get the day off to take her on her first day back, but something has always cropped up to make it imperative I got in for an early meeting. More often than not it was totally pointless, and I sat there fuming while the editor wanked on about extending the programme by two minutes, and I looked out of the window and keened towards home. But today I swept up the drive to Rebecca's school like a real mother, and fussed about getting her book bag and sports kit out. I tried to hold her hand going into school but she hissed, 'Get *off*, Mummy,' and wouldn't let me kiss her goodbye, the ungrateful toad.

Peter Cressingham's mum Caroline (full make-up, new Shogun, flat gold-buckled shoes, husband with

11

millions) caught me just as I was leaving. 'Hellooo – I didn't know you were still at home. I'm having a coffee morning next week – perhaps you'd be able to come along?' Suddenly very thankful that I'm back at work next week

'Sorry,' I said, 'I have to go back to work,' making my mock-sad face.

'Oh, you poor thing,' she said. 'But it must be lovely to have such a *glamorous* job, unlike all of us *housewives*.' All this is said with the confidence of a woman who has the entire day free to play tennis and leaf through clothes shops.

I hate Perfect Professional Mothers whose children never forget their games kit with a huge, loathing vengeance. What she's really thinking is, poor thing, her husband can't afford to keep her. The only equality women like Caroline believe in is being able to dip into their husband's big fat bank account without actually having to contribute anything at all apart from the odd perfect *tarte au citron*. Instead of doing a useful job, they transfer all their competitive instincts onto their hapless children, so apparently jolly get-togethers become a chance for ruthless one-upmanship not only about the perfection of their home but also about the academic and musical brilliance of their vile offspring. It even begins at the baby stage, with cut-throat competitiveness over crawling, toilet-training and first words. 'Josh managed a perfectly grammatical sentence last week,' they crow, beaming fondly at their Osh-Koshed one-year-old. 'Really?' says fellow Professional Mother, looking dispiritedly at her one-year-old, who hasn't emitted anything more articulate than wind.

'I'd so love to join the rat-race like you,' Caroline said with a little tinkly laugh. 'Well, maybe you shouldn't be so thick, get off your arse and do something a bit more stimulating than *shopping.*' No, of course I didn't really say that, although my friend Jill – a part-time teacher, whose two children go to the state school down the road and has an enlightened, if waspish, outlook on life – would have done. I'm not that brave and, to be honest, women like her frighten the life out of me. What is the point of coffee mornings? What actually happens? How do they have the time to spend a whole morning sitting about having coffee? I guess they all get to have a good nosy at each other's houses and say things like, 'Oh, a two-oven Aga. We swear by the four-oven ourselves.' There is a whole ritual of womanhood that has completely passed me by.

Wednesday 14 January

Claire and I are indulging in a 'baby-share' this week, after I've taken Rebecca to school. I am allowed to get Tom up and dressed, and then Claire sweeps in and bears him off for some stimulating play, as opposed to lying on the sofa watching cartoons with me. It should be a harmonious arrangement, allowing me to get myself together, go shopping for new clothes, ring chums at work and gear myself up psychologically towards The Return.

In reality it's more like a subtle form of warfare. I sneak in and grab Tom while she's ironing. (Yes, she irons like an angel as well, and even appears to enjoy it. Weird.) Then she realizes he's missing, trots round the house like our Labrador, Turtle, looking for a bone until she finds him, then sweeps him up saying, 'Let's let Mummy have some time on her own and we'll go out for a lovely walk, won't we, darling?'

But I don't want time on my own. I want Tom. I'm going to be without him for great big gobs of time very soon, and I want as much physical contact with him as possible. Cooking his lunch, we silently wrestle over the cooker with pans of baked beans and mashed potatoes. I know I should just leave her to it, but I am finding it so very hard to let go. After only a few days Tom's babygros are all fluffy and white and folded in his drawers. I'm losing *ownership* of him. To be perfectly honest, half of me *is* relieved to be giving up the bone-numbing boredom of looking after a six-month-old all day every day, while the other half is silently screaming, 'Get off! That's *my* baby,' as Claire fusses over him and calls him her 'little man' (when she does this I have to leave the room for fear of killing her).

Yesterday she buttonholed me in the kitchen, as I was peering hopefully into the fridge looking for something non-fattening but tasty to eat. Impossible. 'I've drawn up a timetable so you'll be able to see exactly what we're up to while you're at work,' she said brightly.

'Umm, lovely,' I said, my mouth full of chocolate mousse (immensely fattening but delicious). I peered down the chart, which she'd carefully divided into days using different coloured felt-tip pens. The list for Monday read:

8.30 a.m. – 9 a.m. Rebecca school (gym kit, recorder, book bag).

9.15 a.m. – 10 a.m. Tom jigsaws/drawing/storytime.

10 a.m. – 11 a.m. Walk with dogs.

11 a.m. – 12 noon. Tom sleep, tidy up and ironing.

12.30 p.m. Lunch.

1 p.m. – 2 p.m. Tumble Tots, village hall.

2 p.m. – 3 p.m. Tom sleep, prepare tea.

3.30 p.m. Rebecca home from school.

4 p.m. – 5 p.m. Rebecca homework, Tom structured play.

5.15 p.m. Tea.
5.30 p.m. – 6.30 p.m. Supervised play, bath.

Tom and I looked at each other agog. If I achieved even one of these things on time I would regard it as a minor miracle. Our family was about to be organized with a capital 'O'. I only just restrained myself from asking if she might draw up a similar list for the dogs.

At least Rebecca hasn't welcomed her with totally open arms, and is maintaining a kind of *froideur* which I think Claire is finding extremely difficult. I am not gaining any private satisfaction from this *at all*, because to do so would make me a very small-minded person indeed. Of course I want my children to love her as much as possible. Only not more than me, please.

Sunday 18 January
Bill and Sue came round for dinner last night and couldn't understand why I was yawning like a giraffe by eleven o'clock. It's all right for them – they don't have any children yet and go to places like Mauritius for their holidays. How does *anyone* have enough money to spend so much on just a holiday? We're being forced to live like the Amish at the moment following my financial blow-out of Biblical proportions at Christmas, but at the weekend I spotted that a 'For Sale' notice has gone up at the farmhouse by the green in the next village to ours, which I've been secretly coveting for ages. It would be *perfect* for us. I may well be indulging in a dangerous fantasy but it's got a small orchard and a stream. A stream! My children can grow up in an Enid Blyton fantasy world. I slipped into the estate agent's to pick up the details this week and the snotty cow behind the desk took one

look at my leggings and milk-stained T-shirt and tried to pretend she'd run out, until I spotted some on the desk behind her. They're currently lodged like an unexploded bomb in my handbag and I keep taking surreptitious peeks.

They were all on for a good session – I realized this when Mike started rooting about with the feverish determination of the very pissed for his old Fleetwood Mac and Deep Purple LPs – but I had to duck out, for fear of falling asleep with my head in the Cambozola. It was actually a relief when Tom started crying, and I could slip upstairs to see to him. I breastfed him – what am I going to do with all this milk next week? – and then the two of us sat in peaceful silence in the dim light of his room. He fell asleep on me, curving his plump little body into my stomach, and for some bizarre reason I felt like weeping. It was probably the gin.

Monday 19 January
A week to go. Claire is now very much In Charge, and I am forcing myself to take a back seat. But when Tom cries I immediately surge forward to pick him up, and Claire and I knock heads. I had a teeny little complain about her to Mike last night over dinner, and he said I was being an ungrateful witch. 'What's the matter with her? She seems fine to me, and the house has never looked tidier.'

I have to say it took superhuman effort not to quietly reach over and pull him tie-first into his pasta. 'Nothing at all,' I said icily. 'That's the problem. What am I *for*, if someone can just come in and, after just two weeks, take over my house and my children and do it much *better* than me?'

As an attempt to find sympathy this scored *nul*

16

points. 'She does seem to be pretty well organized,' said Mike, nodding in agreement.

Not only has Claire turned my baby into Designer Child, she has also sorted out the airing cupboard. Half of me is delighted that all my pillows, sheets and towels are now in neat little piles, whilst the other half is infuriated at the inherent criticism of my own sluttish habits. Memo: I must be more positive and learn to embrace the art of delegation.

Kate rang this morning from work. 'God, I can't wait for you to come back. Nick is being a complete pain and I have no-one to have a really good whinge to.' Just hearing her voice cheered me up and made me feel part of the human race. What is it about really good friends that makes you feel life is bearable and you don't have to commit immediate hara-kiri? I have friends with whom I put up the false front that everything is marvellous, darling – like Harriet, married to Martin who is something-in-the-City and lives in a huge house in the next village, whom I met at National Childbirth Trust having Rebecca. She spends all her time subtly undermining me and we have a constant and totally childish battle, never spoken but always implied, about who has the best life. (Men never do this, do they?) Fortunately I also have the sort of friends I can ring up, like Jill and Kate, and say, 'I hate Mike, my house is a slum and my children are taking no notice of me whatsoever, let's have a bottle of chardonnay.'

When Kate actually rang, I was sitting alone in my bedroom staring in awe at a breast pump. (It was 10 a.m., structured play with wooden jigsaws, I think). The idea is that for the first few weeks I will express milk and leave it in the fridge for Claire to give Tom his occasional bottles. 'You'll have to be quick,' I said to Kate. 'I'm just about to milk myself.' There was a stunned silence at the other end of the phone.

'You are so disgusting. It's high time you got back to real life. Oh, and by the way, Peter's nicked your chair and there are papers all over your desk. We've got a new computer system everyone's making a right bollocks of, the budget's been slashed to hell and the cameramen are threatening to strike. Maybe I'll come and join you in nappyland.' Like hell she would. In her tailored suits and suede platforms, she'd be shrieking in horror at the first sign of puréed cauliflower cheese. She is a woman welded to her mobile phone and Chanel briefcase.

After she'd rung off, I had a good long think about what returning to work will actually be like. At the moment, it seems like an alien planet. Has all that work-type activity been going on while I've been at home? Somehow I imagined them all in suspended animation, frozen at their desks, the daily news programme put on ice while I've been pottering about with nappies and sterilizers. Maybe no-one's noticed I've been away. My job was filled on attachment by an over-ambitious bimbo with a blond bob and perfect teeth. Perhaps they like her more than me. Perhaps I can't actually *do* my job any more. I broke out in a cold sweat. What if no-one speaks to me on my first day?

Since having Tom my brain has felt like blancmange: facts go in, but they kind of sink into the mushy pink gunge and I have to ferret around for ages to find them again. I can't even remember my *children's* names, so how will I ever be sharp enough to cope with the cut-and-thrust of office politics? And, more importantly, will I care? And why does it feel so much harder to go back having had Tom? With Rebecca I was only twenty-seven, and my career seemed like the most important thing in the world. We desperately needed

18

the money to pay for our first house and there wasn't ever a possibility that I *wouldn't* go back. When she was born I felt like we'd been given the world and it was Christmas every day – but I still yearned to return to work almost from her birth. Work was what I did. It was what I am. I'm sure it still is.

Wednesday 21 January
Last night, in despair, I roped Mike in to help me with the breast pump. He sat on the edge of the bed, with his nice clean work suit on after a hard day being an important television person, manoeuvring the funnel onto my terrifying chest while I squeezed. He really is a saint. The milk, instead of dripping into the bottle, shot out at an angle and hit him in the eye. I began laughing helplessly, and he dropped the bottle. 'Jesus,' he said. 'Your tits are positively certifiable. We could be talking decommissioning here,' he said.

'Shut up,' I said, 'and keep pumping.'

To achieve some kind of privacy we'd closed the bedroom door, which is always a red rag to Rebecca, who immediately began thumping on it saying, 'What are you *doing* in there?' Eventually after persevering for what felt like hours, we had about two inches of milk.

'That'll last him about two seconds,' said Mike. 'We'll have to get him to take powdered milk.'

'OK,' I said. 'You try.' And, bless him, he spent all night sitting in front of the TV with Tom, trying to push the bottle into his mouth. Every time he slipped it in one side, he pushed it out the other. I left them to it, and then woke suddenly at midnight, realizing there was an empty space in the bed beside me. Tip-toeing downstairs, I found Mike fast asleep on the settee. Tom was lying prone on his chest, both of them snoring

19

away. The milk bottle, still half-full, was drip-drip-dripping onto the carpet.

Friday 23 January
Claire took Rebecca to school for me this morning, and it was agonizing to see her little white face pressed up against the window as they drove away in Claire's very clean car. I think she's actually getting really anxious about my going back to work, although she refuses to talk about it. Babies are so easy, really – as long as they're fed and warm they're happy with anyone, like puppies. Rebecca is a much more tricky kettle of fish. As well as being a bit cold towards Claire, she's already begun to withdraw from me, refusing to let me read her *The Lion, the Witch and the Wardrobe* last night, insisting that Daddy did it. She knows *exactly* how to hurt me. That's daughters for you. Mike, miraculously, was home on time, so he went in and made her hoot with laughter doing lots of silly voices. This morning she made me go over and over exactly where Claire must meet her when she picks her up from school. Normally so sure of herself, she's asked a million times if Claire knows it *must* be four o'clock.

Once Claire had gone with the children this morning, the house felt unbearably empty. I was meant to be laying out my clothes and packing my briefcase, but instead I mooched about, picking up Tom's clothes, straightening his duvet and rearranging the pile of teddies on Rebecca's bed. The house felt like a haven – warm, domestic, familiar – and everything out there seems hostile and frightening. I've got so used to the rhythm of my days in the house over Christmas – the leisurely breakfasts, with Mike kissing a smeary Tom goodbye in his high chair, me still in my dressing gown, Rebecca in her pyjamas and the dogs stretched out under our feet. Then the gradual tidying-up, pausing to sit down and play with Tom, everything taking an age, but not really caring. Then lunch, and in the afternoon a dog-walk, Tom strapped into his pushchair, craning forward to catch hold of branches and being totally thrilled at being given a stick. I suppose it was rather pointless, but there was a freedom to those days that I loved – not really having any responsibility other than to the children, just having to meet the deadlines of meals and bedtimes. It was Cloud-cuckooland to think it could go on for ever – and to be honest with myself, the reason I've enjoyed this time off with the children so much is because I know it will end. It's like holidays – you enjoy them like mad, but you wouldn't want to be on them all the time. It'll be great to be somewhere where it actually matters where I am every minute of the day and I get to talk to people over the age of six.

Monday 26 January
Hardly slept at all last night. I kept going through all the things I had to tell Claire to do, and whether I'd packed everything Rebecca needed for school today. Book bag, reading record book, recorder, ballet clothes, pumps, tracksuit for games and clean pair of knickers, because you still never know. I had that awful feeling of dread I used to get when I was going back to school. In the end I got up at six and crept downstairs. Tom was still snoring in his cot, clutching his favourite rabbit and looking too adorable for words, but I resisted the impulse to pick him up and kiss him, because I'm not that brave and I was enjoying the peace. Rebecca was firmly asleep in her fierce little way, legs out of the duvet, pieces of paper strewing her bed as she'd been

21

practising joined-up writing, her hair matted into a thick nest.

The dogs thumped their tails at the unexpected early rising, and joyfully rushed out into the frosty garden. I made a cup of coffee, and stood looking out over the lawn. So much to do – those roses need tying up, and that hedge is becoming really overgrown. No time now. The day was no longer mine to organize. At half-seven, Tom's seagull cries began, and I started to get him up and dressed. Then, promptly at quarter to eight, Claire arrived. 'You see to yourself,' she said, taking Tom firmly from my arms, her immaculate hair swinging, and Tom immediately reached up to put a strand in his mouth, as he always does with me. Mike had already gone – his morning meetings seem to get earlier and earlier – kissing me goodbye and wishing me luck. I wish I could talk to him about how I feel, but work is such an integral part of his life, I don't think he could get his head around the concept that it might be considered an option. Which of course it isn't. I just have to get on with it.

'Thanks,' I said, faintly, to Claire.

Rebecca came and sat in the middle of my bed as I pulled clothes out of my wardrobe. 'You look fat in that,' she said helpfully, as I levered on the largest of my suit skirts. My breasts – although I'd already had a quick session with the breast pump – felt uncomfortably large and full, like water-filled zeppelins. God forbid anyone comes near me with a pin. I put on a dark blue silk shirt, and then tried to tame my hair from wild bush into Meg Ryan. My briefcase was already packed: purse, breast pads, Always pads, make-up bag and biros. I've almost forgotten what I need to take to work, and there seemed to be far more Mummy-disaster-avoidance-kit than serious work implements.

At the breakfast table, I hovered nervously away from the children, suddenly aware of the mess a jammy hand could make. My face felt odd – why? – and then I remembered it was because I was wearing make-up. While I've been on maternity leave make-up has been for special occasions – going out for meals, having people for dinner, or simply out of sheer desperation – but now it would have to be a regular morning ritual. How would I find the time every day?

Claire was busying about, fetching Tom's Weetabix and insisting on milk rather than Ribena.

'Rebecca must clean her teeth before school,' I said.

'Claire's already helped me,' said Rebecca.

'Oh. Rebecca needs her recorder today.'

'We've packed it,' said Rebecca.

I hung about, reluctant to leave but knowing I couldn't be late. 'Would you like a coffee?' said Claire.

A coffee? At breakfast time? Before the children have finished their cereal? We're talking serious luxury here. 'Lovely,' I said, and then drank it standing up, hopping out of the way of Claire clearing up my plates, already mistress of my home.

I edged towards the door. Tom immediately let out a huge yell, stretching out his little arms like a bush-baby. Rebecca, who was trying to be so cool and collected, realized that I really was going, and hurtled towards me, sobbing bitterly into my skirt. Of course I should have just *left* and let Claire deal with it, but I couldn't resist going back over to Tom, lifting him out of his high chair and holding him close, closer than I felt I've ever done before. After a few moments I mouthed at Claire, 'You take him,' and tried to hand him over to her. But he clung to me like a barnacle, his shrieks reaching a crescendo. Rebecca was also stapled to my legs, and I gently tried to prise her away from me. 'I have to go, darling, you know I have to,' I said.

'Don't,' she wailed. 'Don't!'

'Oh darling,' I said. 'I'll see you tonight.' I managed to push her away as gently as I could, and Claire, who now had a screaming Tom in one arm, tried to hold her too. I slid towards the door, wrenched it open, and almost fell through it. My heart was beating wildly as I ran towards the car and I felt a deep, sharp pain inside me, almost as if I had been physically hurt. The old Volvo estate looked nude without Tom's car seat, which was now in Claire's car. I'd cleaned it out the day before, as part of the bright shining new me, but as I put my briefcase into the well of the passenger side, I found I'd missed something. One of Tom's soft shoes. I tucked it into my briefcase, next to the breast pads. Putting on the radio, I tried to distract myself. But I sobbed all the way to work, trying not to catch people's eyes at traffic lights. I felt like a large part of me had been left behind.

Tuesday 27 January
Quelle journée. I am absolutely *exhausted.* I felt absurdly nervous when I pushed my way through the swing doors to the newsroom. There'd been a bit of a hassle getting into the car park, because the passes had changed and no-one had thought to tell me, so I immediately felt wrong-footed. I'd also spent ten minutes reapplying my make-up to try to cover up all signs of sobbing. *Not* very professional. Everyone seemed to turn and stare at me as I walked in – I must have looked like a pink-eyed rabbit. Thank God I managed to catch Kate's eye, who realized I'd been crying and gave me a hugely sympathetic smile. Predictably, my chair had been swapped for the one with the broken back, but after a short but vociferous argument with Peter I managed to get mine back. Then I tried to

switch the computer on – and a completely foreign screen appeared, not the old system I had just about mastered. I hissed, 'How do you get in?' to Kate, feeling completely helpless. My hands were like great flappy fish and I couldn't get used to the noise of the office.

It was even a relief when the morning meeting was called. News editor Nick made a big point out of welcoming me back and Georgia – the blonde bimbo who'd replaced me on attachment – gave me a very smarmy smile. What has the management promised her now I've come back? She must hate me. No, I Must Not Be Paranoid. By eleven o'clock, I was on the phone to Claire, hunched over so no-one could hear I was ringing home. 'Hi, just me. Everything OK?' Falsely bright and unworried tone.

Claire sounded irritated when she picked up the phone. Tom was crying in the background. Crying? Why? He never cries. I could almost *hear* her sighing with annoyance at my interference. 'I'm just changing his nappy. Everything's fine, and no, of course, I won't forget it's four o'clock to pick Rebecca up. Don't *worry*. Really, Tom's *perfectly* happy. We were just about to go out for a walk and we must go, mustn't we, Tom darling? Bye.' She put the phone down very sharply. Neurotic Working Mother Syndrome. Don't worry? How could I not worry, so far from home, helpless to influence matters? Let go, I told myself. You're being absurd. Then, At least if he was crying I know he's still *alive* . . .

As the morning wore on I began, slowly, to enjoy myself. I rang lots of old contacts and said I was back, and did they have any stories for me, and then enjoyed a long, gossipy, child-free, grown-up lunch with Kate. How nice it is to be able to talk (OK, bitch) about other people instead of endlessly about children. Nick has put me on planning for the first few weeks, 'to ease me back into the swing of things', which is a long way from the stress of churning out items for the programme. He's been regarding me with a kind of wary suspicion all day – perhaps he thinks I'll suddenly whip Tom out from my briefcase, lob out a terrifying boob and breastfeed him there and then.

I'd brought Tom into the office to show everyone when he was about three months old – I remember pushing my way through the doors holding Tom very tightly, somehow uneasy about this merging of my mummy-self and my work-self. I felt so beamingly proud of him, but at the same time very off-balance – as if I'd walked into the office naked. Predictably it was all the women who crowded round me to exclaim over his cuteness – the men just came over and harrumphed a bit, looking me over cautiously as if I'd sprouted feathers. Nick slid out of his office and peered hesitantly at Tom, as if he might suddenly explode. Honestly. He has two children of his own, but I bet his wife makes sure they're all tidied away like toys when he comes home from work.

It was great to be so *free*. No-one said, 'Muuuuum,' in a long whiny voice. People listened to what I was saying. I was making things happen. I could go to the toilet on my own. The first time I went in the morning, I automatically left the door unlocked, so Rebecca could wander in as usual and ask me long complicated questions about dinosaurs and volcanoes. But then as I settled down something struck me. Silence. There was no-one else in here. I was a grown-up person in a grown-up toilet, and I was sitting having a wee with the door open. A little eccentric, don't you think? I had to lunge forward mid-wee and slam it shut, hoping to God that smarmy Georgia wouldn't wander in at this moment to give her bob a quick respray and check

26

there wasn't the teeniest smudge of her mascara under her eyes, whereby catching large whale-like person stranded on toilet with outstretched feet. Thankfully, she didn't.

Out of the loo, I gave myself a quick once-over in the mirror. Snug was the word which sprang to mind about my suit. Very, very snug. The worst thing about working in television is that it's full of groovy twenty-year-olds wearing Lycra mini-skirts and huge clumpy platforms at the ends of their skinny legs. I will either have to lose vast amounts of weight and have a serious style up-date (how fashions have moved on while I've been in domestic limbo) or accept the fact that I have become my mother.

2

FEBRUARY

Sunday 1 February

I had forgotten what a bloody nightmare it is trying to cram all domestic activities into the weekend. It was a blur of activity, and tomorrow I shall creep thankfully into work for a rest. Instead of being able to shop during the week, I had to do a full week's shop in one go. With The Children. No day off for me. I'd asked Mike repeatedly during the week to be around to look after Rebecca and Tom, so I could get to the supermarket, the dry-cleaners, the pet food shop to pick up dog food and the garage to fill up with petrol and hoover out the worst of the debris. Then in the middle of breakfast a terrible hunted look came over his face, and he admitted he'd promised Bill he would have a game of golf. Much recrimination ensued, but he said he just couldn't let Bill down. What about letting me down?

It meant I had to force my way round the supermarket with a six-month-old trying desperately to climb out of the trolley and lunge beneath its wheels, and a six-year-old disappearing shrieking down each aisle singing 'Doh a dear' at the top of her voice. Then Rebecca insisted on weighing all the fruit carefully by hand, attracting smiling, approving glances from all the old ladies, which meant I couldn't swipe the bananas from her hands and pull her off by her hair. By the time we reached the till, my head was throbbing and I gave in immediately to sweets.

We then moved into one of those speeded-up cartoon days as I frantically rushed to get to the dry-cleaners before it closed at lunch-time (why? Do they close early as a ritual form of torture?) and then spent all afternoon buying tiny but apparently essential things from a variety of shops which involved getting Tom and Rebecca in and out of the car what felt like a million times, before returning home to throw huge bundles of washing in the machine. Mike came home at eight, and collapsed on the sofa. 'God, I'm exhausted,' he said. 'Really,' I said, politely. 'I feel as fresh as a daisy.' Then I fell asleep with my mouth open.

Wednesday 4 February
Complete disaster at work today. We play the local radio station in the office — basically so we can nick their stories — and one of the features had the sound-effect of a baby crying. Oh dear. Red alert to my chest. Baby crying. Tom crying. Feed Tom. Imperative feed Tom NOW. There I was, harmlessly working away at planning our election coverage, and my tits turned into Vesuvius. The ensuing spurts completely drowned the thin little breast-pads and soaked through my shirt. Bending double, I rushed puce-faced to the loo, clutching my jacket around me. In the safety of its marble confines, my worst fears were confirmed. There were two huge, spreading stains on the front of my shirt — the sort of stains which couldn't be casually explained away. 'I tripped and spilt two cups of coffee down myself — simultaneously'? 'I had a nasty accident with an exploding tap'?

29

I then had to spend half an hour in the loo, frantically mopping away at the stains before having to bend over in a most uncomfortable manner in front of the hand-dryer, attempting to dry my shirt, which, predictably enough, dried with two big round marks like polos. My bra was also soaked, but I couldn't risk taking that off, because then my tits would plummet like a lift. What kind of madness happens to breasts when you have children? For twenty-seven years I had two perfectly normal, firm, not-too-big globes, with nipples which sat in the middle, pointing quite respectably upwards. I have to say I'd never really thought about them much. There they were; they had to be put in a bra every morning, but after that I more or less forgot about them; they were just a part of my body, like knees. My first hint that I was pregnant with Rebecca came when my nipples felt like they were going to burst from my breasts. Gradually, during my pregnancy, they began to swell . . . and swell, like great barrage balloons. At first Mike loved the novelty – at the time he said it was like being married to Dolly Parton – and I had to constantly slap away his fiddling hands. Then, towards the end of my pregnancy, they began to explode on him at unexpected moments – i.e. orgasm. It's very nice to know your wife is having an orgasm, but vaguely alarming when her chest erupts.

Once Rebecca was born the problem intensified, and often we would both wake up in a big lake. Then, once I stopped breastfeeding her at nine months, my breasts went away too. I mean completely. One moment they were vast melons, the next little limes. And they had moved, too. 'You look a bit like an African tribeswoman,' said Mike kindly as I surveyed my much-changed naked body in the mirror. In my normal bras, they were like little lost puppies. I became obsessively interested in the promise of the Wonderbra, which would at least bring them up to somewhere near my armpits.

Once I got pregnant with Tom, however, miraculously they came back. Where had they been? Round the back somewhere? Mike was happy once more. It doesn't take much to keep men amused, does it? If men had breasts, they'd never have to go out at all. Anyway, now I'm going to have to start bringing in a change of clothes for work. Here I am, a top-notch television reporter with a mind like a steel trap, lumbered with the body of a wet nurse. Why can't my breasts leap into the 1990s? How can I be a serious career woman when I've got amazing exploding breasts? I should be able to turn breastfeeding on and off, like a tap. The answer of course is not to have breastfed Tom at all in the first place and put him straight on the bottle, but that seems so clinical, doesn't it? I shall deny you all of those essential antibodies and what-nots because I am shortly to abandon you to a complete stranger. I had to spend the rest of the day crouched over my desk, and, Sod's Law, the heating was turned right up in the office. Kate wandered by and said, 'You look a bit hot. Why don't you take your jacket off?'

'It's a long story,' I said. 'And one which will put you off motherhood for ever.'

Friday 6 February
Our mornings are forming a distinct pattern. At seven, the alarm clock goes off and we all fall out of bed. All: that is Mike, me and Tom. Tom's siren calls at the moment are waking us at about six, when Mike humorously nudges me with his foot and says, 'Your baby's crying.' I try to restrain myself from falling about laughing, and exact revenge by crawling out of bed, dragging the duvet with me. If I do not do this, then

Mike simply swathes himself in it like a maggot and goes back to sleep. I spend a futile five minutes trying to persuade Tom to stay in his cot because it isn't morning time, but he is not fooled and so I compromise by bringing him up to bed with us. The best thing about this is that a) I get to go back to bed and b) Mike is inconvenienced too.

At least Tom does sleep in until six. When Rebecca was about two she developed the sadistic routine of waking up at five. This lasted for about a year, until her little body-clock clicked back on to Human Time. She was too young for me to allow her to roam unchecked around the house, so there was a whole ghastly year of having to heave myself out of bed, stumble blearily downstairs to put on a video, and then attempt to doze on the sofa, which of course is quite impossible because once you're up, you're up. There's nothing quite so strange as those twilight mornings, when you are convinced you're the only person awake in the whole world, and you know there is a normal packed day stretching ahead of you. It seems quite monstrous that you can be expected to get up this early and survive. Thank God she grew out of it, because otherwise I think I would have been forced to kill her.

For the next half an hour or so we try to sleep while Tom crawls over our heads. Having a morning-nappy bottom stuck in your face is a reasonable incentive to get out of bed. Mike bags the first shower, while Tom and I play. I love having him in bed with me: he's fat and squashy, and so cuddly – far more cuddly than Rebecca ever was. Then I try to shower while Tom crawls around the bathroom, selecting a variety of interesting objects to play with: razor blades, Tampax, nail-scissors. I often find it's easier to have a bath, because then at least he can come in with me and I know where he is.

The next task is getting Rebecca out of bed. At the tender age of six, she has already achieved all the qualities of teenage angst and regards her bed as her sanctuary. So I begin my gentle entreaties to the mound under the duvet with, 'I think it's time to get up now, Rebecca.' 'Rebecca, it's half past seven now, you're going to be late for school.' 'REBECCA, IF YOU DON'T GET UP NOW I AM CALLING THE POLICE.' Eventually a skinny white leg will appear and she slinks off to spend half an hour sitting on the toilet, gazing aimlessly into space, before getting off and forgetting to flush it. Half an hour later I will find her happily humming to herself wearing just her vest and knickers, carefully pressing Spice Girls stickers into an album, without a care in the world. Then I go back to my room to survey the joys of my wardrobe. I either chance on what I want to wear immediately, or clothes begin to fly out of my cupboard as if by invisible force. I put on mascara, while Tom sits heavily on my foot, or tries to climb up my legs, seriously endangering my tights. I have still not changed his nappy. I think perhaps that joy should be left for Claire. All the time I am waiting for the sound of her key in the door, when I can be absolved of all parental responsibilities. Mike meanwhile has got himself out of the shower, dressed, and made himself a cup of coffee. I mean, give this man a medal. He's done all that all on his own, with no mummy to help him. 'You know your problem,' he says, bobbing his head round the bedroom door to say goodbye, immaculately shaved and laundered in his suit and stripy shirt. 'Lack of organization.' Then he is gone, before I can throw either Tom or my make-up bag at him.

Rebecca hears him heading for the door and is out of her room like a shot, yelling 'Daddy!' He turns to pick her up and swing her round, before he leaves, whistling, quite unstressed and ready to face the day. When Claire arrives Tom squeals with joy at the sound of her voice and I shoot down to hand him over. Our mornings are all about timing. If Claire is ten minutes late, I'm ten minutes late, which means I have to crash into the morning meeting with a red face and unzipped skirt, while all the men smile at each other and think, Women! I can imagine myself standing with a stop-watch by the door some days, so obsessed am I at Claire getting here on time. When she does arrive she gives me that little forgiving smile which says, quite clearly, that I am the most incompetent mother in the world.

'Poor Tom!' she says. 'We'd better get that nappy off you *right now*, hadn't we, little man?'

Wednesday 11 February
There are rumours in the office that a new job is in the offing. It is Assistant Editor (Planning). I love the BBC. When the head of regional broadcasting gets bored with playing with the model aeroplanes on his desk, he decides to entirely reshuffle the regional manage-ment structure, so that everyone is permanently paranoid and no-one ever has a real job. One minute you're sitting there all secure, with Editor (News) on your door, the next you're being booted out to set up a news web-site in the Department of Twenty-four-hour On-line Broadcasting in some dim and distant corner of the labyrinthian Hell that is Television Centre. These crab-like sideways movements are called attach-ments, but basically they exist so people the current HOB (Head of Broadcasting) is fed up with can be shunted off and never seen again to do a job that no-one gives a monkey's about. That's what's so great about the BBC – it's so big you can just lose staff. For

ever. Eventually someone will remember they're there, stick their head round the office door, say, 'How's it going? Marvellous? Very challenging? Good man,' and then leave them to gather dust for another year. The backwaters of the BBC are full of middle-aged men playing cricket down the corridor with rolled-up bits of newspaper.

They've been shunted aside to make way for twenty-five-year-old women with Ally McBeal haircuts, mini-skirts, fierce expressions and degrees in Communication and Media Studies. There's never been a better time to be a woman – but perhaps on balance I think I'm probably much safer staying here as a reporter. Foot-soldiers are far less likely to be sacked or shunted about unless they actually want to move. But part of me is thinking, Hmmm, it would be quite nice to move into management. After all, Mike is now Executive-Whatnot at Midlands TV down the road, and I don't like him getting too far ahead of me in the career stakes. It gives me marginally less ammunition in the I-do-the-most-work-so-I'm-the-most-tired round of arguments as we compete for the sofa once the children are in bed. I don't know what Mike would think about it. It would mean more money, but it would also mean more responsibility and – eek – more time in the office. I'm already working four ten-hour days (thank God for having Fridays off), but this would be five ten-hour days, with the possibility of evening meetings. But I know they are looking to persuade more women into senior management, and, well, I am a woman so I'm halfway there. We could certainly do with the money (crafty farmhouse-plot begins to boil and bubble in my mind) and I know Nick rates me, which is why I've been put in charge of co-ordinating our election coverage, even though he is slightly wary because I am also a Mother. Poor old Nick. He's such a dinosaur. Women to him are only women until they have children, and then they become Mothers. He can't cope with the idea of working women at all.

Kate immediately messaged me saying: *Go for it! You'd be great! If you don't Miss Perfect-Knickers Georgia will and she'd be your boss.* Hmm. Good point. That really would be unbearable, especially as she's ten years younger than me and has never even heard of a parish council meeting or magistrates court, leaping as she did in one graceful and seamless bound from media studies course to BBC TV without having to soil her hands in the grind that is local newspapers. How would I cope with the interview? What questions would they ask me? Of course what I am *really* thinking is, what shall I wear?

Saturday 14 February

I am going to have to be much more firm about the Division of Labour. After last week, I felt completely stressed out and would ideally have spent the entire weekend lying in an aromatherapy bath listening to calming whale music whilst sipping chilled Sauvignon Blanc, with no children within a hundred-mile radius – especially children carrying small squeaking penguins who want to get in with me. Today Mike magnanimously said he would get the children up and give them breakfast. All on his own. Hurrah! I thought. I shall have another hour's sleep. Did I? I did not. I lay there, tossing and turning, looking at the patch on the ceiling Mike missed with the paint-brush when we did the cottage up, thinking about how big our overdraft is, how much I want the farmhouse (I still haven't dared mention it to Mike), and how we could possibly pay for that and still employ Claire.

What can we sell? *Who* can we sell? I found myself

eyeing up poor old Turtle the other day – he is after all a fully trained gundog and the most under-used dog in the world – but I doubt he'd fetch much more than six hundred quid. And then he put his head on one side and pricked his ears forward. You can't sell a dog with such an appealing face. How much would we get for this house? There is a big demand for old houses in our village and boy, is our house old. If you slam a door particularly hard bits of it drop off on your head. It was ideal for just Mike and me and Rebecca; we still had a spare room and, with Rebecca going to nursery, it didn't feel like the house was ever uncomfortably full. But now with Tom, and Claire here most of the time, I feel that we're all falling over each other like a Tom and Jerry cartoon. And there's nowhere to put the pushchair, except the hall, so every time you try to squeeze past it, it bites you.

I want more space outside too and the garden is tiny. We'd need practically to double our mortgage even to attempt to put a bid in on the farmhouse. Not sleep-inducing thoughts, as you can imagine. So I lay there in a cold sweat for about an hour, before an eerie silence from downstairs propelled me out of bed. I love it when Mike takes the children, but then I can never resist popping in to see what they're doing – just to make sure they're making clay models or playing chess, rather than lying on the sofa in a big heap watching *The Little Mermaid*. It's OK when I let the children watch videos, because it's only temporary before we skip on to another brain-enhancing activity, but when Mike does it it's child-care avoidance.

Sure enough, what they were actually doing was lying in a big heap on the sofa with the curtains closed, watching football on the satellite channel. What can those men with horrible cornish-pasty hair *say* about football at nine o'clock in the morning? Isn't there a danger they might even bore themselves? I think sports programmes were invented to give all men the length and breadth of the country the excuse to absolve themselves completely of any family responsibilities and pretend they are watching something *frightfully significant* when really they are just asleep.

Rebecca was thoughtfully painting her toenails bright blue with some nail varnish Jill gave her (I'm working out my revenge – her daughters are ten and five so I may well buy them a make-up set each) and Tom was lying flat on his back on Mike's chest, in the process of taking his socks off and throwing them at Angus the retriever, who was snoring in front of the telly. 'Is that it?' I said. 'Child-care of the nineties?'

'It's the Carling-premiership-first-round-knockout-tie,' (or something) said Mike.

'Well, as long as you're going to be gainfully occupied,' I said, and swept up Tom and Rebecca to get dressed. Mike then firmly closed the door of the TV room, and went back to lying on the sofa. So far as I could tell, he'd only managed to stuff them full of cereal before collapsing, exhausted.

He spent the rest of the day lying in the Stygian gloom, skilfully repelling all attempts to integrate him into family activities. How can men remain inactive for so long? If I sit down for more than five minutes I start to feel guilty. There's always something I should be *doing.* I kept sending Rebecca in with little tasks for him, like taking the rubbish to the tip, but she kept being spat out again, like a screw in a hoover. I think, on balance, he needs to spend a week alone with the children. But I know exactly what he'd do: he'd wait quietly until I'd gone and then ring his mum, who would run sobbing hysterically to his aid. How could a man be expected to look after children all on his own? I know my mother never ever left me and my two sisters alone with our father. I think she seriously believed he would either murder us, or completely forget we were there and go out. We're talking about a man who still does not know, as we approach the Millennium, how to use the kettle. That's how 'modern' my parents are. My mum's way of coming to terms with the fact that I aimed to have an ongoing and successful career after marriage was to tell me to smile a lot and always look as pretty as possible to impress the boss (who, inevitably, would be male).

Mike's parents are the same although his father is possibly even more feudal. He calls me 'the Career Girl'. 'How's the Career Girl?' 'Fine, thank you. How's Medieval Man?' Mike's mum is constantly examining the children for signs of neglect whenever they come to stay for the weekend, and makes a point of washing their hair and cleaning their fingernails – jobs I can never bring myself to do because they involve far too much drama, and after work I'm all drama-ed out. Unless, of course, I can get Claire to do it.

Sunday 15 February
Today I decided, in the wake of Mike's lack of activity yesterday, that we were going to have a Family Day Out. You know, the sort of day when a smiling mummy and daddy pack up the car with a gorgeous picnic to head off to the nearest zoo. They drive there singing their heads off and at the end of the day a contented pig-tailed child turns to them and says, 'That was smashing. Thank you so much for being my parents.'

Of course we woke to a day of pouring rain. Mike peered glumly out of the window and said, 'We may see ducks and we may see penguins but I think the leopards will be inside watching telly by the fire.' But Rebecca was so excited at the thought of going out with *both* of her parents – we normally run a split shift to minimize the aggro – that we couldn't bear to let her down. Trouble began as soon as we tried to get the children into the car. I bundled Tom into so many clothes he looked like a Russian doll, and then strapped him firmly into his car seat. He hates this at the best of times, and began yelling and struggling. Mike meanwhile stood by the car, tapping his feet and looking at his watch, having managed once again the Herculean task of getting himself ready to go out and checking he had his wallet.

I managed to catch Rebecca and force-feed her into a coat and wellingtons before she darted back into the house to find an essential travelling companion, her smallest toy rabbit, which had been lost for days. We eventually found the rabbit under her bed covered in dust, whilst Mike's foot-tapping reached a crescendo outside. Apologizing profusely (why?) I pushed Rebecca into the car, just managing to foil another back-to-bedroom trip for a lost sequinned purse. 'Perhaps now we can go,' said Mike, starting up the Volvo's engine. We pulled out of our driveway towards the Cotswold Wildlife Park, and I felt the tension beginning to seep out of me. 'I need to wee,' said Rebecca.

And no, we didn't sing, because Mike was listening with that curious male intensity to sport on the radio. All the way I kept peering up at the clouds, mentally willing the greyness to lift, but the drizzle remained constant. When we turned into the car park, it was almost totally empty. Normally when we come here, there are huge lines of cars, with frenzied mums stuffing toddlers into pushchairs and garrotting overexcited five-year-olds who are attempting to rush off immediately to see the monkeys' bottoms. But today the car park was just a vast, eerie, empty space. 'Is it open?' I said, half hoping the answer would be 'no'. But towards the end of it we spotted several other dispirited-looking cars, and in the booth an elderly and bad-tempered crone was hugging herself to keep warm.

'Any chance of half-price?' said Mike cheerfully.

'No,' she said firmly, so Mike handed over vast sums for the family ticket. He had the slightly desperate look of a man who would far rather be ensconced in a warm and convivial pub with a pint of beer in his hand saying, 'Now what I really call a tackle is . . .' to a group of like-minded fellows, but instead is bravely willing to escort his little band around a rainswept and empty zoo.

In the end, though, it was an excellent day. Rebecca jumped into lots of puddles, so she went round the entire zoo with flappy wet socks but didn't complain once; Tom took one look at the giant tortoise and went straight off to sleep, so he got his money's worth; and Mike thoroughly enjoyed himself over-exciting the marmosets, to the delight of Rebecca, who loves her dad being daft. I just liked being with them all, and having Mike's full attention.

Even in the evenings, I can tell that Mike is still mentally preoccupied with his job. He's getting harder and harder to talk to – when he does come home, I have to barrage him with questions, like the Spanish Inquisition, otherwise we'd never actually say anything to each other at all. Our conversations now seem to consist of me asking him endless questions about the minutiae of his day while he says, 'Why are you asking me all these questions?' He's been facing a lot more pressure since he became Head of News, and he seems increasingly unable to leave work at the office. In the evening, the phone calls come thick and fast, and quite often I'll wake at two in the morning, and he'll be lying reading, unable to sleep.

I must be less of a witch to him. But then, I'm the one who carries around huge lists in my head, and has to remember if we've run out of butter and whether Rebecca has recorder today. Often at work I'll be sitting in a meeting talking about the news prospects for tomorrow, when half of my mind is dreamily trying to work out if we have enough sausages for supper. At least his brain can run on one track during the day, instead of the thirty that my brain seems constantly to career down. But today it was so lovely to see him relaxing, heaving Rebecca up onto his shoulders, jogging her up and down, making her laugh hysterically. She adores him so much. Men with children are so sexy, aren't they? They seem to think that what women want are huge penises, but what we really want are men who love children. The image of Mike holding Rebecca to him, pressing a kiss she didn't notice on the side of her head while she laughed at the antics of the spider monkeys, made me long poignantly and fervently for the early days when Rebecca was just born, when we were so less-rich (or at least less overburdened with *things*, like big mortgages) and our jobs were less pressurized, and we had the time to have so many more days like this together. We felt much more of a proper family then. We were both home by six every night, and weekends were free from work. We even went shopping in the supermarket together, before it was officially declared a Mike-free zone. All too often, Mike now pops into the office on Saturdays; he logs onto the office computer from our home PC most evenings and on Sundays, as well as monitoring rival output on the telly. It's like living with Bill Gates without the handy cash.

The divisions between our working and home life seem to be blurring, I thought, and we're coping by farming our children out to a stranger whom we pay.

But then I shook myself, and reminded myself firmly that everyone moves on, everything is always changing and you just have to adapt and make the best of it. After the zoo, we (extremely bravely) went for afternoon tea at one of those chi-chi small hotels in Burford, full of crusty old fellows in blazers and tweedy-wives wearing pearls. It's amazing how you can clear a space around you with a grubby baby and a noisily excited six-year-old. I positioned myself well away from Tom, so Mike had to deal with the sticky hands and spilt drinks. Why do babies want to cover themselves in gunk all the time? Rebecca sat on the edge of her seat being very grown-up, and making disapproving faces at Tom. Normally she regards him simply as an inconvenience – I think she bitterly resented us presenting her with a brother at the age of five – but out of doors, in the presence of other people, he becomes a severe embarrassment to her. 'Mummy,' she hissed at me. 'He's got the *sugar*.'

'It's all right,' I said. 'He won't be able to open the packet.' Small ripping sound. 'Well, it'll keep him quiet,' I added, as he dreamily made big circles with the flat of his hand amidst the sugar and the spilt orange juice and the bits of egg mayonnaise sandwiches he'd been gumming. I imagined the staff would have to get an industrial hose to wash it down after we left. We drove back slowly in the fading light, Spice Girls on the radio to please Rebecca, and the shadows of tomorrow's work for once were held at bay.

Wednesday 18 February
'You know your problem,' said Kate at lunch-time, toying with her parmesan and chorizo salad in the trendy café near to the office. 'You've got too much time on your hands. You should take up a hobby.' I'd been

43

having an extended moan to her about how I felt I never had any time to myself any more to do anything. What a sensible person would do, of course, is keep Claire on for half an hour after I got home to get at least some breathing space to de-stress, have a bath or just read the paper, and ask her to come much earlier before I was due to leave the house in the morning. But I feel so guilty about leaving the children at all, I time things so that as she comes into the house, I hand over a (usually half-dressed) Tom like a kind of baton in the relay race and, with a final yell at Rebecca to get off the toilet, steam out of the house. At night, I come home and immediately want the children all to myself. And . . . Oh, I have to admit this to myself. Claire is *really* irritating me. She has this way of making what seem like completely innocuous statements that I *know* are veiled criticisms of me, my life, and the way I run my house. A relationship with a nanny is so bloody tricky. You rely on them so desperately because without them you could not work, so you have to be constantly nice to them for fear they'll turn round and say, 'I'm off,' leaving you appallingly in the lurch. You are paying them, so you should have some control, but you can hardly treat them like a servant, can you? I cope by being exaggeratedly nice, which I'm sure makes Claire think that I'm a complete push-over. Mike certainly says that instead of moaning to him about the fact that Rebecca is becoming appallingly cheeky, I should tackle Claire about it. I can't. I'm too much of a coward.

At the moment, I'm not getting home until about half-seven, so the children are fed and often bathed by the time I get there, but at least I can read them their stories. Last week Nick introduced this sadistic ruling that we all have to stay behind to discuss the programme immediately after it's gone out, so that has put another twenty minutes on my day. I sit there, poised like a gazelle, on the edge of my desk, as Nick picks a fight with the graphics department and witters on and on about the lateness of captions, with all the surety of a man who knows his supper is in the oven and his children are safely tucked up in bed by someone else. Once he's eventually finished, I'm off the starting blocks as all the men and single women in the office slowly pick up their bags and say, 'Time for a beer?' While the likes of Georgia and Kate are convivially sipping gin and tonics in the BBC Club, I'm haring homewards at the speed of light, screeching round corners and knocking over pedestrians in my haste to get home. Through the door, I fling down my briefcase and hurtle towards the sound of their voices. Tom is in the bath, kicking up the water with his fat little feet, and Rebecca is under her bed making a den for her Barbie. Seeing her face light up when I come in the room makes all the petty niggles of the day fade into what they are: bollocks. Even if I've made a balls of things, or I've had row with Nick, or someone has been snotty about a story I've covered, none of it matters any more once I hold her in my arms. She doesn't care if I'm the world's most brilliant reporter, or the saddest duffer ever to grace a screen. I'm just her mum, and that's all she cares about. She loves me anyway.

Claire carries Tom into Rebecca's room, and hands him over as he keens towards me, his little face wreathed in smiles. He is sweet-smelling and warm from his bath, solid, *real*. He clutches hold of my hair in the way he always does, and we sink to the floor for a collective cuddle. Then by the time I've got Tom into his cot and sung him a song, it is time to hear Rebecca read. This is a very exhausting process. All the time she's slowly pointing out the words and saying them, I'm mentally willing her along, agonizing if she gets stuck. But she's coming on very well – the exorbitant fees must be paying off, thank God. She always wants me to lie on her bed while she goes off to sleep, which is pretty fatal because all too often I doze off too, before waking with a stiff neck and a start, realizing it's after nine o'clock and Mike still isn't back. Once she's asleep, I can kick off my high-heeled shoes and finally have a read of the paper. I can't face cooking, so I guess Mike will once more enjoy seafood tagliatelle, cooked by someone else, of course. Thank God for ready-made food. Mike gets home, a quick glass of wine and then we are both ready for bed. Mike has worked out that he can have sex if he catches me just as my book starts to droop out of my hand. A second later, and I am irretrievably gone.

As I described all this to Kate, she kept pulling totally horrified faces. After a gin and tonic at the Club, she drives slowly home to the strains of Classic FM (Rebecca would be screaming for the Spice Girls), then runs herself a deep and soothing (childless) aromatherapy-oil bath. Oliver, her boyfriend (they've been living together for five years, but far be it from me to say he's a commitment phobic), has already been home for several hours from his job as a graphic designer, and brings in a large glass of Châteauneuf-du-Pape. Then they sit quietly and eat the meal he's cooked, or they go out for a meal. Whenever they like. On a whim. Oh, let's go out. Fine. Fine if you have a joint income of five thousand pounds a month and NO KIDS and fine if you don't have to ring fifteen-year-old Samantha down the road and say, in a falsely bright voice, 'Hi, Samantha, I just wondered if you could babysit tonight? You can't? You have a new boyfriend? How lovely. Never mind. No, really, we weren't going anywhere special. Thanks, 'bye.' So I put down the phone and Mike says, 'Well, I may as well go down

the pub for an hour, then. Fancy an Indian take-away?'
and I line up another stimulating evening on the sofa,
to mull on the curious fact of life that ringing baby-
sitters is *always* a Woman's Job, like cleaning the loo.

Anyway the upshot is that Kate reckons we could get
a free deal (press) at a smart new health club which has
opened up nearby, and if I could persuade Mike to look
after the children for a day at the weekend we could go
and de-tox, and I could completely pamper myself. I
can but ask. But I quite like being toxic . . . Will I like
a non-toxic me?

Friday 20 February
Our bank statement plopped through the letterbox this
morning, just as I was leaving for work. I thought,
bravely, I'll open it now. But then I thought, Nope, I'm
not that brave. It can just sit *there*, behind the plant
pot, until I get home, and I can open it with a large gin
in my hand. I can never see those square white
envelopes with the crinkly hole for the address without getting a chill up my spine. Is anyone ever
pleasantly surprised by the contents of their bank
statements? Does anyone peer into the little pink box
and say, 'Look, how lovely, we're a thousand pounds
better off than I thought we were, I *must* spend more
money on clothes this month.' I bet Harriet-no-job-
huge-house and her husband Martin are. They're so
careful they have PEPs and building society accounts.
They thought ahead and set up a school-fees plan for
their two sons, Arnold and Sidney, as soon as they
were born. Poor fellows, what names. I don't really
know why I'm still friendly with Harriet. At first I
thought we had lots in common, and she seemed very
jolly. It was only later that I discovered her sole *raison
d'être* is to make me feel inadequate. Her house –

five-bedroomed, stone flags, family paintings – is full of the effortless style achieved by having a very rich husband and lots of time to fart about buying tapestry cushions and concocting huge and beautiful flower arrangements. When she brought Arnold round to my house, she picked her way very deliberately round Rebecca's litter of crayons and model horses. 'What a lovely little cottage,' she said. 'I've always thought how sweet these cottages in this village are. Did you know they used to be alms houses?'

When I got home and opened the damn thing – I should have done it there and then because I had a sick feeling of dread all day – the contents of the bank statement were catastrophically worse than usual. *Massively* overdrawn – way over our limit! What do we spend it all on? Why is it that as two grown-up people we cannot work out the simple equation that every month we spend more than we earn? Dammit, I need to think we have loads of money to skip into shops with a light heart and a nice flappy credit card, because let's face it, that is the *only* thing that makes life worth living. We are still over a week away from respective salary days, so that gives us – quiet, let me think – no money at all for the next week. It therefore seems unfortunate that I have promised to pay Claire a week early, as she needs to pay for some tickets for a ball. A ball! I can't remember the last time I went to a ball.

She is deliberately mysterious about her social life. I think she still lives with her parents (which presumably is why she can afford to be a nanny on my pitiful wages) but is able to afford, somehow, a brand-new car (which we can't) and to go out most nights of the week, judging by her lengthy phone calls from our house to friends with names like Fiona. A couple of mornings this week she has seemed very bleary indeed, although trying desperately to hide it. The phone bill arrived yesterday and, like Sherlock Holmes, I tracked down the number of phone numbers I didn't recognize and added them up. More than we spent! I haven't dared tell Mike, because he, unlike me, would tackle her about it, and I couldn't face the hassle.

How can I broach the subject of moving to Mike if we are so overdrawn? How could we possibly – and yes, I have worked this out in the still watches of the night – double our mortgage and survive? But I want it, I want it! I've taken to driving to work every morning via a slight detour so I can go past the farmhouse, just longing and longing. I've already mentally moved in and am welcoming surprised and impressed visitors, *especially* Mike's mother. The 'For Sale' board is still up so it hasn't been sold yet. Every day at work when I feel depressed I whip the details out to have a soothing, dreamy read about stone flags in the downstairs hall and a walk-in fireplace and a *larder*. I know I will be a grown-up person if I finally own a larder, and it will turn me into the kind of mother who makes jam and her own bread. I will prepare lots of meals at the weekends and store them in the large chest freezer (kept in the boot room), so Mike and I can eat home-cooked food during the week, instead of plates of steaming E-numbers. I will make apple pies from our own apples in the orchard, and I will learn from my mother how to make pastry which does not resemble a heavy blanket. I am going to be strong. I am going to mention the house to Mike tonight. The matter of the overdraft is but a trifle. Did Michelangelo think of the cost of paint when he started on the Sistine Chapel ceiling? He did not. To own a place of such beauty should not come down to the mere baubles. It is Our Destiny, and if Mike doesn't agree I will cry very loudly, which he hates.

When I really think about it, I think I want to move so badly because I want – or need – it to herald a change in our relationship. Marriages are such strange things. From the outside, to other people, they appear static and concrete – there you are, you're married, you're permanent – but inside them, there's this con-stant private swirling of such conflicting emotions: love, passion, anger, hurt, bitterness, jealousy. Marriages are like small children: if you take your eye off them for a moment, they run off and do something awful. As Jill says, if people could really see how appalling she and Pete are to each other, they would suspect they should be housed securely in an insti-tution. Certainly, no-one would ever speak to them again. One minute you're standing on what you think is solid ground, and you know and can trust each other completely, the next, it has abruptly shifted from beneath your feet with just one remark and you are left hanging in mid-air.

God, it is so exhausting. Anyone who smugly tells me there is such a thing as a happy marriage is clearly *not* married. The other night Mike came home from work, tired as usual. I'd only just persuaded Rebecca that she really had to stay in bed, after the fourth time she'd appeared in the kitchen wanting something. The first couple of times it was quite endearing when she pushed her teddy's face round the door and made him ask for a drink, but by the fourth demand from Teddy I was ready to commit tedricide. Mike opened a bottle of wine for both of us and I took the heated-up pasta out of the oven. I began to relax. Elbows on the kitchen table in the fading light, I thought how lovely it was that we had each other to talk to about the small tribu-lations of the day, and felt a faintly smug rosy glow descending. 'Rebecca's driving me mad,' I said. 'She was so naughty this evening, she would not go to bed.

And, God, I could have killed Claire this evening when she said—'

'Carrie,' Mike suddenly cut in. 'I don't care. I have spent all day locked in battle with the bloody union about the changes I am being forced to make to the technical staff's rota. Why can't you get organized? The last thing I want to do when I get home is hear you whinge about bugger all. You're doing a job which is nowhere near as demanding as mine, and still you're complaining you haven't got enough help and every night we have to eat this ready-made crap. You've got everything you want on a plate, and it would be great if just once you could think about me instead of this constant obsession with what's supposedly wrong in your life. You're so bloody *selfish*.' Then he picked up his glass of wine and stormed out.

I sat there at the table, feeling like I'd been run over by a bus. One minute we were having a chat, the next it was World War Three. Suddenly my feelings were unimportant compared to his. Here I was, trying to make life as comfortable and as easy for him as I possibly could, and now he was calling me selfish. How dare he? Who is the person who organizes all the child-care? Who is the person who gets up in the middle of the night with the children when they cry or need the loo? Who is the person who constantly worries – but admittedly, never quite gets on top of – the amount of food in the house and if everyone has clean clothes? I loathe it when he suddenly assumes this head-of-the-household-my-needs-are-most-important role. It makes me think that I work for nothing.

I sat there and seethed before pointedly going up to bed leaving the plates and glasses on the kitchen table and without turning out any of the lights. I made sure I was very determinedly asleep when he did come up to bed, but he foiled me by getting into the spare bed in Rebecca's room, which meant I couldn't show him how very little I was affected by the row.

Saturday 21 February
Diplomatic relations were resumed only following a bunch of flowers which arrived on my desk at work, and tonight I plucked up courage and poured us both a huge soothing glass of Merlot. As we sat in the cramped and messy kitchen, festooned with Rebecca's drawings of dinosaurs and Tom's hand- and footprints in paint, courtesy of Claire, I said, very quietly and calmly, so he wouldn't smell a rat, 'Mike, how do you feel about this house?'

'How do I *feel*?' he responded, eyeing me up as if I was totally barking. 'It's fine. We love it. I mean, that's why we bought it. What are you talking about, Carrie?'

'It's just that now, with Tom, and having Claire here as well, it just feels a bit, well, *small*,' I said, turning my glass of wine round and round in my hands, trying not to go bright red in the face. He immediately knew I was up to something. He always knows when I have a plan. No Question Is Ever Asked Entirely Innocently. It always means I want him to do something for me, and it's usually something he doesn't know he wants to do – *yet*. This is what happens after seven years of marriage.

'What have you seen?' he said, beginning to smile.

'Oh,' I said, 'it's just a whim. The – um – farmhouse by the village green. You know, the one with the stone gateposts and the big willow in the front garden and the orchard at the back, and the paddock so Rebecca could have a pony and the stone flags in the hall and the *four bedrooms* and the . . . Oh, look,' I said, 'here are details in my handbag! I'd completely forgotten they were there!' I skipped out to check on the kids, leaving the brochure tantalizingly under Mike's nose. I know he won't be able to resist looking at them. He's as much a sucker for big old houses as I am.

When I came back, I found him deep in thought. 'Yeees,' he said. 'It does look great, but how much is it?' (The price wasn't printed at the end. It had one of those very fishy 'price on application' notes instead, so I knew it was going to be a stonker.)

'I really don't know,' I lied. He then admitted he had seen the 'For Sale' notice as well. Aha! I knew he'd like it. He was brought up on a big rambling old farm and I know he has always rather hankered after the Good Life. What is it about men and vegetable gardens? There's a bit of the Percy in them all. Anyway, he actually agreed that we could go and see it, possibly next weekend. 'Not tomorrow?' I asked. Not immediately right now at eleven o'clock I'm sure they'd still be up?

'Not tomorrow. I have some work to do. We're going to need every bit of both of our salaries if this harebrained scheme of yours ever comes off. Now let's go to bed.'

How *could* I refuse?

Sunday 22 February
Went round to see Jill and her mob, with Rebecca and Tom in tow. Tom loves it at her house because she has a cat which allows him to stroke her without immediately disappearing. My suspicion is that this is because it is actually clinically dead. We tried to drink our coffee in a civilized fashion, but the girls kept running back into the house to ask us to watch them doing handstands, and Tom then refused to be put down onto the floor, so I had to hold him slightly away from me

while I manoeuvred my coffee cup to my lips. 'I'll have him,' said Jill. 'I love holding other people's babies because it reminds me that I must never have any more children.'

She agreed that it was imperative we buy the farmhouse, so she could visit us on a frequent basis, if not actually move in.

Mike can't quite see the point of Jill. He tends to warm to women who think he's wonderful. Jill isn't quite so easily bowled over, and I know she thinks he takes advantage of me. She rules Pete with a rod of iron; as we chatted, he staggered past us with his arms full of washing. 'Don't forget to separate the colours,' she said, while Rebecca stared at him in amazement. A man doing the washing? 'How's work going?' Jill said.

'Hectic,' I said. 'What about you?'

'Wonderful,' she said, sarcastically. 'I took our special needs group on Friday, as a favour. One of them stabbed himself with a pencil and two ate their rubbers. One, I could understand. But two?'

Wednesday 25 February
Just before lunch Nick casually wandered down towards my desk from the Golden Heights that are his office. Oh Lord, I thought. What have I done? Maybe the parents of the four-year-old excluded child (the youngest child ever to be excluded from a reception class) I so brilliantly persuaded to talk to camera are suing us for harassment. Ungrateful beasts. To get that story, I spent over an hour sipping thick brown tea out of mugs rimmed with grime perched on a sofa which they later told me they'd had to get the council in to de-rat. Maybe he has seen my plans for the local election coverage and has worked out that to implement them would bankrupt the entire Midlands region.

He casually perched his ample rear on my desk and, with blushing face (he really cannot talk to women), asked if I might be interested in applying for the new job, Assistant Editor (Planning). I said, rashly, that I might be (coquettish smile, oh for goodness sake, Carrie, forget your mother). 'Well,' he said (relieved smile, difficult task of talking to woman over), 'that's fine. I'll expect it on my desk in the morning.'

Oh gee. Now I suppose I'll have to go for it after all. Actually, I feel rather perkily excited. It would mean running the entire planning department – eight staff, including three men older than me, ha, ha – and would give me access to High-level Meetings with Senior Management (they get coffee in silver coffee pots, not big urns like the rest of us, and *chocolate* biscuits). I didn't immediately think what it would mean to Mike and the kids. I thought what it would mean to *me*. It would be so great to ring my dad and tell him I was now an Assistant Editor at the BBC. No matter that the BBC is crawling with Assistant Editors, all frantically clawing at the door of the beleaguered Editors who know that the days of playing slip in the Television-Centre-international-corridor-cricket-championships are just around the corner.

As I stared at my computer, trying to work out the introduction to a story which involved murder, a sex change and satanic rituals (someone's been busy), I mused: Who do I do things *for*? Do I do them for me, for the family, or for my parents? A lot of my ambition is based on my own relentless urge to succeed, to do well, to be praised. But also – OK, honesty-time now, Carrie – it is to put two fingers up to my dad. Look, Dad! I may be a girl, but look where I've got to! It is also to keep my end up, so to speak, in our marriage, as well as bringing in much-needed cash.

Mike has always been so ruthlessly ambitious, and

one of the things that attracted him to me in the first place was that I was successful at work too. A lot of his friends, after university, were going out with girls who were nurses, newsroom secretaries and typists, all clearly desperate to chuck in their dull jobs once they got that ring on their finger, and could fulfil their destiny as Susie-homemaker. He was proud of the fact that we both did the same job (reporters on a local newspaper), and that we could compete on equal terms.

We could talk about our work because we knew exactly what each other meant. In the first year of our marriage – before Rebecca came along – we were like two mates who happened to have excellent sex, going down the pub together, taking turns to load the washing machine, shopping together after work. None of the domestic tasks then were any big deal: if they needed to be done, fine, one of us did them. It only really changed when Rebecca was born. Why? Why did I let it happen? Suddenly, there I was, exhausted and vulnerable, bringing home this tiny and helpless baby – do we really have to look after this all alone? – and our roles abruptly shifted.

He became obsessed with work, obsessed with paying the mortgage, obsessed with his role as hunter/gatherer. But within three months, I was hunter/gathering as well, only I was hunter/gathering after getting up at six to shovel cereal into Rebecca, get her dressed and hurriedly throw yoghurts, made-up milk bottles and nappies into a bag before rushing her to nursery, and then screeching in to meet the beginning of my shift with a flushed face and milk-stains on my shoulders.

When I left university in the early eighties, we were the generation of women who really would 'have it all'. We could have a successful career, a family, run a home. All we needed was good child-care. Simple. It took less than a month of slogging Rebecca to nursery every morning to realize that child-care was *not* simply the answer. Struggling out of the car with her in her babyseat, bag bashing on my hip as I wrestled her through the door, trying to find a member of staff who wasn't examining her nails or chatting holding a steaming mug of coffee to take her from me. And then her agonized little face as she realized I was leaving, peeling off her little shrimp fingers as her face creased with the desperation of loss, and turning to run out of the door, not looking back as I knew she would be howling, wriggling and struggling to find my face and my smell as I left the boundaries of her existence. And yet I persevered. I persevered with the nursery for two years, until the penny finally dropped that she might be better off at home with a nanny.

Work equals respect. So what I thought was the answer was simply to find better child-care for Rebecca, which we did. Problem solved or so I thought. It's funny, but I've never talked to Mike about any of this at all.

3

MARCH

Monday 2 March

Went to see the farmhouse yesterday. I am writing very
calmly, but inside I am squeaking with excitement.
Mike had been gardening in the morning, hurling dead
sticks in the garden onto a bonfire (why are all men
pyromaniacs?) and looked up at me in surprise when I
came to get him, all dressed up in a long flowery silk
dress. Tom was resplendent in an Osh-Kosh red all-in-
one (this is only ever put on him the second before we
leave the house, and is generally reserved for mother-
impressing visits), and Rebecca was gorgeous in a
pie-collared flowery number too. (Guess who bought
it? Mike's mother, of course.)

'Why are you lot all done up like dog's dinners?' said
Mike, wiping a smear of ash across his face, looking
sexy and gorgeous in ripped jeans and a heavy blue
cableknit sweater. I love men doing outdoor things. No.
Correction. I love men doing *anything* at all, even
unloading the dishwasher.

'Because,' I said, 'appearances count.'

'Bollocks,' he said. 'Cash counts.' But at least he did
go inside and get changed, into a very acceptable pair
of smart trousers and the new orange stripy shirt I
bought him for his last birthday.

The house was out of this world. As soon as I ducked my head under the low, oak doorframe, it called to me, a low siren call. 'This is your home,' it said. I went round from room to room in a kind of trance, hugging Tom to me, trying to keep Rebecca from bashing minute and rather ghastly ornaments off nests of tables. Mike asked sensible and grown-up questions, while I wandered about with my mouth open, noting the stone mullioned windows, the well-worn door lintels, the air of peace and calm. As we went up the stairs – creaking under frayed old carpet – I kept pinching Mike until he turned and hissed at me, 'Stop seeming so *keen.*'

In the orchard it was all I could do not to gambol about like Julie Andrews in *The Sound of Music.* It was all so perfect. There was even a hen house. The old couple who lived there were the frightfully decent sort: children had left home, old place now a bit too big, sad really, because the house had been in the family for three generations, but now all the children, including the two gels, had careers in London and were unlikely ever to come back to this neck of the woods. Too dull, they say, after London. They'd had masses of interest in the place, but no-one had seemed the type who'd take care of it. One fella up from London in his BMW had offered them over three hundred thousand, but they hadn't liked the look of him. *Nouveau.* I tried desperately to look 'old money' and said 'yah' a lot, and thanked God I was wearing a long dress instead of a Lycra mini.

The decoration was hideous: trestles of roses climbing up the living-room walls, brown carpets, Formica units in the kitchen. But it was still lovely. We drove home in silence, while I beamed quietly inside. That night Mike and I sat down in the kitchen to another serious chat.

'We can't afford it,' he said.

'I know,' I said. Silence. 'But . . .'

'We can't afford it,' he said.

'I know,' I said. Another long pause, as I took a slug of Sauvignon. 'Could we ask your mum and dad?'

'No!' said Mike, horrified. He'd never ask his father for a penny, not even for Rebecca's school fees.

'What about *my*—' I said.

'No way!' he said. 'I'll talk to the bank in the morning.'

'I love you,' I said. The storm seems to have passed. I knew the house would make things better and I feel so much calmer and happier.

Thursday 5 March

SEX. Sex is becoming An Issue. It was actually a bit of a joke between us for a while after Tom's birth, that Mike was going around in an agony of frustration, but now I think he feels it is getting *beyond* a joke, and he wants us to get back to the way we were pre-children. But it's very hard to get worked up about sex when you know you look like a performing elephant in frilly bra and pants.

We had just had what I thought was a perfectly acceptable shag last night, mission successfully accomplished for both of us, when Mike said, 'Carrie, we have to talk about this.'

'What?' I said, just about to drift off into mindless oblivion.

'Our sex life,' said Mike.

'We've just *had* sex,' I drowsily pointed out.

'I have,' said Mike. 'You haven't. You were just *there*.'

Oh jeepers. I know I have got very lazy. It's just that I still feel so big I don't really want to raise myself from

60

the prone position, because at least my stomach is vaguely flat when I'm lying down. Lie on my side, and it lies next to me. Lie on top of Mike, and it threatens to engulf him, like a tidal wave. I can't believe he actually wants to *see* me when we're making love now.

When we first met, in our mid-twenties, it was sex, sex, sex all the time, but then it's perfectly fine to prance around the bedroom exciting your partner with your sexual wiles when your stomach goes straight down from breast to hip.

I'm still a bit sore after the episiotomy. I know it was over seven months ago, but I still feel like I've been zippered. We did just about manage to resurrect our sex life between having Rebecca and Tom, but sex becomes a very different matter, doesn't it, when you have a child? First of all you're so knackered all the time that bed only means one thing: sleep. Then if the urge does suddenly take you during the day, you have to condense twenty minutes of sex into five panting ones, simulating passion while you keep a radar ear out for sounds of footsteps on the stairs, because you know at any moment the small one will become bored with watching *Bambi* and will come to see why Mummy and Daddy have sneaked off to their bedroom.

How often have we lain like two pink naked rabbits with the duvet pulled up to our chins, squeaking, 'Hello, Rebecca. Mummy and Daddy are just having a little cuddle and we are so cold we got into bed.'

'Why,' Rebecca would say in a very stern little voice, 'are your knickers on the floor?'

'Because we're going to have a bath, aren't we, Daddy?' Mike by this time would be completely under the covers, his erection dwindled irretrievably to a tiny fledgling bird.

When I was pregnant with Tom I felt remarkably randy, but Mike wasn't so sure. He felt it was rather a

61

strange way to introduce himself to his new baby, and I guess I can see his point. There is also the Similarity Factor. This is something known to all married couples, in that once you know what works for both of you, you tend to do it over, and over, and over again. It becomes a bit like driving a car: first gear, second gear, and then suddenly up into fifth, with the smoothness of well-oiled machinery. I know Mike finds this very dull indeed, and longs for us to have sex against the Rayburn, in the potting shed, out in the fresh air – anywhere which might make it a bit *different*. I don't think men ever grow out of giving themselves Brownie points for the number and variety of their shags.

I try to disguise the fact that I can't be bothered to *do* anything different by making different *noises*. Well, it's one kind of a change, isn't it? The thing is, I'm sure I used to be very good in bed. No previous boyfriend ever complained, and certainly in the early days Mike was very enthusiastic about my wantonness. It's just that with children, wantonness becomes less of a positive attribute than the ability to clear up sick speedily and effectively.

'What can we do about it?' I whispered, guiltily, to Mike.

'Well, you could be a bit more enthusiastic, for a start,' he said. 'Why can't you ever initiate it?' Because I never really want it that badly, is the truthful answer but not, I surmise, the one he wants to hear. 'You're Carrie. I'm so proud of you. I love you. I love making love to you. I just want you to want me.' I do, I think, miserably. Just not quite as often as you seem to want me, and at such inopportune moments. 'Couldn't you buy some stockings or new underwear?' says Mike. I think sadly of the heap of greying and tattered bits of cotton and nylon that is my underwear drawer.

'Yes, I will,' I lie.

Monday 9 March

This is a Red Letter Day. A missive from the bank arrived this morning saying that our new mortgage has been AGREED (largely due to the increase in Mike's salary) and that our Personal Mortgage Adviser is Nancy. We are borrowing right up to the limit, almost three times our joint salaries, and I think it's probably better if I don't think about the hugeness of the sum AT ALL. So Mike then had to ring up the estate agent to put in the offer, which made him late for work. I rang work and said my car wouldn't start. Hurrah for cars. There are some advantages to driving a car which looks like it should belong to the Beverly Hillbillies – everyone believes you when you claim it has broken down.

While Mike made the call we all hung round the stairwell with bated breath, until he made shooing motions for us to go away so he could be grown-up. They said they would call us back later. Later! How can I wait until later? Mike was very cool about it, and said we must not get over-excited, although this was a bit like closing the stable door after the horse had bolted, literally, because I told Rebecca last night that if we got the house she could have a pony. This meant she had been hopping about like a tightly coiled spring ever since she got up, making neighing noises and galloping up and down the stairs. Claire seemed pleased too, I guess because it will give her far more status to be the nanny to the family who live at Lawn Farm, rather than Grove Cottage, which sounds like you've only given it a name to be posh. It is clearly a house which has been around for quite some time, and can be slipped casually into the conversation *à la* 'Do pop down to Lawn Farm. We're having a small drinks party,' etc. Am I already getting ideas above my station?

At work I found it very hard to concentrate, and

frantically messaged Kate who had the air of someone who knows she should be very pleased for her dear friend, but is actually a teeny bit jealous and trying hard not to show it. Why is it that when our friends do well or buy something that we really want, it's so much harder to cope with than when people we loathe do? Mike didn't call until well after three. Then when he did, he said, 'I've got good news and I've got bad news. Which do you want first?'

'The good news, the good news!' I squeaked.

'They've accepted our offer,' he said.

'The bad news?'

'Now all we have to do is sell our house and pay for it.' Pshaw to that. Like Scarlett O'Hara, I will think about that tomorrow.

Wednesday 11 March
Got home at nine tonight, knackered. I had to ring Claire at seven to say it was very unlikely I would be home on time, and could she stay on to baby-sit? She said yes, but sounded very tight-lipped indeed. Rebecca grabbed the phone from her and said,

'When are you coming home, Mummy? I got a star today for reading and Charlotte Parsons fell over and her knee bled all over me. Then I—'

'Rebecca,' I said, gently. 'Mummy's rather busy at work at the moment, so could you tell me all this later?' Two trains had collided in a small station just outside Birmingham, and my six-year-old daughter was telling me in her tiny, breathy voice about minor playground accidents. Nick had put me in charge of co-ordinating the coverage, while he sent the day producer to the scene, plus the satellite truck.

It was complete mayhem in the office, with the phones ringing constantly, London wanting a feed, punters offering information, worried relatives trying to find out what was happening. We put out a special long bulletin at four, only just getting the piece edited on time – it was like *Broadcast News*, with me hurtling down the corridor waving the Beta tape, leaping over prostrate colleagues and hurdling the tea trolley to get it into the gallery in time. Even though I say it myself, I am particularly good at staying calm in the face of chaos. I think being a parent is very good training for this. If you can maintain your equilibrium while one child is having a hysterical tantrum and another is threatening to throw itself down the stairs, then you can cope with a small train crash.

At the end of the day Nick came up and said, 'Well done,' to all of us, but gave me a special mention. Quite a few people came up and said, 'That was great! You were brilliant!' and I felt exhausted but extremely chuffed. It's great to matter, isn't it? I also felt that our team did a rather better job than Mike's lot, which of course is something I won't point out to him tonight. Not. Mike didn't get home until well after midnight, and then he couldn't sleep, he was so exhilarated. We sat up in the kitchen, swilling glasses of wine we knew we'd regret tomorrow.

Saturday 14 March
Rebecca has been very martyred with me since the telephone incident. I made a special point of getting up extra early on Thursday morning so she could read to me and show me the star in her book, but it didn't wash. Her initial coldness towards Claire seems to have waned, and she's gradually beginning to rely more and more on her instead of me. Yesterday she brought home a picture from school. It was of a big red house, with a huge green path leading up to it, and lots

of billowing black smoke coming out of the chimney. In front of the house, gambolled her (Rebecca's) three-legged pony. At the top it said 'Claire'. Not 'Mummy'.

I didn't find it until I was tidying her room this morning, and saw it propped up on top of the desk my mother had stripped for her last Christmas. 'This is lovely,' I said.

'It's for Claire,' said Rebecca without looking up, intently plaiting her Barbie horse's tail.

'Oh,' I said. 'Nothing for me?'

'Nope. We had to do lots of spellings,' she said.

'Where is your spellings book?' I said, suddenly aware that in the rush and haste of work, I hadn't checked her spellings with her at all that week.

'In my bag, where'd you think,' replied Rebecca, bored. I found the little blue book, and saw she *had* done her spellings every night – with Claire. Ditto her reading book, initialled 'C' after a neat entry every day.

I suddenly realized that I hadn't actually talked to Rebecca's teacher for over a month. I am becoming disconnected from my children. Every morning Claire drives her to school, fusses about with her book bags, her sports holdall, checks she has her recorder, and then kisses her goodbye. It was to Claire that her teacher spoke about her lack of willingness to go out and play in the playground, her success at reading level five, the fact she wouldn't eat semolina. Claire didn't pass any of these messages on to me – I suppose there wasn't any real reason why she should, as she could deal with them. I only found out about these problems embarrassingly, at the parent's evening. Rebecca has all but stopped hassling me about the whereabouts of her gym shoes and her tie – if anything's lost, she says, 'Claire knows where it is.'

This week I'd had to work late almost every night,

caught up in the buzz of a frantically busy news time, obsessed with meeting deadlines. I hadn't even thought about the children or the house, I was just swept up in a maelstrom of immediacy. Nick said at the end of the week that if I kept this up I'd walk the job interview, which happens in a month's time. Bloody Georgia has applied as well, which makes me doubly determined to get it. Her lack of experience really showed this week – she went out to do some interviews of survivors and seemed only to be able to ask one question, 'How do you feel?' It was bone-crushingly bad. She may look as pretty as a picture, but she sure is dumb.

'Let's do some reading now,' I said.

'Nah,' said Rebecca. 'I read to Claire last night and I want to watch telly.'

Sunday 15 March
This morning did not get off to a great start. Knackered after the week at work, it felt incredibly difficult to grind myself up to cope with all the tiny, tiring disasters that accompany looking after two small children. Tom spilt blackcurrant juice from his Tommee Tippee cup all over the floor at half-eight in the morning, and Rebecca then announced loudly that she was not going to go to her swimming lesson, although it was her grade test and I'd carefully packed all the paraphernalia that goes with getting her there. I completely lost my temper, smacking Rebecca hard and yelling at Tom, who burst into loud and terrified sobs. Nobody ever shouted at him. Immediately I felt a total witch and, as Mike walked into the chaos, I burst into tears and ran out. 'What the hell's the matter with you?' he said to my rapidly retreating back, picking Tom out of the sticky mess and soothing Rebecca who

was curled up on the floor, crying and saying, 'I hate my mummy! I want a new one!'

In the bedroom, I stared at myself in the mirror. I was shaking, and my eyes were red raw. Why had I hit Rebecca? I could cope, I could always cope. For goodness' sake, I'd coped with getting up to breastfeed Rebecca three times every night when she was Tom's age, because she was such a lousy sleeper, and worked a full five-day week. I'd never lost my temper like this. What was happening to me? When she had said she wouldn't go, I'd literally felt my blood boiling. All this effort for her and she couldn't even be bothered to help. My hand had whipped out like a snake and I'd hit her hard on the leg before I even realized I was doing it.

The trouble with working full time is that you paint an impossibly rosy glow around your children and forget how bloody irritating looking after them really is. I wanted desperately to lie down, but I couldn't, because Rebecca usually refuses to go into the men's changing rooms with Mike, which means that whenever we go swimming I have to take her. I couldn't not go, either, because we'd already missed two of the lessons and I'm sure the swimming teacher has me marked down as Totally Incompetent Mum.

We're always late for the lessons, hurtling and skidding over the tiles to the side of the pool, Rebecca hastily pulling up the straps of her swimming costume, me trying to give her a hug while Tom attempts to dive head-first into the water. Then I go up to join all the other mums to watch, who sit chatting, perfectly calm, cool and collected. And they all seem to know each other. Why is this? Is there a vast mummy mafia that I haven't been invited to join? I suppose it's the network of school/rainbows/swimming lessons which inter-links them all. When they drop their children off at school, they have time to have a good moan to each other about the little trials and tribulations of coping with young children. I don't have that luxury – I have 'real things' to deal with, which tend to push the niggles and irritations of bringing up children aside.

Rebecca is certainly testing the boundaries at the moment, trying to play me off against Claire. A frequent refrain is: Well, Claire lets me. 'Claire lets me have sweets after school.' 'Claire says it's OK to watch television before school.' 'Claire lets me watch *Neighbours*.' 'Claire doesn't make me go to bed straight after Tom.' 'Claire is not your mummy,' I retort. 'I make the rules in this house.' 'No you don't,' says Rebecca. 'You're never here. I heard Claire say "bugger" after you said you'd be late on the phone. I wanted you to be home on Thursday because I hurt my foot at PE and I wanted to show you the bruise, but Claire wouldn't let me stay up till you got home. She was very cross with me and made me go to my room while she watched telly. I cried and nobody came.'

When I crept back downstairs Mike had efficiently resolved the situation. He'd told Rebecca off for being rude to me, cleaned up Tom and the mess and said that he'd look after Tom so I could take Rebecca on her own, even though he had promised to go and see Bill about borrowing his mower, because we're putting the house on the market this week. Rebecca was sulky all the way to the pool and refused to speak to me at all, but managed to pass her grade. I paid my fiver, got the badge (which I really, really will sew onto her costume, when I find time) and bought her some Skittles. I knelt down to give her a hug, but she turned her face away.

Wednesday 26 March

We have had hordes of people round the cottage since last weekend, which was initially lovely but is now driving us mad. An irritating bloke with a (very new) Discovery, mobile phone and stripy shirt came round from the estate agent's to value it, and was extremely upbeat and positive, and said he thought we'd have no problems at all. 'It's a shame I'm not looking for a house!' he said. (I don't suppose he's ever said that to anyone else ever.) He suggested an asking price lower than the one we wanted, but we said that wouldn't be enough for us to get the house we wanted. He chewed on the aerial of his mobile for a bit, and said he'd see what he could do. Bloody shark. The thing with estate agents is that it doesn't actually make much difference on their commission if we sell for the price we want, but the lower we price it, the quicker it sells, and the faster they make their money.

For the millionth time I wondered if we are doing the right thing, or whether it will all go horribly pear-shaped. For the first lot of viewers, I did all the traditional things like sticking a (bought) loaf of bread in the oven to make the kitchen smell like I'm the type of woman who makes her own bread, and put on some freshly ground coffee. But they were complete peasants, and stomped round the house pointing out all the defects, of which of course there are many. I tried desperately to emphasize its good points (there must be some) while they wrenched open the airing cupboard and peered in, tutting. Such a shame a large piece of plaster fell on their heads. Mike too was very cheery at first, but by the fifth lot on Sunday, he'd decided that inverse psychology was clearly going to be the answer. And it kept him amused. 'This is a horrible little shed,' he said as we all picked our way through the mud of the garden. 'Far too small, and the roof leaks.' 'What kind of central heating is it?' 'Oil. Very, very expensive,' he replied, while I stared at him with my mouth open.

Rebecca is becoming paranoid at the thought of leaving her bedroom, and I found her sobbing in her bed on Tuesday night. 'What's the matter, darling?' I said, sitting down and putting my arms round her.

'I don't want to leave this house!' she wailed. 'It's our house! My bedroom won't be the same!'

'Pony,' I said. The sun came out once more.

Saturday 28 March
Mike said, 'I've got some good news for you.' He was lying in bed this morning with an amused look on his face as I attempted to haul myself into my pre-Tom jeans. Tom was propped up in front of *Postman Pat* in his playpen downstairs, and Rebecca had stayed the night at Jill's house – she and Jill's daughter Susie are complete soul mates; they spend all their time giggling and pinching each other.

'What?' I said, rocking backwards and forwards to achieve enough momentum for a roll onto my front. Maybe I could get to my knees . . . ?

'Steve at work has a place in the Rockies he lets out for holidays. He wondered if we wanted to go for a week after Easter. The ski-ing's supposed to be fabulous.'

'Great,' I said. 'But how much will it be?'

'Well, he's said we can have the house for free, because it hasn't been booked that week, and I reckon we could swing it on air miles . . .' A small bubble of excitement was growing in my stomach . . . Whoopee! A real holiday!

'The kids will love it,' I said, enthusiastically. 'Rebecca can learn to ski and I'm sure Tom would go in a back-pack and if not he'll just love playing in the snow and . . .'

'Carrie,' said Mike. 'I wasn't thinking of taking the children with us.'

Oh. Oh *heavens*. A *grown-up* holiday. We haven't had one of those since Mike whipped me off for a fabulously expensive holiday to France after Rebecca was born, and I pined all the way round the Dordogne, rushing into mysteriously complicated phone boxes, fighting my way through incomprehensible French directions to speak to my mother, who would invariably say, 'Everything is fine, darling. Just go off and enjoy yourself. I managed to bring you lot up successfully, didn't I?' No, I'd think grimly, how we survived is a miracle, before padding back to the car, where Mike sat tapping his fingers on the wheel, smiling indulgently. 'Nobody dead yet? Your mother not managed to set fire to the cottage?' All very well for him to laugh, but he doesn't *know* my mother like I do. She gives the impression of being a completely normal person – apart from her tendency to chat in an animated fashion to herself – whereas she is in fact an alien from another planet.

'Who would we get to look after the kids? Your mother?' NO. Not that again.

'Claire.'

'Of course!' No problem.

'We'll just pay her extra, because she'll have to stay over.' Mike is smiling so happily I stride over to him with legs straight out in front of me like a robot, to give him a very careful cuddle. Ouch! I made the mistake of trying to bend in the middle. I will need a block and tackle to get down the stairs, or perhaps one of those disabled stair-lifts. But the button is done up. If I concentrate very hard, I'm sure they will loosen up during the day.

'And, Carrie,' said Mike, 'it'll give us a chance to have a good time *on our own,* for once.' Oh, I think. Sexual Olympics. Still, I'll be safe. I'll never ever manage to get these jeans off ever again.

Monday 30 March
Breaking the news about the ski-ing holiday to Rebecca was not easy. 'Daddy and I have something to tell you,' I said, bravely. 'We've been given a house to go and stay in, just for a week, but I'm afraid it's very cold there and not the best place for children, and you'd be very bored. You'll get to stay here with Claire and have lots of lovely outings and then I'll take you up to Granny's when I get back—'

'NO!' yelled Rebecca, horrified. 'You're not going away without me! You're always leaving me behind! Every day!' Then she ran to her bedroom and slammed the door shut.

'That went well,' observed Mike.

Claire did not seem very thrilled at the prospect either when I asked her this evening. 'I've been meaning to ask you,' she said. 'You know the hourly rate we agreed? Well, I was talking to my friend Helen – you know, who works with the Hendersons – and she's getting much more than I am per hour. Would it be possible to increase my wages slightly, because I'm finding it a bit hard to manage . . .'

A bit hard to manage? She's driving round in a brand-new car, she lives with her mum and dad, she seems to spend all of her salary on new clothes and make-up and she wants *more*! Completely unreasonable. 'Fine,' I said. 'We'll put it up from this month. Now, do you think you could manage the week? I'll put the dogs in kennels and if you get stuck I'm sure my mother would help—'

'No,' she said. 'I'll be fine. But would you mind if my boyfriend came to stay? I'm actually . . . living with him, not my mum.' Aha! Really! All this time I've thought she was the last surviving virgin in Oxfordshire and in reality she's shacked up with some Hooray Henry farmer-type!

'No problem,' I said, 'as long as you can look after the children OK . . .' I resolve privately not to let this little detail slip to Mike. I have a sneaking feeling he would be a bit funny about boyfriends in our house . . .

Tuesday 31 March
'Right,' I said to Kate this morning at work. 'You know that health farm you were on about? Well, I have two weeks in which to lose a substantial amount of weight in order not to look like a barrage balloon on skis. Fix it up for next weekend if you can.'

'Hooray!' said Kate, 'you're being allowed out to play,' before swishing off in her latest grey silk suit. The last thing she needs to do is lose weight.

Memo to myself: I *must* get some fat friends.

4

APRIL

Thursday 2 April

Health farm weekend looms, and my cellulite is marshalling its defences against being massaged out of existence. My money's on the cellulite. It's been there a long time and we're talking *cunning* here. Kate booked our little treat straight away and it seems ruinously expensive, as the free press weekend idea has not materialized. I think it was a ruse to get me to agree to go. I have deliberately rounded down the cost for Mike and just hope he does not decide to check our credit card bill this month, which has a very nasty habit of listing exactly where you've been frivolously spending money.

He has agreed enthusiastically to look after the children this weekend – 'You need a break from all of us' (blimey) – but has demanded an elaborate back-up system just in case a crisis blows up at work and he needs to swoop in like Batman. Why do men need to feel they are so indispensable? Whenever Mike goes anywhere he leaves a whole battalion of phone numbers and addresses and fax numbers, whereas I am just so delighted to be away from work I jump in horror at the sound of the telephone and refuse to read newspapers in case there is an advert in bold letters saying,

'URGENT MESSAGE FOR CARRIE ADAMS: YOUR HOUSE HAS BURNT DOWN AND YOU ARE BEING SUED.'

I think men like to feel they have a get-out clause just in case the holiday proves too boring/child-orientated/stressful. Just to keep the peace and allow myself to get away on my own – something I feel very guiltily excited about – I have asked Jill if she can come to the rescue if necessary. She is a bit tight-lipped about the whole venture because she desperately wants to come along to the health farm, but I just cannot see Kate and Jill together. I know I would feel like a bone being pulled in two very different directions. At least Kate and I have work in common, Jill and Kate have practically no common ground at all, apart from both being women. Anyway, I want to feel like a glamorous single person just for once, and the thread that binds Jill and me is our children, so we would inevitably end up talking endlessly about schools and what more can be done to turn our children into prodigious readers.

Kate horrified me yesterday by saying she hoped there would be some fit men at the health farm (it isn't one of those women-only places, eek) because she thinks Oliver deserves a good scare (she is coming round to the commitment-phobic way of thinking I have long suspected about him). The thought of attractive men sent me into a complete panic, because I cannot cope with men at all since I got married, *especially* attractive ones. Mike is profoundly jealous. In fact the nearest I ever came to leaving him was when he threw a complete strop at a wedding of one of my friends, when he realized the very interesting and funny man we had been chatting to for the past half-hour was in fact an ex-boyfriend and had therefore had *intimate knowledge* of me – something he cannot bear to think about at all.

I really think he would have liked me to have remained a virgin until my wedding night but since we were both teenagers in the seventies this was a pretty unlikely concept, and if I *had* been a virgin with white lacy pie-collars, flat shoes and an interest in Bible readings he wouldn't have fancied me anyway. I actually find meeting his old girlfriends fascinating, unless of course they are tall and slim and more attractive than me. The ugly ones I like.

If I do fancy someone now I am rendered completely inarticulate and go bright red like a teenager. I find it very hard to believe that men could fancy me these days anyway, so if anyone does ever come on strong I start pointedly brushing back my hair so they can see my wedding ring. I seem to have lost the art of flirting – I can't play the game any more, so God knows what would happen if Mike and I ever broke up. I'd have to join one of those rural dating agencies which pairs you up with a mentally subnormal farmer who has three ears due to generations of inbreeding.

I suppose my biggest fear is that I *might* be tempted by some glamorous man and then where would that leave our marriage? Mike and I give each other a pretty long leash at parties, and it's so wonderful to know that you don't have to try and pick anyone up – you know whom you're going home with. If I think Mike is spending an over-long period of time with a woman I judge to be dangerous stuff then one long, hard stare seems to do the trick, as does a subtle arm slipped around the waist and a murmured, 'Do you think we ought to ring the baby-sitter to check everything's all right, darling?' Pretty effective. I don't *think* Mike has ever given me cause for concern, but how do you ever really know?

Already this week I have waxed my legs, a job I had been putting off for weeks and weeks because it is not only tiresome but also extremely painful. I realized the time had come when I looked down at my legs whilst climbing into the bath and saw they had begun to resemble those of a llama. I have bought an extremely expensive new type of conditioner being promoted by yet another celebrity hairdresser, which made me feel very happy indeed. I have also painted my toenails a daring shade of cherry red, am foregoing all dairy and wheat products, have given up alcohol (temporarily) and am drinking a gallon of water a day. It may make your skin glow, but it also condemns you to enforced lengthy periods in the ladies toilet. The chocolate machine at work is also looking lifeless and dusty from the loss of my daily caress. I am sure it will all be worth it when I emerge like a thin butterfly from the cellulite-ridden cocoon which has been masquerading as my body.

Friday 3 April
I woke this morning at five, my brain in a fever of confusion. There is so much to remember. Does Mike know Rebecca's swimming costume is hanging on the rack in the kitchen and that the lesson is at eleven on Saturday? (I have made her promise to go into the men's changing room – if she won't he will have to stand by the door of the ladies' and yell.) Does Mike know that the catch on Tom's pushchair is faulty and will not snap automatically into place, and if not jabbed severely with a knee will suddenly catapult Tom into orbit? Will Claire remember to take Tom's baby seat out of her car and give it to Mike, otherwise Mike will have to drive with Tom wedged between his knees? Have I told Mike that Rebecca is going to her friend Eleanor's party on Sunday and that the present is on the windowsill by the telephone and that Rebecca

must write the card herself so that Eleanor's mum can see how well-formed and mature Rebecca's handwriting has become? Does Mike know where Eleanor's house actually is?

I tried to give him a long lecture last night on all the things he needs to remember about the minutiae of the children's lives at the weekend, but to be honest, I don't really think he gave me his full and unqualified attention. In fact, as soon as I began to talk his eyes started to glaze over and although he appeared to be listening, I knew he wasn't. It is the look that comes over his face when I try to give him directions – men do not believe women can tell them how to get *anywhere*. Still, he's a man who runs a large and successful news station so he must be able to look after two small children on his own for a weekend, mustn't he? Mustn't he?

Last night I spent a joyful half-hour packing my small bag, humming to myself as I tucked away all kinds of things I never would if I was going away with Mike and the children – things like bath oil and face cream and a large romantic novel, which I imagine I will have lovely, long, luxurious and undisturbed hours to enjoy. I am determined that I am not going to spend all weekend wondering about how Mike is coping and whether the children are missing me. This weekend is for me, although of course its ostensible purpose is to make my body lithe and lovely for our ski-ing holiday. Hmmm. Still not sure how I feel about that, despite Mike's evident enthusiasm, to which I can safely attribute his willingness to look after the children this weekend. All part of his plot to get me on my own and turn me from an earth mother into a sex goddess.

Sunday 5 April

My skin is soft and peach-like from the application of so many expensive unguents, and I feel curiously indolent, like a three-toed sloth. Kate and I immediately rendered ourselves inarticulate and helpless from our first meeting with receptionist Samantha, who was a dead ringer for Claudia Schiffer until she opened her mouth, when out came an approximation of gentility masking pure Essex girl. We had parked Kate's snazzy new Golf prominently at the front door – the car park was full of Porsches and even a few Rollers – and swept up the front reception as to the manor born. We had mutually decided in the car that for the benefit of strangers we were both going to be actresses this weekend, called Tiffany and Laetitia, just to make life a little more interesting.

The health farm was one of those completely over-the-top stately homes which the owners (who according to the brochure had become multi-millionaires after working their way up from a small ironmongers in Preston) had furnished in a manner they presumed to be appropriate to a period country house. Everything which could be swagged and tailed was, coupled with those ruched curtains which look like a hen's bum. The final touch were the paintings of the owner and his wife in period costume, hung prominently in the mock-grandeur of the flocked-wallpaper dining room. Samantha showed us round while describing our health regime this weekend, which she clearly took very seriously indeed. I have to say that we didn't, and were immensely cheered by the sight of an oak-panelled 'bar and rest area'. Yippee. Booze. After our tour of the 'lounge and beauty areas', courtesy of Samantha's strangled vowels, and listened in horror to the length and complexity of our 'beauty schedule', Kate and I felt impelled to order champagne from room service to be enjoyed in our pale yellow chintzy twin bedroom with 'gold' taps on the bath. Not a good start to a weekend of Spartan self-denial.

Naturally enough, I phoned Mike to say we had arrived safely *before* I began imbibing, because he has certain views about myself and alcohol – i.e. that I become immediately helpless and likely to be ravished if I take as much as one sip without him being there to protect me. He can spot immediately from the sound of my voice if I have been drinking, no matter how carefully I articulate.

The phone rang for what seemed like an inordinately long time, and was eventually answered by a panting Rebecca. In the background was what sounded like a loud roaring and swooshing noise coming from the direction of the bathroom. 'Daddy's bathing Tom,' said Rebecca. 'He's getting very wet.'

'How are you?' I said. 'How was school?'

'Fine,' Rebecca said, artlessly. 'Claire was in a big rush to go, and she took my book bag with her in the car.' There was a pause, and then a big, breathy sob. 'I miss you, Mummy! I want you to read my story because Daddy says I have to tidy my room first and you know I can't lift my duvet!'

'It's all right, darling,' I said, trying to be soothing, while Kate made a mock-tragic face and waved the glass of champagne at me encouragingly. 'Don't bother to bring Daddy to the phone, just tell him Mummy got here safely and I'll see you all on Sunday evening.'

'Daddy's taking us to Legoland tomorrow,' said Rebecca, brightening up.

'How lovely,' I said. Then an awful thought struck me. 'Did Claire remember to give Daddy Tom's car seat?'

'I didn't see her give it to him,' said Rebecca.

'I love you,' I said, and hurriedly rang off. 'Give me

the champagne,' I said to Kate. 'Now.'

After the champagne it was downhill all the way. We were the most noisy people in the dining room by a *very long way* and choosing deliberately from the 'red' (for caution) menu, we rattled our way through two bottles of expensive plonk and ended up in the 'oak-panelled' bar, being chatted up by two merchant wankers called Rupert and Miles, who'd sidled over. They had suspiciously pale bands around their third fingers. They were staying as part of an up-market stag do, and gormlessly took in the whole Tiffany/Laetitia thing. I found myself adopting the language-*à-la*-Samantha and told them I'd recently had a small part in *EastEnders*. They were exceptionally impressed but I became rather concerned when one of Rupert's toned thighs began to press against my own on the 'chaise longue'. Eek. Perhaps he really thought I fancied him.

I sobered up very quickly and told Kate – who was by now leaning forward none-too-wisely in a very short red satin halter-neck dress, nose-to-nose with Miles – that I was going to bed. I then spent a long time meandering up and down the very long corridors which all looked the same, occasionally bumping into the walls and hiccuping gently to myself. When I did locate our room I owlishly inserted the key while giving myself an animated running commentary of my movements, and then the bed very kindly came up to meet my descending form.

I lay there trying to stop the room spinning and shivered at the memory of Rupert's thighs. My last conscious and consoling thought at what I had escaped was, Better the willy you know. I didn't hear Kate come in at all, and I rather suspect it was closer to morning than night-time. Shameless hussy. I for one am too old to snog in corridors.

On Saturday morning we viewed our muesli with

something less than enthusiasm. Ahead of us was a highly organized day, about which we were feeling rapidly more and more paranoid. There was nothing to do, but we were late for everything. 'It's nearly ten! We should be in aerobics by now!' one of us would howl, as we lingered over cappuccinos in the 'rest and relaxation area'. Aerobics with a hangover I would not recommend, and the instructor did not have the nickname 'Tarzan' for nothing. Clearly gay, with a highly impressive Lycra pouch, he was taking extreme pleasure in pushing all of the leotarded ladies who lunch through a punishing schedule. I positioned myself carefully at the back next to the fattest woman I could find, whereas Kate immediately went into competitive mode at the front, and ostentatiously put two squares under each side of the step so she'd have to work harder. How masochistic can you get?

At eleven we each had a 'treatment'. We hung about feeling self-conscious while a team of white-coated beauty therapists who all looked and sounded like Samantha filed in to collect their 'ladies'. I had opted for the algae thalassotherapy bath, because it claimed to be the instant cure for cellulite. This proved not the most sensible activity for someone with an intense hangover either. Instead of being able to drift off gently to sleep whilst being massaged (although I do worry about this as I have a tendency to snort while asleep in inappropriate places) I lay like a steaming kipper in a very smelly bath of seaweed. I'm paying for this? After half an hour of this whelk-like experience, the therapist hauled me out of the bath like the monster from the black lagoon. She then wrapped my slimy, slippy, green body into a huge piece of tin foil. At some point this must become pleasurable, I thought to myself as I lay alone on one of those high narrow orthopaedic beds, basting gently and making loud, crinkly noises whenever I dared to move. As she removed the foil, I realized what it must feel like to be *en croûte*.

She then proceeded to give me what I can only describe as an up-market bed-bath, involving exfoliating grit and a hand mitt. The entire process took almost two hours, and I emerged feeling like I had been de-scaled, with a pervasive and noxious whiff of the briny. 'What happened to you?' asked Kate, who was glowing and relaxed after her aromatherapy massage.

'I have been to the seaside,' I said, 'and I'm never going again.'

Lunch was a sad concoction of green things followed by brightly coloured fruit things, and then more 'treatments'. I had a facial, and completely alarmed my beauty therapist when she asked what beauty products I normally used. 'Water and a bit of soap?' I ventured back, carefully.

'Dear, dear,' she said. 'Your skin is extremely dehydrated.' My face then went glub, glub, and thirstily drank up an entire pot of very expensive moisturizer to make up for all the years of being starved of Estée Lauder night cream etc. I must give it more to drink, I thought musingly before drifting off to sleep, only to be wakened by the sound of myself emitting a loud and deeply embarrassing snort.

After the previous night's excesses, dinner that evening was a more restrained affair, and I must say I was beginning to feel a little restless. Being without the children is all very well, but I think the anticipation of such an event often far exceeds the actual enjoyment of it. While Kate is a complete love, I was beginning to find her a bit self-obsessed. It took her ages and ages to get ready and she seemed genuinely anguished when she accidentally mussed up one of her newly painted nails. I am now trained to get ready in about half an hour – any longer and Mike begins to rev the car and threaten to go without me. And I do not think I have updated my make-up technique since my older sister and I learnt to highlight our upper lids with white gloss which came free with our teenage magazine. Ordinary make-up is lipstick, eyeliner, mascara and blusher – extra-special make-up means the addition of gold eye shadow.

Kate also went on and on that night about her relationship with Oliver. (A bit rich seeing as I had prised out of her the fact she *had* snogged the Miles character who thank God had taken Rupert and his City pals back to London on Saturday morning in a succession of Porsches and Jaguars.) She also, on much closer inspection, seems slightly neurotic – something that had never struck me about her before, because she is always so full of confidence at work. Her clothes may well be immaculate and she does have everything I seem to spend so much of my life longing for – all the time in the world to have long, dreamy baths, the money to buy hoards of designer clothes and a house which wouldn't have looked out of place in *Homes & Gardens*. She can leave a room and know it will remain exactly as she's left it – something I can never do, as the minute a room is tidied, Rebecca zooms in and creates a wave of chaos around her, trailing beads, Barbie clothes, felt tips with the tops off and floating pieces of brightly coloured paper in her wake.

'It's just that I don't have anyone to do things *for*,' Kate said, as we aimlessly pushed bits of Italian lettuce around our plates on Sunday lunch-time. I wanted to go to the pub down the road and have beer and steak and kidney pie, but Kate wouldn't let me. Cheating. 'You're so lucky. You've got Mike and the children – you've *done* all that. And,' she continued, not quite meeting my eyes, 'Mike is *so* gorgeous, you're really lucky to have him. I've got it all to come, and now I'm thirty-four, it seems more and more of a remote possibility. I really wish I'd got on with it in my twenties like you did.' (I seem to remember she was slightly snooty at the time, as if marriage was rather plebeian and not what we career women did. When I told her Mike and I were getting married – we were all working together in radio at the time – she was totally taken aback.)

'I've got every *thing* I want,' said Kate. 'So why do I feel so hopeless, as if the future's just a big void? Of course, marriage is so old-fashioned, but it would be nice to be *asked*.' My secret thoughts on this matter are that if Oliver did want to marry her, he would have asked her straight away, like Mike did with me, not wait five years to pop the question. You either know if you want to marry someone or you don't, and if you dither, then I for one wouldn't rush out and set up a joint account. Also he's on to an excellent number in that Kate has created for him an extremely beautiful home, a perfect social life, and presumably the sort of riveting sex life involving minute silk underwear that Mike can only dream about. There's also something slightly precious about him, with his Boss shirts and his Armani suits, slip-on loafers and Japanese-sports-car-like-a-penis. I just cannot see him picking up a small grubby baby, or humping bin-bags full of used Pampers out to the rubbish bin. To me, he seems the sort of man who will take to golf in later years, wearing all the latest checky yellow outfits, and become extremely fussy about club rules.

But of course, I lied. 'I'm sure he sees you and he as a permanent thing – you've bought the house together, haven't you?' I said reassuringly. 'He's probably just scared of putting you off, because you've always made such a big thing about not wanting commitment and being so keen on your career. Does he have any idea you want children?'

'I'm scared to bring up the subject, to be honest,' Kate said. 'It just comes out as so neurotic and insecure, as if I'm scared of losing him. So whenever friends ask us when we're going to get married and have kids I just laugh and say there's loads of time and we're enjoying ourselves too much. But there isn't and we aren't.' She stared morosely down into her salad and picked out bits of garlic croûton. 'And what if I can't have children? I don't want to end up some mad bat of forty-five on endless IVF.'

I put on my deeply sympathetic face and tried not to look smug. I've got my family at home. Just thinking of them gave me a warm, rosy glow, and suddenly I wanted to be far away from here, from this chintzy, fussy dining room with its gilt-lacquered chairs, back to our messy, comfy sitting room. I may not be a tiny size any more or have thighs as smooth as dolphin skin, but I do have a family.

Monday 6 April

It was worth going away, just for the home-coming, I reflected as I drove to work this morning. Kate and I had perhaps foolishly booked another treatment on Sunday afternoon, because by then I'd had enough of lying like a beached whale on a narrow uncomfortable bed, and had a strong urge to yell, 'Get *off* me!' when yet another white-coated Tracy came at me with her hands covered in detoxifying massage oil. Totally unused to lying still for longer than five minutes at a time, I felt disorientated and urgently wanted to plunge myself back into reality. Staying at a health farm is like being incarcerated in a lunatic asylum. Everyone wears white coats; you spend the day in a dressing-gown; you are forcibly removed from the real world; forbidden to leave, and everything you put in your mouth is controlled. You become absurdly obsessed with the minute rituals and timings of the day, as you have nothing else to think about. It is excellent preparation for life in a geriatric home as well.

Kate drove me home, and we chatted in a desultory fashion, lulled into a torpor-like state by all that massaging and indulgence. We said goodbye on a slightly falsely bright note: 'It's been wonderful, I've really enjoyed myself. We *must* do it again soon,' Kate said, leaning over to close the car door.

'Yes, it was fabulous. Thanks so much for arranging it. I'll see you tomorrow.' As she drove away, I felt a profound sense of relief. Kate seemed to want me to confess my problems with Mike (I suppose we all like friends to dish dirt of this kind) but somehow I felt it was rather unfair to Mike, who wasn't there to defend himself. It never felt quite so disloyal unburdening myself to Jill, because Mike doesn't rate her opinions much anyway. But Kate's he does, and somehow it felt not on to have revealed just how much of a selfish bastard he could be at times – especially as he is being such a poppet at the moment. So I know I'd disappointed her by muttering vaguely that he could be rather unhelpful but really we were fine, honestly, although I found working and looking after the children exhausting.

Spending such a long time together highlighted what was different about each of our lives. How much we need similarities and shared experiences to cement friendships. Away from the common ground of the office, Kate and I were as un-alike as fire and water. Maybe she wouldn't want to go away with me again. Maybe I did imply that Oliver was a hopeless case and she'd be better off looking for someone else to nest with. Either way, I hope it won't affect our friendship, as I do need her at work to keep me going against the Georgias and the Cassandras. Friends are a very useful convenience, like food.

Opening the front door, a gorgeous smell of cooking cream, wine and roasting meat assailed my nose. After a weekend of inanimate green objects, I was ready to kill for anything with real calories. It was by now half past seven, and I anticipated finding a still-dressed Tom and Rebecca hurtling about a bomb-hit house, with toys and clothes strewn everywhere and the prospect of bath and stories still to face. But there was silence, with just the sound of bubbling pans on the oven, and a gentle murmuring coming from Rebecca's room. I went in to Tom first, and there he was, tucked under his blankets, fast asleep, his hair fluffy and his face glowing from his bath. There's nothing I like quite so much as a clean sleeping baby. All his clothes were neatly put away, and his books filed away into his little bookcase.

Tip-toeing into Rebecca's room, I found Mike lying on the bed with his arm round her, as they giggled at Winnie-the-Pooh. Rebecca too was fluffy, clean and night-dressed and – total amazement – her school uniform was neatly folded and ready at the end of her bed. 'Wow,' I said, walking over to kiss them both. 'How was it?' I asked Mike.

'Piece of cake,' he said, pulling my face down so he could kiss me properly – just in time for me to see how tired and puffy his eyes were. Good.

'I shall have to go away more often,' I said. 'Don't push it,' he said jokingly, giving his full attention once more to Piglet's fear of the Heffalump.

In the kitchen everything was tidy and clean, a casserole could clearly be seen through the oven door and even the dogs' blankets were folded in their baskets. Better still, a bottle of wine was open and warming by the oven, and I gratefully poured myself a big glass. Outside, the pale light was fading over the apple trees at the bottom of the garden, and the light from the kitchen lamps made small, amber pools on the terracotta pots outside. *Home*, I thought. If anyone comes at me with an exfoliating mitt now, I'll stab them.

Wednesday 15 April

I have been going to the gym at lunch-time from work. Pause to give myself a small round of applause. The beneficial effects of the health farm lasted about a day, after the vast feast Mike had prepared for us and the two bottles of excellent wine we felt compelled to consume. Mike admitted he had really enjoyed being with the kids, and why didn't I leave him alone with them more often? Because you usually make such a palaver about it, was the real answer, but I didn't want to say anything to knock such a perfect atmosphere and said, 'Well, if you feel like that, I will.'

'Why don't you take up a hobby?' he said. 'You used to love going horse-riding. You should make time for that.' By this stage I felt like leaning over to feel his forehead, but he was being completely genuine.

I think a weekend alone made him realize just how much I do do for the children – and that it isn't all tiny, meaningless, invisible tasks that he used to think I frittered my time away on, while he does big, manly and visible things like mowing the grass and clearing out the garage. I may not have had the time of my life at the health farm, but it seems to have given our relationship a kick up the backside.

However, the lithe and lovely butterfly is still some way off, hence the gym. We are due to depart for the Rockies (why are they called that? Are they wobbly?

Might I fall off?) on Saturday, and the past week and a half has passed in a blur of frenetic activity and attempts to make myself look sinuous in a pair of ski pants. I have been slightly hampered in this cause in that I cannot afford to rush out to the big sports shop in Oxford and buy myself the full monty due to the fact that we have no money. We seem to have even less money than ever before. The health farm weekend dug a big chunk out of our budget, as did Mike's trip to Legoland with the children, which they totally adored. No-one as yet has put in an offer on our house (hardly surprising given Mike's off-beat selling methods) and I had already mentally assigned a chunk of cash from the sale to pay off our ever-increasing overdraft.

The Gowers at Lawn Farm are being complete angels and not letting anyone else look round the house now they have accepted our offer, although of course they are perfectly within their rights to do so because we haven't sold our cottage. It is yet another thing for me to be paranoid about, but I can't see them letting any-one else gazump us.

Anyway, the upshot is that I have had to borrow a ski-ing outfit from Jill, who is, bless her, slightly larger than me and not exactly Kate in her approach to *haute couture*. The jacket is OK – red and puffy – but the bottoms are very, well, baggy. I've rolled the waistband over several times but I still cannot achieve the ski-chick effect I'm seeking. At the top: Michelin man; at the bottom: Max Wall. I shall just have to buy one of those fluffy headbands teamed with designer shades, and huge Yak's-feet boots.

I am very excited at the prospect of the holiday, and keep bouncing in my seat at work. In the run-up to it I am being extremely organized *vis-à-vis* the washing and Mike is constantly surprised to open his under-wear and sock drawer to find said items present. The only fly in the ointment is Claire, who does not seem exhilarated at the idea of being left in total charge of Rebecca and Tom for a week, despite the extra money we're giving her. Rebecca is working up a mammoth sulk and is constantly tugging at my heart-strings by finding pictures of snow scenes in magazines and asking pitifully, 'Is this what it will be like on your holiday, Mummy? You will send me a postcard, won't you? Will Father Christmas be there?' I actually think that Claire is rather worried about being left alone with them for such a long time, which is making me rather anxious too. She has asked if she can have my mother's telephone number as a back-up, which makes me very worried indeed, as my mother has all the child-minding skills of Herod.

Friday 17 April
This morning Nick called me into his office. We'd had the interviews for the new job (or 'boards', as the BBC bizarrely calls them) on Monday, and everyone involved had been hanging round with bated breath ever since. As well as a number of internal candidates – including smarmy Georgia, who'd been going round saying it had been a doddle – there had also been some rather impressive people from the independent stations, presumably desperate to catch what is still seen as the gravy-train of the BBC. I sidled in to Nick's office with drooping mien, having convinced myself that I'd done an incredibly bad board redeemed only by the fact that I hadn't actually been physically sick on the carpet.

'Sit down,' said Nick, smiling. (Smiling! A good sign.) 'It's good news. The job's yours. It was a pretty impressive list of candidates but you were the best. Great interview.' It was? 'Now, as I said at the outset, it's going to mean a lot of changes to the management structure here, so there will be some reshuffling and a few noses out of joint. You'll be in charge of overseeing the planning team for television and radio both here and in the East Midlands, so there will be some hopping about, and you'll effectively be taking over Alex's job in the East. You can talk to personnel about salary, but presume we'll be generous – oh, and you'll get a car too. Well done. Happy?' I nodded rather dumbly, feeling as if I'd been struck from a great height by an unexpected thunderbolt. I didn't know if I was happy or not. 'How does Mike feel about the longer hours? No problem with the family?'

'Oh no,' I said, finding from somewhere a smile to stick on my face to indicate confidence I didn't actually feel. 'We've got a nanny now, as you know, and I'm sure she'll be quite happy to work a bit longer.' Will she? 'Thanks a lot, Nick. I'm really going to enjoy it.'

'Thank *you*,' he said. 'You've made a big difference to the team since you got back from . . . erm . . . the baby thing . . . and I really admire the way you soldier on.'

I strongly resisted the urge to stand up and salute, but said instead rather lamely, 'That's marvellous,' and wandered out.

Kate gave me an quizzical 'good or bad?' look and I dredged up a big smile which clearly said, 'Good.' She punched the air, and quite the best thing was Georgia's crestfallen face. Maybe she hadn't done the right thing after all in putting on her very shortest mini-skirt and leaning forward a lot.

Back at my desk, I had to force myself to pick up the phone to ring Mike. He'd been very encouraging about the idea of applying for the job, but I don't think he really thought I'd get it. I had also rather sidled round the issue of longer hours and more travelling, while talking up the good bits about more money and the car. We could say goodbye to the old Volvo, and the new salary would be extremely useful for the mortgage on Lawn Farm, if only someone would make an offer for the cottage. I got through to Mike's secretary (Oh God), who did her Mike's-rather-tied-up-but-I'll-just-see-if-he-can-be-interrupted twaddle before putting me through. I could hear the sound of Mike's deputy Peter and the advertising manager Steve in the background, so they were obviously having a meeting.

'Hi,' said Mike, in his tense I'm-very-busy-make-it-short voice, which immediately put me on the defensive.

'I got the job,' I said. Long pause.

'Well, that's great, isn't it?' he said. 'More money and a car. Brilliant. Look, I'm very tied up at the moment but I'll bring champagne home. Clever you. 'Bye.'

If I was a very brave and sensible person I would have talked through all the implications of the job with Mike while we consumed the Piper Heidsieck this evening. But I'm not and I didn't. The chaos of packing for both of us, with fuzzy champagne-brain, took most of the evening, as did the list of instructions for Claire to be left on the kitchen table, alongside the wodge of cash we were giving her to enable us to leave.

When I went in to kiss Rebecca, she was tear-stained and awake. 'Don't go,' she said, wrapping her arms powerfully around my neck. 'I don't want Claire to look after me. She gets cross if I make a mess. Why can't I go to Jill's?'

'Because Tom would be all alone with no-one to play with,' I said. 'You can go and see Susie whenever you like. It'll be fine. I'll ring you as soon as I get there and Daddy and I will bring lots of lovely presents home.'

Claire is due to come at six in the morning, so Mike and I can get to the airport in time. All bags are packed, and placed in a very organized fashion by the front door. Turtle and Angus are hiding under the kitchen table, traumatized by the sight of suitcases. At least with Claire being here they don't have to go into kennels, which means they come home with no bark and fleas.

I crept in to give Rebecca a last kiss just before we went to bed several hours later. She was fast asleep, one leg out of the duvet, hair damp with night-sweat and arms tightly clasping her moth-eaten teddy. She'd started to make a little card which was lying on the bed, with a big reindeer with wonky antlers and Christmas trees on the front. Inside it said, 'I love you Mummy and Daddy. Tak this with you to see Father Chirstmus.' Her cheeks were still damp as I kissed her.

Sunday 19 April

I cannot *believe* this place. It is so far removed from the sphere of my normal existence that I feel like I'm on the moon. It's all so . . . Somewhere there is a perfect descriptive word but all I can think of is: *big*. As we drove in our hired four-by-four from the airport towards the mountains, I couldn't get over how incredibly gorgeous the mountains were, and sent Mike mad by wittering on about the colour of the trees and the beauty of the landscape, constantly exclaiming, 'It's so lovely!' But alas men are not big on scenery. The house is like an up-market log cabin, with roaring fires and even bear-skins (yeah, a bit kitschy) on one of the walls. Like everything on this continent, the kitchen's full of the very latest gadgets like juicers and egg-slicers and coffee-grinders, which I have had to play with immediately. Mike's friend Steve – who was out here ski-ing last week – has been incredibly kind and left the fridge full of the most delicious and foreign-looking food.

As soon as we arrived and dumped our bags on the patchwork bedspread, I made us both a steaming cup of coffee which we took out onto the terrace. It overlooks an awe-inspiring view of trees, mountains and lakes, and we can even see the cable-car at the ski resort, which is only three kilometres away. (I'm getting the lingo.) We sat down in two rocking chairs, swathed in our thick anoraks, and smiled gleefully at each other. Just us. No children, no work, no ties. Mike reached over and took my hand. 'Isn't this brilliant?' he said.

'Certainly is, Mr Adams,' I said.

'Say,' said Mike, in an awful attempt at a Canadian accent, 'fancy a roll under the old moose-head?'

'Sure thing,' I said. And roll it was, as we both totally let go of all inhibitions, with no risk of tiny hands knocking gently on the door with urgent demands. After about an hour (something of a record for us) I struggled up from my prone position in Mike's arms (shagging on the floor gets much harder as you get older) and got a big heap of bread, ham, tomatoes, cheese and beer from the fridge. Sod the diet, I'm now thin enough.

It felt so natural to be able to wander about naked, and later that night, lying together in the big old bed, I felt we were so tuned in to each other and completely at peace. 'I'd better ring home,' I said eventually.

'Don't,' said Mike. 'Just leave it. They'll be fine. Come here.' So I didn't ring, and turned back once more to rekindle the flames of our romance. It was like living in a Danielle Steel novel, although I don't suppose any of her heroines ever accidentally farted mid-shag.

Monday 20 April

When I woke this morning, Mike was still fast asleep beside me, his arm lying heavily over my shoulders and his legs curled into mine just as we'd slept after making love, like two spoons. As I opened my eyes, swimming slowly to the surface from a deep and voluptuous sleep in this hugely comfortable bed, it took me several moments to remember where I was. Instead of looking out on the old apple tree at the bottom of our garden, I was looking at a stunning vista of trees, mountains and snow. The old bed was pushed up close to the window, so you almost felt you were part of the mountain. And it was so *quiet*. No Tom chatting happily to himself, making his cot-toy sing the tinny little tune he found so comforting; no discordant recorder-playing coming from Rebecca's room or purposeful footsteps on the stairs. I yawned and stretched, savouring the bliss of not having to drag myself out of bed to change nappies, administer Weetabix and boot the dogs out into the garden. At home, waking up is immediately followed by the pressing need to get up and *do* things. Here, I could just lie still, and think.

I pushed my toes down to the bottom of the bed and turned towards Mike, moving his arm off me. He moaned in his sleep, and readjusted his arm to curl around my back. In his sleep, he looked so vulnerable, so unlike the completely-in-charge-authoritative-person he is when he's awake. The side of his tanned face nearest the pillow was creased with sleep, his hair flopping down over one eye, which made him look like a young boy. How beautiful he is, I thought, smoothing it out of his eyes. I tend to take his looks for granted — when you've lived with someone for so long you forget to notice what they look like; their faces are so familiar it's almost impossible to make an objective judgement. But just occasionally, when I see him walking down the street towards me, his jacket over his shoulder and other women turning to catch another glimpse of his blond hair and broad shoulders, I think, God, he is good-looking, and my stomach does that funny fish-flip it used to when we were first going out.

I wonder if he ever thinks that about me. He used to tell me I was beautiful when we were first together – he'd pull back the sheets to the bottom of the bed so he could gaze at my naked body as I lay, half-excited, half-embarrassed, while he traced his fingers around the contours of my shape, which were rather smaller than they are now.

When we were dancing late at night at parties, and we were both exceedingly pissed, he would go on and on about how much he loved me. I always treated it as a bit of a joke that he adored me so much, because he was so good-looking, whereas I could just about muster pretty. Never beautiful. My face was too round, my curly brown hair too wayward – some days pre-Raphaelite, other days loo brush – ever to be called beautiful. Blonde was beautiful, with long, skinny legs, and a wide, full mouth. I had freckles and a tiny button nose (which Tom has inherited) and I was always too loud, too keen to be one of the lads and have a good time, to be cool and interesting.

I always imagined that Mike should be with a willowy, controlled blonde with a name like Aurelia, rather than a small lively person like me with a tendency to eat a plate of pasta and drink a glass of wine too many. But he was the first man who really seemed to want me, who enveloped me in an almost obsessive cloud of love. When we met I had a huge circle of friends, from university, from growing up at home, whereas he had had a much more restricted upbringing – sent off to boarding school at seven, straight to university and then on to his first newspaper. He had friends, but he didn't seem very close to them, it was more jokes down the pub, mates on the rugby field. He kept people at arm's length. He appeared to envy my ability to make close friends of both sexes, but when I tried to assimilate him into my group of friends they didn't immediately warm to him. They found him slightly reserved, aloof – cold, even.

It was only with me that he let his guard down, as if my friendliness and openness allowed him to reveal his real self, perhaps for the first time. His parents are rather posh and upper-class, and I'd never seen his mother kiss him. He always shook hands with his father, who was very much 'Father', never 'Dad'. It must have been the emotional trauma of having been sent away to school at such a young age – he'd never before allowed himself to show his emotions, or even really admit that he had any. With previous girlfriends, he acknowledged, he had been a bastard. At the time of our marriage, there was much envy that I had 'caught' him, although in reality he'd been much keener on getting married than I was. I think he envied me my family – although my mother is completely mad she has always been very openly loving with myself and my two sisters – and he loved the warmth of our house, although we had far less money and style than his parents.

When we first had the children, I had to teach him how to show love, by giving them constant hugs and kisses, and telling them I loved them all the time, outwardly, openly. Slowly, slowly, he'd begun to be more demonstrative, and now I hear him whispering to Tom and Rebecca that he loves them every night. I don't think his parents ever told him they loved him. To Mike, I have always been this special person who opened the door into the real world, who unlocked a world of love. But more and more now – maybe it's the pressure of his job – I see glimpses of the old Mike coming back, the don't care Mike, whose reserve and snappiness create a chilly barrier around him, and make him unreasonably bad-tempered with the children. I can cope (most of the time) with their squabbles and yells when I've been working all week, so why can't he?

Sometimes I feel I don't really know him any more, and that scares me. Am I enough for him now? Is he getting bored with our life? Would he like me to be more glamorous, more in control, more – heaven forbid – like his mother? I know my inability to stem the tide of mess annoys him, but how can he have a successful working wife, which he claims so much to admire, and have the kind of creature comforts with which his mother surrounded his father? It just doesn't work like that. He does seem to want to make love to me – practically all the time – but is it just because I'm there and he's used to me?

As I stroked his face, one eye flicked open. 'Good morning,' I said.

'God,' he said, stretching over, squashing me to reach his watch on the bedside table. 'Is that the time? I slept like a log. We should be up and ski-ing.'

'I know,' I said, wriggling my hands down to touch him. 'But it's so cosy in here. Don't get up yet.'

'Too late,' he said, 'I'm already up,' and, lifting the covers with a Tarzan-roar, he rolled over on top of me. I put my demons back in their cupboard. When we're on our own, without the children, we get on so well. Why do I sometimes feel that we're not a real family?

Wednesday 22 April
When I did ring home yesterday – having bravely left it until then as Claire had our number at the house in

the event of disasters – she sounded slightly twitchy and nervous. It was at eight o'clock English time, and in the background I could hear the thump of loud music. Clearly her boyfriend had arrived, and they were having something of a party. 'I'm not interrupting anything, am I?' I said, fishing for details.

'Of course not,' she said. 'I've just put Rebecca to bed and Tom's fast asleep. We were out all day and they're both tired out. Are you having a good holiday? How's the weather and the ski-ing?' I could sense the wild gesticulation of her arms to make someone turn the music down. There were sounds of muffled laughter, clearly indicating there were more than two people present.

'Have you got some friends over?' I asked casually.

'Just my sister and her boyfriend,' replied Claire. 'Really, everything's fine here. Rebecca was a bit weepy after you went but she's OK now. We went swimming today after school and they both had a really good time. Harry' – the boyfriend – 'took her up to the top of the big slide and she was really brave.'

The big slide? The big slide *Mike*'s afraid to go down? I quelled my beating heart. But what if she had an accident? It would take us almost a day to get home and she could be dead by then. And what if Tom hurt himself? He's so little and prone to sudden and unexpected topples. All kinds of horrible thoughts filled my head. 'You will be . . . careful,' I said to Claire, trying not to sound neurotic or accusing.

She picked up immediately on my tone of voice and said, rather abruptly, 'Look, there's no problem at all. This call must be costing you a fortune. Honestly, I'll ring if even the slightest thing goes wrong. See you on Saturday. 'Bye.'

The phone went dead, and I stood for quite a long time in the hall of the cabin, staring into space, feeling helpless. So what if she was having a small party? The children were in bed; no harm had been done. Why did I feel so uneasy? Claire hadn't actually been rude, just a bit abrupt, but then I had interrupted her having a good time. Somehow, the gloss was tarnishing on my holiday. I wished I hadn't rung at all. When I went back into the living room, I didn't dare tell Mike about the party, because he would have blown a fuse. 'Everything all right?' he said. 'Fine,' I said. But for the first time since we got there I was beginning to count the days until we could go home.

Thursday 23 April

'Come on, Carrie,' Mike shouted enthusiastically through the bathroom door. 'I want to get out on the slopes early today. I want to try that run we saw on the map yesterday – you know, the red run that takes you down into the valley. If we leave now, we can be back by lunch-time and then we should have time to do that run we did yesterday. It's fabulous weather. Come *on*. What are you doing in there?' What I was doing was sitting on the toilet in a contemplative manner. I'd awoken feeling tense and nervy, and couldn't stay in bed. Great, isn't it? I long and long for lie-ins and the one time I am away from the children I can't stay in bed. I think I need the children about me to achieve that feeling of complete exhaustion which makes bed such a haven. This morning it felt like there was something bad lurking in a dim corner of my mind, but I couldn't quite grasp it, pin it down, sort it out. It was just a nebulous *worry*.

'I'm coming,' I said, pulling up my ski-ing trousers – even more baggy than ever – wishing that Mike wouldn't constantly try to rush me from pillar to post, and that we didn't have to accomplish something all the time. I wanted to mooch about hanging onto Mike's arm, look in the shops, have a long lunch and talk, not go for the Olympic record of how many runs you could ski in one day. I wanted us to be close and romantic. We had so little time together normally, I wanted to have all of him.

Sure, we were having lots of sex, but we weren't really talking. To Mike, sex seems to be all the communication he needs, but I want – no, I *need* – more. I need the reassurance that he still finds me funny and interesting, not just a reasonable lay after seven years of marriage.

Outside in the warm sunlight, Mike threw his arm round me as we walked towards the car, carrying our skis. 'Cheer up,' he said, his face creasing into a frown as he saw my worried expression. 'What's eating you?'

'I'm just a bit tired,' I said, trying to smile. I didn't want to ski down the red run at all, but I knew he'd get bolshy if I told him. I might fall, and what would happen if I broke a leg? Who would look after the children? How would I drive to work? I didn't have the confidence Mike had on skis and this was potentially too dangerous.

'Look, Mike,' I said, 'why don't we skip ski-ing this morning and have a look around the town? I've seen a great place we could have lunch.'

'I didn't come here to shop,' said Mike, tetchily. 'You know I've been looking forward to this.You'll be fine.' There was an edge of impatience to his voice. 'What is the problem? I'll help you down the steep parts. We came here to ski, didn't we? I don't want to ski on my own. It'll be an adventure. Don't be such a wimp.'

'I'm not being a wimp,' I said, 'I just don't fancy it. If you want I'll stay here and meet you at lunch-time. I don't see why it's a problem.' My voice rose with anger.

It was such a little thing to be arguing about, and I couldn't understand how what had been light-hearted banter was now in danger of becoming a full-blown row. Mike suddenly slewed the car into a lay-by and savagely pulled on the hand-brake before turning to look at me. 'We came here to have a good time, but you've had a face like a smacked arse ever since you got up. Are you worrying about the children? That's it, isn't it? You're scared of doing anything remotely exciting because there is the *faintest* possibility you might hurt yourself. Why can't we do something a bit daring? I want to remember this holiday.'

'No,' I said, turning to look out of the window. I was not going to let him do what he wanted to do all the time. Why shouldn't we do what I wanted to do? 'You go alone.'

'I wish I'd bloody come here alone,' he said, angrily. 'I didn't realize I'd dragged you out here against your will. I didn't realize you'd much rather be at home with the children and that one phone call would put you in such a bloody awful mood.'

'Mike,' I said, struggling to keep my voice very calm, 'it really isn't worth having a fight about this. I love being here with you. I don't wish the children were here. Go off and have a good time. I'll meet you later.'

'I won't be back by lunch-time,' said Mike, starting the car and pulling back out onto the road.

Why was he being so unreasonable? This was pathetic, and I was not going to give in. When we reached the car park by the cable-car, Mike unloaded both our skis from the roof-rack in silence. 'I'm not ski-ing,' I said, carefully. He let my skis fall to the floor with a thump.

'Well, I'm not going to sit around all morning wait-ing to ring home,' he said.

I exploded. 'This isn't about that! Stop twisting

everything! You're trying to force me to do something I don't want to do and when I say no you're behaving like a ridiculous child! I have the right to make up my own mind,' I shouted. 'Well fuck you,' said Mike quietly, leaning towards me so no-one else would hear. Then he turned on his heel and marched off towards the queue for the cable-car.

'When will you be back?' I called after him desperately.

'Who knows?' he said, disappearing into the sea of ski jackets and woolly hats. The warmth of the sun had gone and been replaced by a cold chill, wrapping itself around me. In that crowd of people, I felt intensely alone and vulnerable. I wanted to go home.

Sunday 26 April

Home. I am sitting surrounded by the debris of a week's washing, with two small suitcases as yet unpacked and looking at me accusingly. The plane journey and trip home from the airport seemed to take for ever, with the tension between us almost visible. We'd tried to make it up, that Thursday night. Mike had come home in the early evening, his face tanned, his clothes smelling of clean, cold air. I was in the kitchen half-heartedly making a casserole, having spent a miserable day mooching round the shops looking at things I couldn't afford and eating a lonely cannelloni whilst keeping one beady eye on the restaurant door which had remained resolutely Mike-free.

'We're eating in?' he said, his eyes avoiding mine. At least he was speaking to me.

'I thought we ought to, to save some money,' I said.

'I don't want to think about money,' he said.

'Did you enjoy your day?' I said, relenting slightly.

'It was incredible,' he said, his eyes glowing at the

memory. He was full of child-like enthusiasm.

I walked over and put my arms around him. 'Why were you so awful to me?'

'Carrie,' he said, turning to place a careless kiss on my cheek, 'drop it.' And I did drop it. I dropped it like a stone, because I couldn't face another row. But I felt like a tiny piece had been taken out of the jigsaw of our relationship.

When we got home, early on Saturday evening, Rebecca catapulted herself down the hall towards us. Tom, in Claire's arms, wriggled and strained towards me, and clung fiercely to me when Claire handed him over. She was rather non-committal, and seemed to avoid my eyes when I asked if everything had been OK. Rebecca told me breathlessly about the slide at the swimming pool, and their trip to the zoo today. As soon as we were back, Claire shot off in her car. Mike put the children to bed while I carried the suitcases up to our room. Oh. Our duvet cover looked suspiciously neat – not at all as I'd left it – as if someone had been sleeping in it and exaggeratedly tried to hide the fact. I had politely asked Claire if she could use the bed in Rebecca's room, and Rebecca sleep in the bed in Tom's room, but it looked as if she and Harry had availed themselves of our king-size bed . . .

As I stuffed one load of washing into the machine, Mike ordered a take-away. I then opened a bottle of wine, and he hunted for glasses. 'Why are there only two in the cupboard?' he asked.

'They must be in the dishwasher,' I said. They weren't.

'How the hell could Claire lose twelve wine glasses?' asked Mike.

'I really don't know,' I said, trying to sound vague and unconcerned. I also didn't like to tell him about the cigarette burn I'd found on the sofa and the large red stain on the sisal under the table in the dining room. I didn't really care as long as the children were safe and happy. However, I did think Claire could have told me about them rather than just zooming away. On Monday night, I would mention it. Definitely. No more pussy-footing around. Who was in charge here?

5

MAY

Friday 1 May

'So, how was the holiday?' said Jill, lolling back on the settle in our kitchen. Friday mornings she tends to swoop in on me because it is my one day off work, which very soon I will lose. I generally like to use the morning to catch up on shopping and washing with only Tom to keep an eye on, but I can never resist the opportunity to off-load on Jill, who only teaches part-time and, with both her own children being school-age, is far more a lady of leisure. 'Was it all cold snow and hot sex?'

I regarded her quizzically over a large pile of washing which seemed to consist largely and unfairly of Mike's shirts. Men's shirts are expressly designed to be a pain in the arse to iron. One of these days I'll go out and buy him lots of drip-dry non-iron shirts which he will never wear. 'It was great,' I said vaguely, the memory of our row still too tender a spot to touch upon.

'And how did the angel Claire cope?'

'OK, I think,' I said, and then mentally weighed up the pros and cons of telling Jill about the appalling argument I'd had with her on Monday night. I had to tell someone. I'd been literally boiling with the rage and hurt of it ever since. I couldn't make myself talk to Mike, because we were still cautious with each other and because he thought I'd got the issue out of proportion in the first place, and if he knew what Claire had said to me he would make me sack her, which would drop me totally in the shit. With Jill, I gave in.

'We had a massive row when I got back,' I said.

'Cor,' said Jill, brightening up at juicy news. 'Why? I mean, I know she's so annoying about running your house like a military base and all the "little man" business . . . but what did she do that was so awful? We popped round after school and she seemed to be getting on fine, although there was some great big Hooray Henry type here too.'

'Harry,' I said gloomily. 'He's supposed to be at college, but he spent all week with her.' I plonked the washing down, made us a cup of coffee and told her all.

When I'd got home on Monday night, Claire had already put the children to bed. As I walked into the kitchen, she turned her back to me and made a very pointed show of filling the dishwasher. 'Claire,' I said carefully and as calmly as I could to her frosty shoulders, 'we're really grateful you looked after the children for the week and they seem to have had a really lovely time. But' – I had to pause here to get my breath, I'm so bad at telling people off – 'I just thought you might have told me about breaking the wine glasses and the mess on the dining-room carpet and the cigarette burns, and when I rang, the music did seem very loud with the children in bed . . .' She seemed to freeze. Then she suddenly turned and I was alarmed to see that tears were running down her face. Oh God. I'd gone too far and really upset her. 'Look,' I said hastily, desperate not to let this escalate from a civilized conversation, 'it's not a massive problem, but I just wanted to mention it to clear the air—'

'That's so unfair!' she said, her face flushed and angry. In that moment, I didn't know her at all. I'd never seen her remotely lose control and for the first time she looked much younger than her twenty years. 'I look after the children perfectly! The house was a total mess when you went last week and I had to spend days cleaning it. OK, we did break a few things accidentally and I was meaning to tell you about it, but I was waiting for you to say thank you in the first place for helping you out. I never get enough time off, I'm absolutely exhausted. Harry says I should be earning twice what I'm getting and all I get are little comments about what I haven't done. I'm here twelve hours a day for your children, and all you care about is getting to work on time. Rebecca is so spoilt, I only stay because of Tom. You don't deserve him! You're always ringing up saying you're going to be late and can I just do this and that and you *never* think that I have a life too! You treat me like a bloody . . . servant!' Then she snatched up her handbag and ran out of the house.

I sat down, stunned. What had I done to deserve all that? All I'd meant to do was show her that we couldn't be walked all over and that although I appreciated how she cared for Tom and Rebecca – and I'm sure I did stress that – she should have told me if she'd damaged the house and not just taken advantage of us. And I'd paid her extra to look after them for the week and she'd only just had her wages increased. Why didn't she say if staying on some evenings was such a problem? If she had felt like that, why hadn't she said so ages ago?

My brain was reeling. How on earth were we going to speak to each other now? She clearly didn't like Rebecca. How could I leave my daughter with someone who thought she was spoilt? She was only six, for God's sake. And to say I didn't deserve my children . . . I poured a glass of wine with a shaking hand. Should I tell Mike about all this? He was due home very soon, and if I did tell him he'd make me sack her.

Turtle came and lay on my feet, and Angus put a trusting fat buttery-yellow paw onto my knee. I didn't want to keep Claire. How dare she be so rude to me? But how could I find anyone else at such short notice? And with this new job . . . I needed someone the children knew and trusted. Holding Angus and trying not to cry (which Mike would spot), I resolved to take the coward's route. Not to tell Mike and try to build bridges with Claire. Presumably Rebecca hadn't sensed that Claire didn't like her and Tom obviously loved her . . . Oh God. I could really do without all this.

Jill listened with an increasingly open mouth. 'So what happened next?' she said. 'Why on earth is Claire still here?'

'I gave in,' I said. I wasn't very proud of myself at all. Instead of standing up for myself and gaining the upper hand, I grovelled. On Tuesday morning Claire swept past me looking nervous and embarrassed, and took Tom off into the kitchen. I slunk out of the door without even saying goodbye. Well, I had to get to work. Then on Tuesday night I got home a bit earlier than usual and plucked up courage to say, 'Look, Claire, I'm really sorry we spoke like that. I was tired after the holiday, and it was just a bit of a shock to find those little things had gone wrong after we trusted you with the house, but I won't mention it again. You don't have to pay for them. We're really grateful, honestly we are, for the way you look after Tom and Rebecca. I'm really sorry if you think I've taken advantage and if you do have a night out planned please tell me, and then I won't be late. And . . . I've been offered a new job so

I was going to talk to you about working on a Friday as well. Of course we'll pay you more money. You will stay, won't you?'

There was a long pause. 'Yes,' she said, confidence returning to her eyes. 'But I've been thinking and there are a few things I'd like to sort out too. I don't think I should have to do any cleaning, none of my friends do, and I think you should give me a petrol allowance. I don't want to do any baby-sitting and I don't want to work after seven more than two nights a week. I don't mind helping out with holidays again but not every time so I don't get a holiday. I didn't mean that about Rebecca, she's lovely, but she was really hard while you were away – she missed you a lot and she won't always do things for me.'

She looked me straight in the eye and tried to smile. 'I do like working here. I love the children. I don't want to leave.' As she said the last bit, her voice started to break and tears filled her eyes. She does love them, I thought, and the realization shocked me. How can someone else feel as emotional as I do about *my* children? It sent a small shiver through me, but outwardly I smiled, and, propelled by a clumsy urge, I leaned forward and kissed her on the cheek. She put her arms up and gave me a brief, embarrassed hug, like an errant daughter would a mother, before picking up her car keys and opening the back door. 'Thank God,' I thought, as she drove away. 'I won't have to find anyone else.' It was only later that I realized she now had us totally over a barrel.

Sunday 3 May
Three difficult issues had to be broached to Mike this weekend, at a time when we were still at the icily polite stage. We hadn't made love since the holiday,

Mike turning away from me with a sigh that clearly said, 'God, I'm so exhausted,' every night. Funny how two people can be in one bed and yet so far apart. Firstly, we were going to have to pay Claire more. Secondly, my new job would mean I had to work Fridays as well and there would be some evening meetings, so I'd need him to get home from work and take over from Claire. And thirdly, my mother was coming down next week because it is Rebecca's half-term. I told him about my mother first, and he reacted in a very childish manner, by pretending to slide off his chair, clutching his throat. 'Get up,' I said sternly, 'you're a grown-up person.'

'But she's mad,' he said.

'She'll starch your collars,' I said. 'And think of all the lovely real food she makes.'

'True,' said Mike. 'When's she coming?'

'Next week,' I said. 'Can't you tell? I've cleaned out the fridge.'

The subject of Claire and the job was more tricky. 'They want me to start the new job next month,' I ventured.

'Wonderful,' he said. 'We can start thinking about selling the car, then. Why are you looking like that?' I was trying to look calm, poised and confident, but I knew my face was beginning to suffuse with a telling pink hue.

'I haven't told you yet because I thought you might not like it but they're insisting I have to work Fridays and that means keeping Claire on and paying her more. And' – at this point I paused to refill my glass for Dutch courage – 'I'm going to have to work some evenings as well so I'll need to know that you can get home on time to take over.'

'Just ask Claire to stay longer,' said Mike, in a reasonable voice.

'I can't exactly do that,' I said and, without wanting to give him a full blow-by-blow account of our row, I told him she wanted far more rigid hours.

He flared up immediately. 'Well that's bloody marvellous,' he said. 'She's expecting us to pay her more money but she isn't prepared to be flexible? She can fuck off.'

'Where would that leave us?' I said, trying desperately to keep calm and not let this escalate into another row. This week, I had had quite enough emotion, thank you.

Mike continued, 'Just be tough with her. Tell her we need her to work some evenings. Jesus, Carrie, why is this such a problem? We pay her, we tell her which hours to work. Just sort it out. Come on, this is supposed to be a celebration. You've got this fabulous new job and this time next week I'll have shirts a man can be proud of. Open another bottle.'

Despite trying to keep calm, I felt like I was exploding inside. Why was everything *my* responsibility and why did he trivialize the problems which were potentially so important and should have affected both of us? Why did I have to sort everything out and deal with Claire and pick up the pieces when the child-care went wrong? Why did I have to rush home like a bat out of hell to make sure the children saw at least one of their parents more than once a day, while Mike just came home when he felt like it, and why did I feel so absurdly grateful when he said he would look after the kids like last month, as if he was doing me a *favour*? They were his children too, for God's sake, and I was sick and tired of carrying this huge burden of guilt and responsibility around with me all the time, whilst bringing almost as much money as Mike into the house and having to worry about whether we'd run out of butter and if we had enough loo rolls and had the

114

dogs been walked that day and had the duvet and sheets been washed and . . .

'I've had enough of this,' I said, very coldly, to Mike.

'What?' he said, his face registering complete amazement. 'Enough of what? I just asked you to sort out Claire. Come on, Carrie, don't make such a big issue out of it. I'm tired. It's been bloody hard work this week and the last thing I need is a row when I get home. Just leave it. If you really want me to talk to Claire I will. I'll sort it out.'

'No,' I said, suddenly horrified. He'd destroy all the careful bridge-building work I'd been doing all week and it would end up with him sacking her. I couldn't face that. 'I'll do it,' I said.

'Then calm down,' he said. 'I don't know what's got into you lately. On holiday you were like a cat on hot bricks about the kids, when it was our first time away alone for ages; you seem to be permanently tired and now you start a row about nothing.'

It's *not* nothing, I thought inwardly, but how could I blame him when I *was* so reluctant to hand over control of the Claire/children situation? That's the trouble with us women. It drives us mad that men won't get involved or see all the little things which need doing and take up so much of our time, but at the same time we're so reluctant to hand over or share all the responsibilities which have traditionally been ours – the home and the children. Whenever Mike did very occasionally do the shopping, he always bought the wrong things and I nearly always did a secret shop to fill in the gaps. When he did tidy the kitchen he always put everything away in the wrong place so I couldn't find it, and when he did look after the children I always had the urge to meddle because I thought I knew best. I must let go more and stop trying to be this mad controlling superwoman person.

If I did want to have control of the situation why should I feel so angry about Mike's lack of involvement? Why did it drive me mad that he could leave in the morning without a backward glance, when I took such an immense amount of pleasure from hanging on to all these tiny, domestic details? My head swam with the effort of thinking about it all. 'Look, it doesn't matter,' I said. 'I think I'm still jet-lagged from the holiday. Let's go to bed.'

'Sure,' said Mike. 'I'm getting a bit worried about you, Carrie. You seem to be getting things all out of proportion.'

Tuesday 5 May

Mum is due to arrive tomorrow. I've taken the week off, which feels like I've been given a huge birthday present, and yesterday Tom, Rebecca and I had the most wonderful day. It was great to be able to stay in bed and snuggle, all three of us, while Mike got up and put his suit on and headed towards the city. Hee, hee. Not us. We had a whole week of staying in bed and making large sticky cakes and going for long walks and I could actually take Tom to the mother and baby swimming class and I'd promised I'd take Rebecca riding for the first time. She's been on at me for riding lessons for ages, but Mike was a bit reluctant in that he thought it would be dangerous, and it's bloody expensive. It'll have to be at the weekends as well, because right now I cannot load Claire up with any more after-school activities, because as it is she has to hang around with Tom for an hour while Rebecca does her ballet lessons, and on Wednesdays there's Rainbows, which don't finish until seven when Tom should really be having his bath. Asking if she could take Rebecca to the riding school which is over five miles away may just tip her

116

over the edge. So it was one more thing I think we're going to have to pack into our weekends, whether Mike likes it or not.

Yesterday afternoon we went for the most wonderful long, windy walk in the fields above the cottage. The spring flowers are still out in profusion, and the bushes full of pussy-willow, which always makes me think of my primary school, taking it in to put on the classroom window ledge. We found a pond which had tadpoles, and Rebecca insisted that we went home right away and found an old jam jar. I tied a piece of string around the lid, very inexpertly, and off she ran up the field, swinging it. I followed, puffing a bit, with Tom in the back-pack, happily holding his hands out to feel the pull of the sharp, stinging breeze. He kept squealing with excitement, and clutching my hair, as if to make sure I didn't disappear. The dogs ran on ahead, delighted to get such a lengthy walk – I don't think Claire takes them very far, because Tom is now pretty heavy in the back-pack and the pushchair can only be taken on the very dull walk at the side of the canal which has a proper path. Turtle can also become a little over-excited, so you can find yourself being hurtled forward at unexpected moments, which makes walks with him on the lead rather alarming.

At the pond, Rebecca bent over in fascination, as the tiny, slippery black shapes darted backwards and forwards by the edge. 'Put the jar in gently,' I said, and she slowly moved it along under the water. Into the slipstream went what looked to me like hundreds and hundreds of tadpoles – would they all grow into frogs? Where would they go? – and a lot of murky green pond-water and slime. Lovely. I took Tom out of the backpack, and with one hand firmly holding him next to me I crouched down by Rebecca. She looked up at me, her face beaming with joy. 'Look, Mummy!' she said, thrilled. 'What will we put them in?'

'There's that old washing-up bowl,' I said. 'But we'll have to put a stone in so they can jump out once they turn into little frogs.'

'Little frogs! Little frogs!' said Rebecca, jumping about with excitement.

'Hang on,' I laughed. 'You'll tip them back in. Do you want me to carry them home?'

'No. I want to!' So she walked home extremely carefully, holding each side of the jar with tense, concentrated little fingers. At home, we found the bowl and filled it with tap water (I'm sure a little fluoride won't hurt them — it'll save on their dental charges) and then poured in the stream of pond-water and tadpoles. We found a space on the window ledge in the utility room, and Rebecca spent the rest of the afternoon standing on a chair, peering in with complete fascination at their darting forms. I was sure they wouldn't be too emotionally traumatized by a hand dipping into their watery home every now and then to give them a gentle stroke. I did have to tell her that lifting them out of the water completely to give them a little tickle in the palm of her hand might not be *exactly* how they wanted to spend the day, however.

Later on, as the evening sun began to fall, it was still warm, so I took a just-bathed Tom out onto the old swing. Rebecca was inside, happily swathed in her duvet, watching *Pingu*. She too was bathed, I had made an elaborate meal for Mike involving reduced sauces and gently steamed vegetables, a bottle of wine was warming on the oven and I felt I had life, for once, vaguely under control. All was relatively tidy, the dogs fed, and I didn't have to drive into work tomorrow.

On the swing, Tom leant his face gently against mine

as we swung backwards and forwards in the beginnings of the dusk. 'Ma - ma,' he said, my eyes in his
face gazing up at me.
    'Kiss,' I said, and he comically pursed up his lips
and pressed them against my face. 'I love you,' I said,
holding him to me, feeling for once at peace, truly
happy, swinging for no reason in the fading light.

Sunday 10 May
The house is gleaming, the children have buffed
cheeks, their finger- and toenails are clipped into perfect half-moons and my linen cupboard is full of very
neat piles of laundered napkins and pillow-cases. My
mother went through our house like a regimental
sergeant major, after I met her off the train at Oxford,
children press-ganged into their best outfits with hair,
for once, washed and brushed. I'd even given them
both matching socks.
    'Darling!' said Mum, enveloping me in a bear-hug
and an over-powering waft of Tweed perfume. She was
dressed as if for a garden party with the Queen, in a
matching checked dress and jacket, her hair set into
a bullet-proof perm (she goes to the hairdresser every
Monday for a shampoo and set, never washes it herself) and shiny high-heeled tippy-tappy court shoes.
'And where's my little angel?' Tom pressed himself
much closer to me, not at all sure about this alarming
apparition bearing down on him. Rebecca, however,
had no such inhibitions and flung herself onto her
granny. They have a curious bond, these two, as they
are not at all alike: my mother with her desire for
everything to be 'in the right place' and not a word
spoken out of turn, and my delightful rebel, who blows
through life like a whirlwind and lives in a permanent
fug of mess. I think the answer is that Rebecca actually

enjoys learning all the obscure card games my mother knows backwards, whereas I refused point blank to learn when I was her age. I think Rebecca just enjoys the attention, because when she wants me to play cards I get fed up and bored after five minutes, and there's always so much to do about the house that I haven't got time.

'I met the loveliest young couple on the train,' said Mum, as I hoicked up the familiar suitcase which had been part of our family for so long, shifting Tom to my other arm. She is very reluctant to throw anything away, ever, as everything has its uses and she sees age as no reason for getting rid of things. Going home is like entering the museum of my childhood because every little thing – from ornaments to the tin she and Dad use for biscuits – is unchanged. 'I told them all about you and Mike, and how *famous* you both are now, and she said she *thought* she'd seen you on the television. Now she was a student at the university, studying English *I think*, very clever and bookish, with *glasses*, and I don't know what the boy did, because he didn't say very much. I told them you'd had an interview for Oxford, but you'd failed and gone to Manchester, which hadn't been quite as good but we didn't think it had made *too* much of a difference. And she seemed very interested in the little booklet I'm putting together of the history of the village – *so* fascinating, darling, all the old place names – and then we chatted a bit about Boswell's department store, the girls there are so willing to help. I told her I had a *boy* on the till at the supermarket last week – she agreed with me it was hardly a job for a man . . .'

In my mind's eye I could picture this poor young couple, pinned down like rabbits in the firestorm of my mother's gunfire delivery, and mentally marvelled at her ability to impart totally inappropriate and intimate personal details of her family's life to complete strangers.

Going into shops with my mother is a test of the steeliest nerves, as even the simplest and most innocent enquiry such as 'credit card or cash?' will send her off into a stream of consciousness about how she doesn't believe in credit cards because she's sure they encourage all this debt, what with hire purchase and all that, and she and Daddy have always relied on cheque books because you know where you are, and she can't get the hang of these hole-in-the-wall things either. I know this for a fact because I have been present while she has attempted to extract money from what to most people is a relatively simple piece of machinery. Not for my mother, who didn't realize you have to remember your own pin number. 'Darling, it wants a number from me.'

'Yes, Mum, they must have sent it to you in the post.' 'But Daddy remembers all those type of things, darling.' After experimentally pushing in a series of numbers at random, the machine promptly swallowed her card. 'Carrie!' she said, while I tried to enter the wall by osmosis. 'It's taken my card! Make it give it back!' She then sailed forth into the bank itself to assail the unwitting staff with immediate demands to ring her bank manager who was a *personal friend*.

All too often I have to walk away from her for fear of placing my hand firmly over her mouth and frog-marching her out of shops. 'Mum, people aren't *interested*.' The thing is, people *are* so polite when she goes on and on at them, and listen with such infinite patience to this stream of information which must mean absolutely nothing to them at all. I think they just think, This is a madwoman, while I hover about behind her shrugging my shoulders and making apologetic faces. The worst thing is that she believes she's being charming.

Rebecca and I gently manoeuvred her into the car, and even though I'd made a real effort to clear out its usual debris of sweet wrappers, crisp packets, cartons of juice and unidentifiable pieces of Lego, she still looked about her and said, 'Really, darling, this could do with a hoover.' Gritting my teeth, I drove home at a snail's pace, because if I don't she has a tendency to grip the door handle.

Once home, she went through it like a tornado, pulling open cupboards, peering into the fridge, lifting the rugs in the sitting room and clucking over the size of my ironing pile and the fact that I don't keep my bleach in a separate cupboard. She spotted immediately that Rebecca's cardigan had a button hanging off, and demanded my sewing basket. Big mistake. This is the sewing basket she bought for me just before I set off for boarding school, and its contents haven't changed much since. They have gradually evolved, over the years, from separate cotton reels, needles, buttons and metal poppers into a surreal congealed multi-coloured mass from which Uri Geller would have problems extracting metallic objects. 'Really, Carrie,' she said. 'How on earth do you sew buttons on and take up hems?'

'I don't,' I said. 'I just buy new things.' She looked at me in horror. All those years of darning my father's socks on a big wooden mushroom and painstakingly sewing on buttons as soon as they fall off from her vast and fascinating button collection kept in the big green biscuit tin have clearly been wasted on her slatternly daughter.

'Now, can I ring your father? It's time he had his lunch and I want to make sure he knows the cake under the screen in the pantry is for lunch, not dinner.'

God. She even controls his eating habits from a distance. Since he retired from his job as a company manager he has taken more and more to the golf course and to his greenhouse, in a totally vain bid to escape my mother's iron grip on his intestines. But they are so sweet together, holding hands as they sit watching television, and pottering together around supermarkets spending hours exclaiming over the range and variety of products on offer. 'Quite a treat,' says my dad, who ten years ago had never been inside a food shop. Maybe Mike and I would end up like this: the thrill of our week being a trip to Waitrose to exclaim over the Parma ham.

At lunch-time I started to heat up Tom's favourite Heinz cauliflower cheese jar.

'What is that?' said my mother, peering over my shoulder as the jar simmered away.

'Tom's lunch,' I said.

'But it isn't real food,' she said. 'You haven't been feeding him *that*. You don't know what's in it.'

'Yes I do. It says on the jar,' I said, quite reasonably.

'What that child needs is a bit of mashed parsnip and some stewed apple,' she said, brushing me out of the way and hurling the offending Heinz jar in the bin. Tom's eyes followed its trajectory sadly. He loved that one. Mum managed to locate a potato and a parsnip from my fridge (I must have bought it for Sunday lunch, it's not a vegetable I can get excited about) and then went to elaborate lengths to boil them up, mash them with a little real butter (throwing away my I Cant Believe It's Not Butter with a contemptuous sniff) and peel and core the apples.

Tom meanwhile was beginning to howl with hunger, because preparing his lunch normally takes me about five minutes, and he's not used to waiting for all this *cooking* nonsense. When Mum presented him with the finished product, he eyed the yellowy goo beadily. What was this stuff? It didn't smell like Heinz. How would he know it wasn't going to poison him? After a number of goes Mum got it in his mouth, and he then proceeded to scoff the lot, happily smacking his lips and making lots of contented greedy noises. 'See,' said Mum. 'They always prefer home-cooked food.' Now he would never touch Heinz food again. Thanks, Mum.

Mum then spent the afternoon teaching Rebecca to sew, having untangled the mass in the sewing box. Tom and I took the dogs out for a long walk on our own, which was bliss because I didn't have Rebecca trailing along behind me complaining that her legs were tired, and could she have a carry, and why did Tom always get to be carried?

At bath-time Mum regaled me with her lecture on the unsuitable nature of disposable nappies versus the wonders of the Terry towelling variety. 'We didn't have nappy rash when you were young,' she said as I smoothed cream onto Tom's peach-like bottom. 'It's all those synthetic fibres.' She also said that Tom was cranky at meal-times because I hadn't imposed a strict four-hourly feeding regime on him, and why didn't I put him out in the pram to have his afternoon nap rather than the cot, because then he'd get some fresh air?

'Because it's raining, Mum,' I replied. 'Put the hood up,' she said. 'You went out rain, snow or shine,' she said. 'I just popped you down at the bottom of the garden so you could watch the leaves on the trees and you never uttered a peep.' I bet I did, I thought darkly. You just didn't hear me, because you were so busy playing bridge.

She insisted on cooking tea for Mike, whom she worships, and while she made the cauliflower cheese, steak and kidney pie with home-made pastry followed by a lemon meringue (we never normally eat puddings), she harangued me about my lack of care for him. 'Darling, you must look after him,' she said. 'Why do you think your daddy's still going strong when so many of his friends have dropped like flies? It's all that convenience food and rushing about. It can't be good for you. You look pale. Are you getting enough sleep? Really, Carrie, I wonder if you can cope with that job of yours. Surely you could work less hours?'

'Mum,' I said patiently, 'it isn't quite as easy as that. I need to work the hours I do. It's a full-time job. I have to be there.'

'I don't know about that,' she said. 'Strikes me your children need you just as much. But then, I'm old-fashioned. It wouldn't have been my scene. Your father would have had a fit if he'd come home and I hadn't been there. Men and children do need *looking after*, you know.'

'*I* need looking after,' I said.

'No you don't,' she said, brushing me aside as she opened the oven door. 'You're a woman.'

Mike exclaimed with delight at the feast Mum laid out for him. She'd even found the napkins and table-cloth stuffed at the back of the sideboard drawer I never opened, apart from at Christmas. At dinner she quizzed Mike about how well his job was going, which made him puff out with pride, and hung delightedly on his every word. Mike kept trying to draw me into the conversation and tell her how well I was doing, too, but she was not to be deflected. The master was home, and his needs were paramount.

After dinner she cleared away immediately, and refused to load everything into the dishwasher. 'Waste of time,' she said.

'But it *saves* time,' I pointed out.

125

'You can't get plates really clean with one of those things,' she said.

'I really like your mum,' said Mike, as we levered ourselves into bed, our stomachs grossly distended with steak and kidney pie and lemon meringue and cream. 'I don't know why I ever thought she was mad. She's charming.'

'In that case I shall go and have a perm and practise my pastry-making skills,' I said. 'And then you can go out and find a job which pays twice what you earn now so we can afford this new house.'

'Oh,' said Mike. 'Point taken. But could she give you the recipe for the lemon meringue?'

'I'll ask her to give it to you,' I said sweetly, turning off the light.

Monday 25 May
Unparalleled disaster. Mike had already left in his usual swirl of Monday-morning paranoia, and I was just applying mascara with Tom pulling himself up on my legs when the phone rang. Claire. 'I'm really sorry,' she croaked. 'I won't be able to come in today. I've had a really bad throat all weekend and now my glands are up as well. I've called the doctor.' There was a long pause while my mind raced with the feverish implications of this news. 'I'm sure I'll be better tomorrow . . . I'll work Friday if that makes it any easier . . .'

'No, of course not,' I said. 'Don't worry. You get back to bed and get some sleep. I'll see you tomorrow.' Oh *God*. What the hell was I going to do now? I had a meeting planned this morning with the team from East Midlands, who were coming over to the Midlands office especially, so we could talk over the restructure ready for next week. This afternoon I'd set up a story to film only I knew about, and we were already one reporter short on the rota . . . and . . . Nick was going to kill me. 'Bugger, bugger and blast,' I shouted, prompting Rebecca to hurtle out of her bedroom.

'What's the matter?'

'Claire can't come today,' I said.

'Great!' said Rebecca. 'You can take me to school!' Her little face was wreathed in smiles. 'I'll go and get ready,' and she wandered off, singing.

Jill, I thought. I'll ring Jill. As she answered the phone, a cacophony of shouts and yells could be heard behind her. 'Jill, I'm in a mess. Claire's just rung and she can't come today and I've got two important meetings and Mike's already gone—'

'I can't,' said Jill. 'I'm teaching today. I'm really sorry. What about one of those nanny agencies? Susie, put the cat *down*. I'll have to go, Susie's killing the cat. See you later. Good luck.'

I couldn't ring an agency – I couldn't let a total stranger come and look after Tom, he'd go berserk. Ring Nick, I said sternly to myself. Ring Nick and tell him that your nanny is sick and you have to stay at home and look after the children.

'Nick?' I said, having waited until half-eight when I knew he'd be in. 'I'm really sorry but I feel awful. I've been throwing up all night and I thought I'd be OK but I can hardly drag myself out of bed' – muffled Tom squawk hastily suppressed – 'could you possibly ask Kate to cancel the meeting for me? I'm really sorry but' – pathetic ill voice – 'I really can't manage it.'

Pause from Nick while he tried to be reasonable but didn't feel it.

'OK,' he said. 'But it's rather awkward. We'll try and fix it for tomorrow – you *will* be in, won't you? It's not an . . . ongoing thing, is it?' Oh God! He thinks I'm pregnant again!

'No, no,' I said hurriedly. 'I'll be in. Definitely.' I'll be

127

in, I thought grimly, if I have to go to her house and drag Claire out of bed myself. 'Get off,' I said to Tom, who was pulling at my tights. I was unreasonably shrewish with him all day, torturing myself with all the thoughts of what I *should* be doing, and how was I ever to catch up?

6

JUNE

Tuesday 2 June

I am quite definitely the king of the castle. I now have my own office, with my name on the door: *Carrie Adams. Assistant Editor Planning (News).* It is only in those grey and black sticky squares though, not a printed plate. Significant? I have access to Nick's secretary if I need any letters typing or tricky things like stamps putting on envelopes, which male bosses are deemed physiologically incapable of doing themselves. And yesterday I chaired my first-ever meeting. I had to find a new kind of face for this, the face of a woman who is prepared to be reasonable but knows she is in charge. As well as the facial rearranging, I also had to do some nervous skirt-pulling down because my only navy tights developed a huge ladder so I was forced to put on stockings and suspenders, which is killingly uncomfortable and makes me feel like I should suddenly throw up my legs like at the Folies Bergère. Perhaps not quite the impression of quiet dignity I would like to create.

Alex, who has effectively been demoted to be my deputy rather than face the sack, is clearly uneasy in his new role. He feels extremely cheated that he didn't get the job – and I think the fact that I am a woman and about ten years younger than him has thrown him even more off balance. He kept staring intently at me throughout the meeting like he was sizing me up for a coffin, and is clearly looking for any little chink in my armour. Whenever I caught his eye I gave him a big, winning smile, just to make him even more pissed off.

I had to outline my proposals for the way this post will work, and how we're going to co-ordinate the planning for the new region – and, more importantly, how we're going to work with shared crews, which is all part of a vast cost-cutting exercise which has heaped even more gloom onto the naturally despondent staff cameramen, whose sole aim in life is to drink endless coffee and moan about incompetent reporters and the chronic inability of the beleaguered person running the camera diary to calculate the length of time it will take them to get to jobs. I'd worked all this out late on Sunday night, while Mike lounged in front of some ghastly Bruce Willis film, occasionally wandering into the kitchen to ask impatiently if I'd finished yet and could we go to bed because he had a busy day on Monday. 'You go to bed,' I'd said. 'I'll be up soon. I need to do this or I'm going to look a complete prat.'

'You'll wake me up when you come in,' he said.

'Mike,' I said, 'do I give you this hassle when you need to stay up working?'

'No, but you sleep more heavily than me. Do it in the morning.'

'And when in the morning,' I said, angrily putting down my pen, 'do you think I should do it? Before six when Tom wakes up, or perhaps in between getting Rebecca out of bed and getting Tom dressed? Or perhaps you would like to get Tom ready before Claire arrives and start their breakfast before you set off for the office? If that's fine with you I'll come to bed now,' I finished icily.

'You're getting awfully prickly,' he said, retreating instantly at this potential threat to his hassle-free mornings. 'You know I have to be in first thing on Monday and hit the ground running.'

'And I don't?' I said, turning back to my work. Mike grunted and disappeared back into the TV room, and ended up falling asleep in front of the film, which meant at one o'clock in the morning I was dragging him bodily off the sofa while he humphed and grumbled. It was almost as if he was making life difficult on purpose because he felt so huffy about this new job and the ensuing effects on him. Jesus. If there was a degree course in ego-massaging, I'd get a first.

Nick did some general introductions around the room while I sat there smiling modestly and trying to keep my knees together so no-one got a flash of dimpled thigh. Then he handed over to me. As all eyes in the room turned towards me, I stood up and attempted to speak. A squeak came out. Everyone eyed me a little curiously. They had hired Minnie Mouse to run the planning department? Who was this girlie? Then my voice came back with a gush and I was off like a train, outlining my plans, talking them through all the changes to computer systems we'd need, working out how we'd run the shared crews. It was breathtakingly brilliant, but I seemed to have no control over it, as if my voice was coming from a long way away. Inside was a small scared person, who desperately wished to be back at her old desk in the chaos of the newsroom throwing balls of paper at Kate and doing the tea run and being part of the common herd. I don't know if I'm cut out to be one of the élite. After the meeting, Nick put his hand on my shoulder, said, 'Well done,' and asked if I would come out for a quick drink with him and Bruce (head of broadcasting, *grand fromage*) after work. The simple answer to that should have been 'No'. I hadn't given Claire any prior warning, and with her temper at the moment I wouldn't dare suggest anything, and I knew Mike had a late meeting planned. My mind whirred desperately. I couldn't just come out and say 'No', because this was clearly what being part of the management team meant, and most of the decisions about the running of the newsroom were made over pints of beer and now presumably, in my case, gin and tonics, rather than at meetings during the day, because then everyone was working hell for leather towards the programme. It wouldn't be a problem to either of them, they wouldn't even think about it making them late home. But I'd promised to listen to Rebecca read tonight, and she was so looking forward to hearing about my new job that I knew she'd be waiting up for me. I could try the we'll-do-lots-of-things-together-at-the-weekend ploy, but she was getting pretty tired of that ruse. Damn, damn.

'I'll see you in the bar at seven then?' Nick said, walking off towards his office. I went into my new office, closed the door and sank my head into my hands. It was only my first day, and already I'd been bowled a googly. Be creative, I thought. Nothing would stop Rebecca from being so disappointed, but I could try and sort out the child-care gap. I rang Jill, who I knew would be home from school. 'Jill!' I said brightly.

'You want something,' she said. 'I know you want something because you've got your creepy nice voice on.'

'You couldn't take your two over to my house at seven and hold the fort until I get back at about eight? Claire has said she has to get away on time tonight and Mike has a meeting . . .'

'Don't worry about me,' said Jill, laughing. 'I'll just hump my kids over to your house when they really should be in bed and mind your children and I bet you're not going to give me any money, either, are you?'

'I'll give you a big glass of wine when I get home,' I said.

'Done,' she said. 'I'll tell Pete he has to get his own tea for a change.'

'I cannot tell you how grateful I am,' I said.

'Bugger off,' said Jill. 'Just don't be too late.' I put the phone down, sighing with relief. But how often could I do this? I couldn't keep asking Jill to disrupt her life to help me out; we were only *friends*, for God's sake. I would just have to spell out to Nick tonight that evening meetings are rather difficult, and that if he wants to arrange something after work he'll have to give me a bit of notice. Even then, it was still going to be stupendously tricky.

Just before the programme, Kate wandered over. We hadn't had a really good chat for ages, and she suggested going for a coffee. In the canteen, she carefully poured Sweetex into her coffee and told me how fed up she was. A new presenter's job was coming up and presenting is what she's always wanted to do – she has the blond bob, after all, so she's halfway there. 'I went to see Nick about it this morning,' she said. 'And he told me they already had someone lined up who's been presenting in Manchester. He was very nice about it, but he managed to imply that it was absolutely pointless. I'm just not going anywhere. There's you, in your new job, and there I am, still stuck on the rota like everyone else.' Poor Kate. Her career is so important to her.

'Look,' I said, in a flash of inspiration. 'Why don't you go and see Mike? I know he's been talking about

133

how fed up they are with that Monica woman – she's been making all sorts of unreasonable demands – and you know him. Even if he can't offer you a job, he might know someone who could.'

'Brilliant!' she said, brightening up instantly. 'Are you sure he wouldn't mind me ringing? He's so important now, I feel like I don't know him any more.'

'He'd love to help,' I said. 'Especially if he could shaft Nick in the process.'

Saturday 6 June

My company car came on Friday and we have all been cooing over it, like a tiny puppy. Rebecca spent at least half an hour climbing in and out and at one point I thought I'd lost Tom completely but she'd put him in the estate bit at the back and pulled the screen across. It does not look like my car; it is shiny and new, and there are no ice-lolly wrappers stuffed in a sticky bundle into the driver's door. The glove compartment is free of beads and stickers, and the area under Tom's seat in the back has not, as yet, filled up with biscuit crumbs and discarded Ribena cartons. Maybe the car is the symbol that my life is going to become organized and free of nasty sticky things.

Mike told me suddenly this morning that he'd arranged for Martin and Harriet to come over for dinner tonight. This came as a complete surprise, mainly because he doesn't even really like Martin (pompous City type) – when did they speak? – and he almost never becomes involved in arranging domestic events. I'm the one who says, 'So and so are coming to dinner,' and he says, 'God, no.' I sometimes think he'd like to build a moat around our house, pull up a drawbridge and never see anyone.

'When did you see Martin?' I asked later. 'I bumped

134

into him in town and we got talking and I remembered we still owed them a dinner,' said Mike, vaguely.

'But what the hell am I going to cook?' I said.

'Just make your chicken and avocado thing,' said Mike, his mind on other matters, judging by his glance at the clock which revealed it was perilously close to kick-off time.

'But the butcher closes at lunch-time and that means I'll have to go to the supermarket and it'll be *heaving*.' I felt extremely disgruntled. Harriet was a cordon bleu cook who'd gone on one of those London cookery courses after school, in lieu of attending university like anyone else with half a brain. When we'd last gone round to their house we'd been given devilled kidneys (barf) and a warm goat's cheese salad, followed by one of those puddings which involves trapping lots and lots of different summer fruits inside a kind of jelly for grown-ups laced with Cointreau. Mike at the time had been effusive in his praise, and Harriet had been very simpery and 'Oh, it's nothing,' but I knew damn well she'd probably been working on it for days. But then you can plan dinner parties properly when you have two children at school and no job. She even has a cleaner and a gardener as well, for God's sake. How can you justify having a cleaner when you don't work? Do you simply pretend that dusting and sticking bleach down the loo is too dirty a job for a lady's hands? We don't have a cleaner and Claire will only do the odd bit, so I spend all Saturday morning frantically hoovering and dragging clothes out from under beds, accompanied by enough dog hair to knit another dog.

A dinner party for Harriet and Martin *should* have taken weeks of planning and careful preparation. I should have had tuna steaks marinating in lime juice for *days* in the fridge, and had the time to choose a gourmet pudding which I could have cunningly disguised as all my own work. I wanted to go to the special cheese shop in Oxford and buy lots of small, smelly, expensive French cheeses which exude the delicate aroma of hot feet, but parking on a Saturday would be impossible. I wanted to splash out lavishly on well-chosen wines, and clean the entire house from top to bottom so Harriet wouldn't have to step over discarded items of clothing in her Manolo Blahnik high heels. I wouldn't even have time to buy fresh flowers, and I'm blowed if I'm paying supermarket prices for them. Bugger, blast and damn. What had got into Mike? Still, at least I could leave the children with him while I went to the supermarket.

After a long and increasingly panic-stricken search for my purse (which was in the bread bin) I opened the door of the television room. 'Mike?' I said. No answer. It was very hard to see him in the dark, as he'd closed all the curtains as usual and the only light was the flickering TV. 'Mike, I'm off now. Can you look after the children?' Silence again. Sod it, I thought, and put on the light. He was fast asleep, and when I approached him he turned over firmly, pulling a cushion down over his face. Bloody marvellous, I thought. Should I wake him and shout? Or should I just take the children with me? We were now speaking to each other in an everyday way after the Great Row: remarks such as 'What time will you be home?' and 'It's pasta for tea, is that all right?' and at this stage I didn't want to rock the boat. There were several favours I needed from him next week – in the form of coming home immediately after work because I had a couple of evening meetings – and there was a much bigger issue to be tackled. Nick told me on Friday he wanted me to go on a management training course at the beginning of next month, in Scotland, of all places. Apparently it was one of these outward-bound team-building things. It sounds like the most awful pile of nonsense but how can I refuse to go? I know Mike will say it's totally pointless and the only way to be an effective manager is by actually doing the job, but I could hardly turn round to Nick and say, 'I'm sorry but I can't do the course because my husband won't let me?' Not very nineties, is it? Mike would never actually say, 'You can't go,' but how can I ask Claire to take on all that extra work so soon after the last fracas? Perhaps Mike might be persuaded to take at least a week's holiday . . . and perhaps Angus the retriever will turn round and ask if he could have a trifle more liver in his tea tonight.

The supermarket, as predicted, was packed, and Rebecca insisted on free-wheeling on the side of the trolley, which caused me to ram an elderly gentleman in the heels, who was understandably most put out. I'd meant to make a list to take with me, but then couldn't find a pen which hadn't dried up or even a crayon which hadn't broken. What happens to biros? I bring hundreds and hundreds of the things home from work, and one by one, they slide away, down the back of the sofa, down the crack between the car seats, into the unreachable gap at the back of the kitchen drawer. The rest just disappear into the ether. I think a kind of mental fog must come over me when I put a pen down, which impels me to hide it in a mysterious place so it can never be found again. Either that or someone in the house is eating them. The worst thing is when some- one rings me up from work and tells me something important, and all I can find to write with is Rebecca's Amazing Disappearing Pen so I scribble down the number only to see it vanish before my eyes. Either that or I write down vital messages in eyeliner pencil.

In the supermarket I went onto auto-pilot. I could wear tram-lines round that shop, and if they ever move

137

anything I whir around on the spot like a malfunctioning Dalek. New potatoes, mange-touts, asparagus (in season but still killingly expensive, especially when you then have to suffer the smell of asparagus-pee in the house for days afterwards), a large piece of beef for *filet de boeuf en croûte* and lots of different types of berries. Now, this pudding was very ambitious. I'd seen this particular recipe in an up-market cookery book I'd snaffled from work – publicists are always sending us freebies, it's the best thing about being a journalist – and I'd been wanting to try it for ages, but it looked fiendishly difficult. However, I always start off cooking with supreme optimism. Whatever I am making will look exactly like the picture in the recipe book, and everyone will gasp in amazement. Inevitably, something goes horribly wrong. I once made a crab soufflé which took hours and hours of whipping up egg whites, prising crab out of its shell and making a delicious creamy sauce. All the ramekins looked OK when I put them in the oven, but after the allotted cooking time, they remained resolutely unrisen. Not so much as a bubble. Zip. So I left them in for another half-hour. Finally – oh joy – they had puffed up splendidly. Jill and Pete were round for dinner, and gasped admiringly as they were ceremoniously brought in.

'How clever you are,' Jill said. 'I couldn't make a soufflé to save my life.' Everyone looked expectantly at her as she dug her fork into the rounded brown surface. It opened with a small crack, and there was an immediate 'whoof' of crab-smelling air. She dug her fork deeper. Nothing. I'd spent two hours producing ramekins full of crabby air. 'Well, it *smelt* very nice,' said Jill, loyally.

Tonight I was going to attempt to make fresh summer berries in mille-feuille pastry with *crème anglaise*. No problem. All you had to do was heat the berries gently in some sugar and gin to make a kind of coulis, and then sandwich them between the sweet, crispy layers of pastry, making an attractive pool next to it with the *crème anglaise*. Harriet would be suitably stunned that someone as un-domestic as me could whip up such a difficult, and delicious, pudding. I would make her green with envy. Even though, of course, Harriet would not use pastry twice. Quite unacceptable, my dear. Sod her.

When I got to the checkout I of course chose the queue behind the lady who had picked out the only bag of peas in the supermarket without a bar code. 'STE-PHEN!' the girl on the till bellowed. 'Check these peas for me, will you?' Now why is it that all male supermarket workers either have a) a physical handicap or b) clinical acne. They are of course lovely, charming people, but it doesn't half take them an age to check out the price of a bag of peas.

It was now perilously close to four o'clock, and not only did I have an entire dinner party to cook, I also had an entire house to clean. Mike would have to put the children to bed. Now, booze. I always mean to buy wisely and carefully, taking note of the price, but when I get to the booze aisle I am always so overcome by longing I grab randomly, and get to the checkout to find I have bought Gevrey-Chambertin and Chablis Premier Cru, which inevitably are priced at around fifteen pounds instead of four. I'd also decided we should have gin on the terrace (if we could all squeeze round our little table), as the weather was now getting wonderfully balmy in the early evenings, and the Bombay gin was around fifteen quid. I would have to put my hand over my eyes when she rang up the final total, and cross my fingers behind my back as my credit card was swiped. Would it go through or would

I be frog-marched into the manager's office for spending absurdly over my overdraft limit? I whistled nonchalantly and developed an extraordinarily intense fascination with the contents of one of my plastic bags while waiting for the machine to go whir whir beep beep as it went through. Thank God it did.

I just wish we had a bigger and better garden to sit in – was nobody ever going to put an offer in on the cottage? We'd had more people round last weekend, and they had seemed quite keen but we hadn't heard anything. Harriet was going to be livid when she heard about Lawn Farm, hee, hee, because I know she's quite fancied a move and it would have been perfect for her family. It will increase our standing no end in the eyes of Harriet-type people.

By seven o'clock, I was a whirling dervish. I'd begun quite calmly, plopping Tom onto Mike's chest when we got home, and telling him to keep them entertained and out of the kitchen for the next hour or so. Clearly feeling guilty for having fallen asleep, he happily concurred. He even asked what I was planning to cook, which is unusual for him as he usually reacts with amazement that I can cook real food at all.

First I had to tidy the kitchen, which was a mammoth task because we hadn't actually cleared up from breakfast, and there were cornflakes congealing in bowls alongside piles of breadcrumbs from the hasty sandwiches I'd made at lunch-time. I wonder if other mothers are such sluts. Sometimes the effort of emptying the dishwasher seems so stupendous I have to lie down and read the paper for half an hour before I can summon up the energy. The *filet de boeuf* was fairly quickly assembled – I'd even remembered to buy shallots instead of boring old onions. Grating the nutmeg into the pan, I also grated in a little finger; hell, it'll add texture. Rebecca kept trying to slide in to pinch the after-dinner chocolates I'd set out on a plate, but was forcibly repelled. 'I want to help you,' she said.

'The best way you can help me is by going and standing at the top of the garden,' I said, meanly. 'Where's Daddy?'

'Playing with Tom outside,' she said, sulkily. 'He never wants to play with me.'

'Of course he does,' I said, and opened the window to bellow to Mike to come in and get her.

Eventually, all was prepared except the mille-feuille. This was making me feel a little tense. It's just ordinary sweet pastry sliced very thinly, I kept saying to myself. The problem was, my hands were so slidy from beating the egg to paint on top of the pastry for the *filet de boeuf*, I couldn't keep the knife still to slice it very thinly, and instead of almost transparent layers they looked more like slices of processed cheese. They'd crisp up in the oven.

A final hurtle round the house, stuffing newspapers under the settee and hoovering up matted piles of dog hair, and I was in the bath by ten to eight. Mike said he'd invited them for eight, but no-one's ever on time for dinner parties. If they're like us, it takes half an hour to leave the house. I was just beginning to comb conditioner through my hair and thinking vaguely about what I was going to wear – and the doorbell rang. 'Mike!' I yelled frantically. 'Don't let them in!'

Sunday 7 June
I have a dull, throbbing pressure at the front of my head. My mouth has a sharp metallic tang, and I have to concentrate very closely on what I am doing. The dinner party was – how shall I put this – not all I would have hoped for, and I do not think Delia Smith will be banging on my door demanding the recipe for

my pudding. The only answer seemed to be to drink vast quantities of wine, and I could only cope with Tom and Rebecca this morning by putting on a video and lying like a corpse on the sofa.

As soon as Harriet and Martin arrived, I leapt out of the bath and dragged on the nearest dress in my wardrobe. I half-dried my hair, and slapped on mascara, eyeliner and lipstick – no time for foundation. Harriet, of course, was glowing. She was wearing a simple, pale yellow silk shift dress, showing off to perfection her long, slim tanned legs. On her feet were pale yellow strappy suede high heels, and her blonde hair fell silkily onto her shoulders.

'Darling.' She bent forward to give me a warm, perfumed kiss. 'We haven't caught you on the hop, have we? I'm so sorry we were on time, because I know how busy you working girls are. The house looks lovely,' she lied, and pressed a bouquet of summer flowers into my hands.

'It's no problem,' I said, following her swaying figure into the kitchen. Why didn't she have a panty line in that dress? Was she wearing no knickers?

Because I hadn't had time to dry my hair properly, it was beginning to dry into a frizz. It really needs a hot brush to make the curls look as if they are curls and not a wild bush. The dress I'd grabbed was uncomfortably tight around my middle, and I realized the hem was coming down at the back. I desperately wanted to get her out of the kitchen, so I could get started, otherwise we'd be eating at midnight. Martin and Mike came in too, and Martin gave me one of his hearty hugs and boomed, 'How's the television star?' He was wearing a raffish stripy bow-tie, and his shoes had those little tassles on. How does Harriet stand him?

Giving them all drinks, I shooed them out of the kitchen, hissing to Mike to take them onto the terrace,

142

because I'd lit some outdoor candles and it looked reasonably inviting. It also meant I could crash pans about and swear without being heard. I confidently reached forward to put the *filet de boeuf* into the oven. It wasn't where I'd left it. It should have been sitting there, its little pastry leaves gleaming with beaten egg. It wasn't. Oh my God! I said to myself. Had I put it somewhere else? I frantically racked my brain. And then I noticed that Turtle was not in his basket as usual, but was a shiny black snout sticking out from under the kitchen table. I peered underneath. Immediately, his ears went flat against his head, his eyes peered up at me and his tail wagged slowly and guiltily. This was his I've-done-something-really-bad face. 'You haven't,' I gasped. 'Come out!'

He slunk out, part dog, part eel. He'd either eaten it completely, or he'd taken it into the utility room. And there it was. He'd obviously pulled the pan down taken a bite out of the pastry. But then, being a well-behaved dog at heart, he'd been overcome by remorse and left.

There was nothing else for it. I took all the pastry off, and threw it in the bin. I delved into the freezer and found some ready-made shortcrust pastry. I scraped off the chopped onions and mushrooms, and I *washed the beef*. What else could I do? I couldn't rustle up anything else at such short notice, and surely you couldn't die from a bit of Labrador slobber? They would never ever know, I thought, as I hastily wrapped it up *sans* onions and bunged it into the oven.

I could just hear the sound of their laughter and the clink of glasses as I toiled and troubled, getting redder and redder in the face. It is simply not fair that I should have to spend the best part of a dinner party sweating in the kitchen. Why the hell had Mike ever suggested this? He could damn well do the clearing up.

I'd managed to make the table look reasonably attractive, but I could tell Harriet was running a practised eye over the slightly smeary knives and forks, the cloudy glasses (yes, I had put them in the dishwasher for speed of cleaning) and the red wine stain I had been too drunk to put salt on at the time. She was sitting next to Mike, and seemed very attentive to him, inclining her head towards his as he told her about Lawn Farm. 'You'll be much nearer to us!' she said. 'How lovely. The children will be delighted.' It looked like she'd be pretty delighted, too. She has this way of flicking her hair back over one shoulder, and smiling from under her eyelashes. Smarmy cow. I must have a go at that in the privacy of my own room.

When I wasn't hurtling backwards and forwards carrying plates, Martin had me trapped at the far end of the table and droned on and on about the new off-roader he'd just bought and the cost of the boys' school fees, as if they worried about money at all. I couldn't quite hear what Mike and Harriet were talking about, because they were leaning towards each other, but I could hardly say, 'Shut up,' to Martin so I could find out what they were saying and then slide him and me into their conversation, which seemed far more interesting than ours. No-one commented on the beef, but to me it had rather lost something in the wash. Whatever Harriet was saying, Mike was finding it very entertaining, judging by his laughter. He leant over to fill up Harriet's glass and then put the bottle down.

'I'd like some more,' I said.

'Oh, sorry,' he said, passing me the bottle instead of pouring it himself.

'Let me do that,' said Martin, gallantly. I drained it almost in one gulp. I had a lot of catching up to do.

Back in the kitchen, I carefully lifted the sheets of

mille-feuille out of the oven, ready to make the layers of berries. Horrors. Instead of cooking into crispy separate sheets, it had merged and congealed into a flat blanket. Oh Christ, I thought, and cut it hastily into four slices. That would have to do, as by now I had had so much wine the finer points of culinary achievement had become irrelevant. I crammed in the berries and poured over the *crème anglaise*. Sod it. I took it in, placed it carefully on the table, and Mike said, 'What's this?'

Harriet smiled up at me and said, 'It looks delicious, whatever it is.'

'It's summer fruits with mille-feuille pastry,' I said.

'Looks more like une-feuille,' said Mike, and Harriet, God rot her, began to laugh.

Friday 19 June

'Mummy,' said Rebecca, wandering into my bedroom as I surveyed the contents of my wardrobe. I had no shirts. No shirts at all to speak of. Well, to be honest, I had lots, but they weren't here. They were in the ironing pile in the airing cupboard. It had got to the stage where I could no longer look into the airing cupboard because the pile had become too big. It was out of control, a huge, towering thing which seemed to be getting larger all on its own. I couldn't try to tackle it because it would be pointless. It would simply laugh and regurgitate more crinkled T-shirts and jeans and shirts. *'Mummy,'* said Rebecca, more insistently. 'I want you to take me to school today.'

'I can't, darling,' I said. 'You know I have to go to work.'

'But we're doing a concert and I'm singing "Puff the Magic Dragon" all on my own. I've been learning it for ages.'

'What concert?' I said. 'I didn't know you had a concert.'

'We had a letter,' said Rebecca. 'I gave it to Claire.'

'Claire,' I said as I shoved on earrings and grimaced at my face in the mirror in the kitchen. 'Was there a letter about a concert?'

'Yes,' she said, laying the table with bowls and spoons and plastic cups. 'Don't worry, Tom and I are going.'

'It's just I didn't know,' I said, unreasonably annoyed as I couldn't have gone anyway, I had to take the train to a meeting in London today.

'You've been so busy this week I didn't want to bother you,' she said.

I had been busy. I'd hardly seen the children, with several late meetings and very early starts. Leaving so early, it seemed much easier not to wake them, and three nights this week I'd missed Tom's bedtime. I was beginning to feel like a real person again, and with all this rushing around, the weight was dropping off me.

'I'm sorry,' I said, dropping my head to give Rebecca a kiss as she spelt out the words on the back of her corn-flakes packet.

'It's OK,' she said. 'As long as Claire's coming.'

I hurried out of the house.

Saturday 27 June

Yesterday the estate agent rang to say the couple who'd seemed so keen had put an offer in on the house. 'Yippee!' I yelled. 'How much?' It was ten thousand pounds below the asking price, but after such a long wait it seemed like manna from heaven. I rang Mike.

'Not enough,' he said.

'But, *Mike*,' I said. 'This is the first offer we've had.

146

No-one might ever offer again. We'll lose them if we refuse.'

'Not if they're so keen,' he said. God, he was so irritatingly *cool*. 'Leave it, Carrie. I'll ring them back. Leave this to me.'

I was like a cat on a hot tin roof all day, by the end of which they hadn't come up with any more money. I could see my dream of Lawn Farm melting away like ice-cream on an Aga. This morning I packed the children into the car to drive round and see it again. We haven't been for ages – it felt like tempting fate with our own house unsold. Our house. The 'For Sale' notice had been taken down, a good sign. 'Please don't let Mike bugger this up,' I prayed fervently. Then Mrs Gower came out into the garden carrying a trowel and I forced us all to lie flat on the seat so it wouldn't look like we were snooping.

Sunday 28 June

The phone rang at nine this morning: Harriet, sounding unreasonably bright and cheerful. She'd sent me a little note to say thank you for the dinner party, which made me intensely irritated, as I always forget even to ring. 'I've had the most marvellous idea. A friend of Martin's – Jeremy – has the most wonderful place with a pool in the Dordogne. You said you two hadn't anything planned for the summer and it would be lovely if we could perhaps all go together. The children would love it, wouldn't they? I mentioned it to Mike during dinner and he seemed very keen.'

Did he? He hadn't mentioned it to me. Still, the chance of a holiday was a chance of a holiday, and not to be sniffed at, even if it meant putting up with Harriet for a fortnight. 'I'll talk to Mike,' I said.

'You can't go with *her*,' said Jill, horrified. She knew

Harriet from an ill-advised offer to help out at the summer fair. It had been dominated by Harriet and her cronies. 'She's *thin*. Just think what she'll look like in a bikini. And she'll make you all do lots of jolly things all the time. It's OK for men to do things on holiday, but women should not have to move. There is a reason, you know, why men are broad at the top and narrow at the bottom. They aren't meant to stay sitting down. We, on the other hand, are built like pyramids which means we should be allowed to sit down for long periods of time. It may only be five o'clock, but I for one am ready for a glass of wine. Are those nachos over there?'

7

Monday 6 July
In the middle of the night Tom let out a piercing shriek.
It wasn't the long steady wail of a baby who's wet and
uncomfortable, but a sudden terrified shout. I shot out
of bed as if stung and hurtled down the stairs. He'd
pulled himself up against the bars of his cot, and his
face was contorted with fear, screaming and then pausing to catch his breath with a series of small juddering
sobs before letting out the next ear-splitting wail.
'Tom!' I said, picking him up and holding him fiercely
against me. 'What's the matter? It's all right, it's all
right, Mummy's here.'

I carried him over to the small bed next to his cot,
and sat gently rocking him, stroking his hair as his sobs
began to subside. He didn't have a temperature – it
must just be a bad dream. Then he suddenly pulled
away from me. 'Mum, Mum,' he said, turning his face
desperately towards the door. 'Mum, Mum!' His cries
were getting louder again, and he struggled in my
arms.

'I'm *here*,' I said.

Rebecca's little white-nightied figure appeared in the
door. 'He wants Claire,' she said. 'Claire tells him she's
his mummy. I've heard her.'

'This *is* Mummy,' I said, turning his face up to mine, but how could I make him understand? He didn't want me. He wriggled, arching his back and his cries reached a crescendo again.

'What the bloody hell's going on?' It was Mike, wandering naked down the stairs, one side of his hair standing on end, his face etched with irritation.

'It's Tom,' I said. 'I can't stop him crying.'

'Give him to me,' said Mike, reaching out to take him. But Tom eyed Mike as if he were a stranger, and strained desperately towards the door.

'What are we going to do?' I said, feeling hysterical tears filling my eyes, as Tom continued to scream and push away from me. He'd never done this before.

'We'll have to take him into bed with us,' said Mike, looking as if he'd rather share his bed with a piranha. 'Christ, I've a hell of a day tomorrow as well. I'll take him.' He went off, carrying the still-sobbing and wriggling little form up the stairs, while I tucked Rebecca back into bed.

'Claire says things like, "Let Mummy do it," to Tom,' said Rebecca, sleepily. 'She shouldn't, should she, Mummy? You're our mummy, not Claire. I love you.' I bent down to kiss her cheek as she turned and pushed her hands underneath the pillow. She was asleep within seconds, and I wandered wearily upstairs. Three hours until I got up to face a horrendously busy day.

Mike had tucked Tom in the middle of the bed and had already gone back to sleep. Tom's little body was still shuddering, his hands clutching the sheet. 'Shush,' I said, sliding gently in next to him, and tucking my knees up under his feet. 'Shush.' I stroked his face and he turned his frightened eyes towards me. But he wouldn't focus his eyes on my face, he was looking beyond me. For the first time, I couldn't make it better.

150

I didn't go back to sleep properly. As Tom slowly, slowly drifted off to sleep I watched his face, the way his lashes swept down over his cheeks, the hands thrown up over his head in the abandoned posture of baby sleep and his mouth moving as he followed his dream. What did he dream? Did he dream about running after Rebecca, as he clung like a mountaineer on a precipice to the furniture? Did he dream of rolling and rolling in the muddy patch at the top of the garden, or eating chocolate all day? Who peopled these dreams? Was it me . . . or was it Claire? I lay still, pondering the fact that so many milestones of his life had passed me by. Coming home from work to hear Claire say, 'Show Mummy how clever you are,' as he proudly made a little tiger face and showed me the first glimpse of a tiny tooth. Rebecca running towards me after work shouting, 'Tom's crawling!' after he'd made his first shuffling movement backwards. The first time he'd uttered a recognizable word – which, rather ignominiously was 'dirty' . . . Moments which could never be recaptured.

Most of the time I told myself it didn't matter, that I'd catch up with him somehow. But now, now it was beginning to feel that simply being with my children was a special event. Every night, Rebecca ran to me, thrilled that I was home. It was a treat for them to have me there. I thought of my own mum, how I clung to her at the beginning of each school day not wanting to leave her because she meant being safe, and how excited I was to see her every day as I ran out of school with my friends. I was always so proud of her. Now she may strike me as being eccentric and vaguely peculiar, but then she was my reason for being.

I have justified my way of parenting partly because all my family took her so much for granted. She was always there, just Mum. But that wasn't really how I felt when I was young. Perhaps I did when I was a teenager, but as a child I loved and needed her with such a passion I couldn't bear to be separated from her. Have I made *my* children independent, or have I dislocated them from their natural source of love and support? I relied on my mum for everything: remembering my pencil case, my ballet clothes, my sports pumps. She always knew what I needed and she made it seem her most important task. But I have handed over these tiny daily rituals of parenthood to pursue the goals in life *I* have made my priority. Parenting has become a sideline.

I turned over restlessly, taking care not to wake Tom, and thought, I could cope, I know I could cope and not feel so torn if Mike would just share these responsibilities and make me feel that we were in this together. Yet it wasn't that he wilfully refused, he just didn't see what needed to be done, and when I had to ask him to help, it always sounded like nagging or demanding a favour. Much easier to get Claire to do it, because, after all, looking after the children is what we're paying her for, isn't it?

I lay on my back, the pale morning light beginning to filter through the curtains as the tractor from the farm up the road trundled noisily past. How would my children think of me when they were adults? Would they think of everyday things, or would those day-to-day memories – so vivid in a child's life – be always associated with Claire? Would I be this slightly glittering figure, this 'Mummy' who was brought out in the evenings and at weekends, not the person who ran their lives? But I can't have everything. I have far more of a *life* than my mother ever did. Or what I *perceive* as a successful life. Nobody wins any prizes or even respect for staying at home now, it's seen as failure. Success is measured only in terms of what job you do.

I gently stroked Tom's face as he slept, making him twitch and snuffle. How can I let him know how much I love him without being with him all the time? It's lovely that he's so comfortable with Claire, that he switches allegiance from me to her as soon as she walks through the door. How awful it would be if he was unhappy – as Rebecca had been at her nursery. I must stop being so mawkish, I thought, as I smoothed his dark hair back off his forehead. I closed my eyes and tried to sleep – I'd be a zombie all day – but everything I was worried about began to flash through my mind: money; the house; telling Mike about the management course; how we could end this stand-off between us; the Claire 'mummy' thing . . . It all swam around in my brain, forming patterns like a child's kaleidoscope and then breaking up. It made sleep impossible, and an unbidden tear slid down my face into the pillow. How could I be so sad inside when everyone else thought I was such a success? Morning felt a long time coming.

Wednesday 8 July
'What's all this about Harriet and the Dordogne?' I said to Mike tonight, as we weebled about the kitchen, trying to prepare some food in a state of after-work semi-consciousness. The fridge this evening contained: one piece of Dairylea cheese; a radicchio which was slowly metamorphosing from lettuce into Bovril; a pot of slightly furry taramasolata; and a can of Heineken. I defy anyone to make a meal from that.

'She mentioned it at dinner and I thought it might be quite fun. I didn't say yes. But wouldn't it be cheaper than going on our own?' said Mike vaguely, as if it were of little importance. 'What's for dinner?'

'There's some pasta in the larder,' I said, hopefully. 'We could have that with tinned tomatoes and capers . . . and I'm sure there's a can of tuna here somewhere,' rummaging about in the (very grimy) back of the cupboard.

'What do you think, Turtle?' said Mike to the dog. 'Would that make an appetizing snack for a hungry man?' Turtle at that moment chose to regurgitate part of his dried dog food and make an awful retching sound. 'Exactly,' said Mike grimacing, and, reaching for the top cupboard, he took down a box of muesli. With the air of a condemned man, he poured the contents into a bowl and flicked open the can of beer. 'There's nothing like home cooking,' he said. 'And this is . . .'

'Nothing like home cooking,' I finished for him, taking a packet of pitta bread out of the freezer to defrost to have with the taramasolata. Christ. We earn all this money and all we have to eat is muesli and furry taramasolata.

'I thought you said you were going to the supermarket at lunch-time,' Mike said.

'I couldn't,' I replied. 'Nick decided we had to have a meeting and I've had a freelance crisis. I couldn't get away. Anyway, why couldn't you go?'

'Don't be daft,' he said. 'How could I get to the supermarket? It's miles from the office and anyway I'd promised Steve a pint.'

'At least your priorities are in the right order,' I retorted sarcastically. There has to be more to life than this. Working flat out all day without time to draw breath, returning home so knackered I can hardly get out of the car, and then facing the prospect of trying to make a meal out of ingredients which would make a starving dog barf. I wondered if now was the moment to tell Mike we'd also run out of milk, so he was going to have to eat dry muesli, which is very like eating rabbit poo in wood shavings.

'I'm going to have to ask Claire to shop for us. We can't keep running out of things.' The trouble is that when I do ask Claire to buy food, she buys the type of things I'd never get in a month of Sundays: packet sauces, frozen portions of fish and chips and sticky chocolate mousses with synthetic whipped cream on the top. I have politely asked if she could try and give the children fresh vegetables and fruit, but all she says is, 'But Rebecca loves her chocolate mousse.' I also know that Tom has sweets most days because I've seen the wrappers in her car, but how can I police it? His daily diet these days seems to be sweets and packets of crisps. Whereas I always buy low-sugar fruit cordial, by mid-week our cupboards are full of Coke and Seven-Up, which I know Claire loves to drink as well. It's like having a greedy teenager in the house, albeit one who has the daily care of your most precious possessions.

Mike opened the fridge and peered in. 'Where the hell is the milk?' he said.

'I really don't know,' I said. 'Perhaps the milk fairy hasn't been.' Mike turned to me, his face registering a distinct lack of amusement. 'Rebecca must have had the last of it for her bed-time drink,' I explained.

'Christ!' Mike exploded. 'Is it too much to ask for us to have milk in the house? Why the hell can't you get things organized! You've got everyone running around after you – Claire to look after the children, now another bloody person to come in and walk the dogs because "Claire can't manage it", you're talking about getting a cleaner we can't afford and now it's too much for you to organize for us to have a pint of milk in the fridge!'

'Mike,' I said, trying not to start a row, 'I got into this

house precisely half an hour before you walked in through the door. OK, you left the house an hour before me this morning, but how exactly was I going to get to the shops and back when I had to get myself and the children up and dressed? When would you like me to *do* all this organizing? Perhaps I ought to ask Nick if I could have a couple of hours off every day so I could go round the supermarket and maybe take your clothes to the dry-cleaners for you? Perhaps I should just miss out on the planning meeting even though I'm actually the editor of it so I can make sure your trousers are clean? I can't do this, Mike. I can't be held responsible for everything. Rebecca was bloody awful when I got home. She wouldn't talk to me at all and she started to scream when Claire was leaving, hanging on to her, which I know was a big act – she just wanted me to feel guilty. I had to deal with all that and get her into bed before you even got home and now you're complaining that we don't have any milk. Well, I'm sorry but that is not currently my number one priority.' I slammed shut the door of the kitchen in tears and ran up to our bedroom.

As I passed Rebecca's room she zoomed out, her face pale with worry. 'Why are you and Daddy shouting?' she said, her mouth working as she tried not to cry. 'Are you sad at each other?'

'It's OK, darling, we just had a little argument, it's fine now. You go back to sleep,' I said, putting my arm round her.

'It's all right, Rebecca.' It was Mike behind me. He gave me a little push towards the stairs. 'I'll put her back to bed.' Rebecca tottered back into her bedroom, and Mike followed her. As he got to the door, he turned to me. 'Go to bed,' he said, quietly. 'We'll sort this out later.'

I lay on the bed, my head swimming. I was starving,

and I still had some paperwork to finish off for tomorrow. I felt numb and exhausted. Mike was so *selfish*. All he ever thought about were his own needs, and if something went slightly wrong with what he wanted there and then he seemed to think he had the right to lash out at me.

How dare he shout at me because we didn't have any bloody *milk,* I thought. So what? So fucking what? I've had enough of taking all this crap from him. If he wants me to work then he's either going to have to take an equal responsibility for everything else or ... and I took a deep breath and realized what I was admitting to myself: I and the children would be better off on our own. The only time I ever get really upset is because of him. If it was just me I *could* cope pretty well, and everything would be quite calm.

It's just when he's here, I raged inwardly, criticizing the fact that I've given in when Rebecca screams for biscuits, telling me I'm spoiling Tom because I pick him up when he cries, and that awful feeling of tension I always have when we go out as a family, that somehow he's about to fly off the handle and I have to divert the drama at all costs. Mike seems to think we can be this perfect family without an iota of effort from him and that I should be able to make it happen, even though I'm just as exhausted as he is. I am sick and tired of being made to feel inadequate. I'm doing my bloody best, and it's a damn sight more than he's contributing. I am getting so fed up with this – *controlling* – attitude that he knows best about everything and that we all have to defer to him and let him decide what we are going to do.

I bet we've lost that couple who wanted to buy the cottage, just because Mike thought he could push the price up a bit more. We aren't living in a partnership. We're living in a *dictatorship.* I mean, here I am, bringing in almost the same money as him, running the house, supervising the child-care and even mowing the fucking *lawn* last Sunday. What is he actually *for*? At least my father had an excuse for his appallingly selfish and lazy behaviour at home – he was paying for everything. What right does Mike have to get away with all this macho crap?

I was just swinging my legs off the bed ready to go back downstairs when he came up the stairs. 'Carrie,' he said, with an irritatingly calm look on his face, sitting down on the bed next to me and trying to put his arm round me. I moved away. 'I'm worried about you. You're flying off the handle for nothing. I really think this new job might be too much for you.'

'This has absolutely nothing to do with my job,' I hissed at him angrily, trying not to shout so Rebecca, who has ears like a radar for our raised voices, couldn't hear. 'You started this whole bloody row about *milk*, remember? I was fine before then. You can't go about causing drama and then back off and have the bloody nerve to say that *I'm* the one who's unstable. I'm not the person who went into a rage because no-one had bought *milk*. You need to think about yourself. I'm not the selfish person here. Why don't you pull *your* finger out and get things organized? How dare you say I'm disorganized when I arrange all the child-care and supervise Claire and try to do all the shopping and the washing? You're the useless person in this house.'

As soon as the words were out of my mouth I regretted them. But why should he have the monopoly on condescension? He needed to face up to the fact that he had to pull his weight more if our lives were to succeed. Mike pulled away the hand which was reaching out to me, and for one awful moment I thought he was going to hit me. His handsome face was cold and

158

hard, impenetrable in a way I'd never seen before. It was like looking at a stranger.

'I have to go to London tomorrow,' he said, turning away from me and walking into the bathroom. I could hear him running the taps for a bath. 'I'll stay in a hotel overnight,' he added coldly. 'It'll give us a break and it'll give you a chance to think.'

When I came up to bed, much later, having finished my work with my head like a nodding dog, he was lying in bed and I thought, asleep. But when I slid in next to him, he turned to me, and ran his hands over my breasts, pressing up against me. Christ, no. He can't possibly expect me to make love to him after he's been so awful. I suppose he thinks that making love will make it all OK. I turned my back to him, and coldly pushed away his hands.

'Carrie,' said Mike in a dangerously quiet voice, 'you don't know what you've just done.'

Oh *shut up*, I thought. Why does he have to be so dramatic about everything? We'll make it up in the morning, I thought dreamily, as I drifted off to sleep.

Thursday 9 July
This morning I heard him rise early and pack shirts into his overnight bag. He'll come over and kiss me in a minute, I thought, and didn't open my eyes. It was up to him to apologize. With eyes still tightly shut, I heard him bring Tom up the stairs, and felt him gently put him into the bed beside me. I opened my eyes then to reach up to Mike – I was even prepared to say *I* was sorry – but he'd gone. There was just silence and space and then the next thing I heard was the front door slam shut. He'd left.

Later the estate agent rang me at work. The couple who'd been so keen on the house were willing to up their offer a little. Understandably, the estate agent stressed the fact that they might not go any higher, and we could possibly lose them if we turned this down. They obviously felt we were the house-sellers from hell, and desperately wanted us off their books. I debated trying to get hold of Mike at the conference he was at in London, but then thought better of it. Hell, I could take this decision on my own. I went into the loo and sat there and sweated for a few moments. This was our future I was trying to decide, and I had no idea how cross Mike might be if I just accepted it. But why should I always let him take all the big decisions? I took a deep breath, went back into my office and rang them up. 'That's fine. We'll accept that,' I said. Then I put down the phone with trembling hands. Oo-er. What was Mike going to say?

Friday 10 July
The sound of a heavy overnight bag hitting the carpet tonight was the signal he'd returned. Rebecca immediately leapt up from her Disney video and rushed out into the hall. 'Daddy, Daddy!' she cried. 'Did you get me a present?' I held Tom against me and felt my heart racing. Mike hadn't rung once in the past two days, and I had no idea where he'd stayed the night. It was the first time he'd ever stayed away from me and not rung to let me know where he was. How could he be so petty? Surely our life and the children was more important than the fact that I'd called him useless? I heard the sound of his bag unzipping, and then a yelp of excitement as Rebecca came running in clutching Princess Barbie. She'd been after this for months – give Rebecca anything pink and plastic and we're talking ecstasy. 'Look, look!' she yelled, almost in tears in her excitement. 'Look what Daddy's brought me!'

Mike walked in and I felt him take Tom from my arms. He said, 'Come and see what I've got for you.' I bent down to stroke Turtle, and I could feel my eyes filling with tears, as Tom tore at wrapping paper and shrieked. I wanted Mike to touch *me*. How bloody annoying that I could be so furious with him and still be thrilled when I heard his key in the door. 'Look, Mummy!' said Rebecca. 'Tom's got Action Man!' Oh great. Why didn't he go the whole hog and buy him a *gun*?

'What did you buy for Mummy?' said Rebecca. I forced myself to look up. Mike was holding Tom in his arms, smiling as Tom made Action Man fly through the air like Superman, and pretending he hadn't heard her. How dare he be so handsome in his dark suit and red silk tie? Thoughts of what he might have been up to made my stomach clench. I felt sick. Where had he stayed, and why had he been so long? How was I going to find out if I couldn't *speak* to him? I couldn't bear not to know. The lavish love and attention he was giving the children was expressly designed to make me feel left out, and it made me furious that he could be so childish about it. Why did he want to keep this row going? Normally after a day he was home with flowers, or he'd ring me at work to say he'd booked a table at one of our favourite restaurants. Not this time. We were obviously digging in for a long battle. Well, if that's how he wants to play it, then fine. I could do a PhD in *froideur*.

Mike took the children off and put them to bed, and I crumbled parsley into the casserole I'd made. Salty tears dripped in amongst the beef stock. We ate it in front of the television, neither of us speaking, and the bottle of wine I'd bought in anticipation of making up stood in the kitchen, unopened.

Saturday 11 July

This morning the phone rang early, while Tom and I were splashing about in the bath. I heard Mike answer it, and then froze.

'My wife said what? I'll ring you back in a few minutes.' Footsteps on the stairs, and then he opened the bathroom door. I tried to sit up and look suitably in control, but it's very hard to muster dignity when you have two small penguins wearing little red hats rowing a wind-up boat on your stomach.

'Why didn't you tell me you'd accepted an offer on the house?' Mike said, making a determined effort not to look at my breasts, which were bobbing about on the top of the water like two humps of the Loch Ness monster.

'You didn't ask,' I said, sounding braver than I really felt.

'We could have pushed them up much higher,' Mike said.

'Oh come on,' I said, reaching out for the towel and causing a tidal wave which made Tom bob about like a cork. 'It's only five thousand less than we wanted and it means we can get going on Lawn Farm.'

'I don't think we can afford it,' said Mike.

Pulling out the plug with my toe, I lifted a protesting slippery Tom out of the water and then heaved myself upright. Mike retreated out of the room. Clearly the sight of my naked body was something he couldn't cope with at the moment. I felt anger rising within me. He was prepared to jeopardize our future because he knew how much I wanted the new house and how much it would hurt me to lose it.

'We've been through all that,' I said through the half-closed door. 'We've worked out that we can just afford it. What's got into you? You were as keen as I was.' Mike said nothing and I heard him go back downstairs.

But I didn't hear him pick up the phone to the estate agent to cancel our acceptance. Hmm. Half a victory. I seemed to have cleared that hurdle, but quite how Mike and I were going to buy a house without actually communicating with each other was going to be interesting. Still, I could get used to not speaking to Mike. In a bizarre kind of way it would be more peaceful. I could just muddle along with work and the children, and not have to think about him. As long as I knew we *were* going to make it up, I could even enjoy the lack of responsibility for him. And I hadn't ironed his shirts for almost a week now. He'd run out soon, and if he wasn't speaking to me, he couldn't ask me to do them, could he?

Tuesday 21 July
Having heard nothing more about this management course, I'd assumed it was all off and I for one didn't want to remind Nick about it, because I've seen *She'll Be Wearing Pink Pyjamas* and I cannot see myself hurtling down a rope swing wearing night clothes. Neither can I see myself yomping across the hills wearing a large pair of boots like Popeye and clutching a compass. I never know where north is either. Doesn't it change whichever way you're facing? I could never quite get my head around that particular concept. And me and tents do not get on well. The thought of being zipped like a maggot into a sleeping bag and trying to sleep while assorted beasties climb up my nostrils does not fill me with joy. It's like shagging on the floor – I'm too old for it. I'm more of a mattress person now. Nor am I excited by the prospect of being herded together with dozens of other middle managers at the BBC and made to work out how to ford a stream using only a pencil. Anyway, these courses are usually only

an excuse to get pissed and sleep with other people, and I have had quite enough of men for the moment, thank you.

I told Jill about Mike and our row on the phone last week (being able to laugh about it with her made me feel a whole lot better), and she and I decided we are going to join a women's commune. We are going to do a moonlight flit and leave our appalled husbands in sole care of the children. Then we are going to sell all our worldy possessions and buy cheesecloth dresses. We are going to paint strange runic signs on our faces, wear long dangly earrings like wind chimes and change our names to something like Enigma and Neptune, and join an artists' colony by the sea. At dawn we will rise to dance our strange, cosmic movements in time to the earth's rhythms and we will kiss trees. We will never have to pair socks again.

'But I don't like cheesecloth,' I said. 'It smells when it gets wet. Can I take my hairdryer?'

'No,' said Jill firmly. 'You must let your hair grow as nature intended.'

'You mean we're going to have to have great furry muffs under our arms?'

'That is one of the sacrifices of becoming at one with nature and living without the burden of men,' said Jill. 'Anyway, I have to go now. Susie's Microchips are ready and I've got a huge pile of ironing. Peace, sister.'

Nick caught me just as I was coming out of the planning meeting. He looked rather embarrassed. 'Carrie,' he said, 'you know that management course I mentioned to you? Well, I'm afraid I rather buggered it up. I forgot to send off the forms in time and now they haven't any places. But I have been asked by Bruce to try to find someone really good to act as an executive producer on a half-hour documentary we're filming in Boston at the beginning of next month. It's on children

164

with dyslexia, apparently they're getting miracle cures at this new centre. Parents in the Midlands are paying over fifty thousand a year to get their children in. Fancy it? It'd be about a week of filming. Let me know if you do want to go, because Bruce is getting very edgy about it. The producer who was supposed to go has broken his arm playing tennis, if you can believe it.'

A week in Boston. All On My Own. It is extremely appealing. After two weeks of the cold war – or is it the phoney war? – I now feel like I am going to explode. Every time I try to talk to Mike, or make a gesture to hold him, he moves away. He has become . . . *elusive*. He knows all too well that I cannot bear to be apart from him, and that this lack of contact is torture for me. It's certainly brought home how much I physically need him, and not being able to discuss anything with him is driving me mad. I just hope it's as much torture for him, that's all. I certainly can't remember what it's like to sleep with him, and the thought of being warm and jokey again seems impossible.

He's not sleeping in our room. The first night after his London meeting he stomped out of the TV room and into the spare room and slammed the door. I think he expected me to grapple with the door handle or turn up mewing at the window. I bet he even put a chair under the handle so I couldn't get in. How ridiculously childish. Far be it from me to peer through the keyhole to see if he'd blocked the door, or even hunt for a key downstairs so I could lock him in so he couldn't get out to go to the loo. Would I stoop so low? Of course I would. It is all so infantile. I even found myself lying in bed last night plotting what I can do to make his life awkward. Honestly, if people could see what couples do to each other in the privacy of a marriage they'd think both of them were at least two sandwiches short of a loaf. In a rare moment of frankness Harriet once

165

told me she'd had a furious row with Martin in the car. He was on his way to work for an important meeting and she was driving him to the station. He was so foul to her she slammed on the central locking, activated the child locks and flew past the station. She then drove furiously into the depths of the countryside, slammed the brakes on and tried to push him out of the car. A puzzled lad on a tractor was then treated to the bizarre sight of two very well-dressed people wrestling in the front of a Land-Rover. Eventually she said even *they* were struck by the ludicrous nature of the situation and burst out laughing.

I'm sure one of us sooner or later is going to have to say, 'This is pathetic and we'll sort it out.' But the longer it goes on, the more entrenched our positions seem to become. Mike isn't coming home until late (where is he going?) and I found that the only thing which stems the agony a bit is a bottle of white wine, which helps the feeling of tragedy along nicely.

Nick says he needs an answer today, so I rang Claire first. I've promised her two weeks off in August, as I've told Harriet we will go with them to the Dordogne. Is this wise? 'Darling, that's wonderful. It'll be such fun. Now is there anything I can do to help, as I know you're *so* busy?' I could *smell* the Arpège wafting down the phone as she breathed into it, running her finger no doubt along the exquisitely clean surface of her maple-topped pale green Christiansen kitchen unit. Maybe if I asked her very nicely she'd come and *pack* for me. On second thoughts, no. I am deeply ashamed of my suitcases. I keep meaning to buy new ones but it's such a boring thing to spend money on. However, we are getting to go away for practically nothing. We only have to find the money for the ferry and petrol. At least Mike will *have* to speak to me if we're with another couple. If we went on our own, I can see us spending an entire fortnight communicating through Rebecca, like using a mini ACAS rep.

If I am going to Boston I must have a serious wardrobe-update. The house sale looks pretty certain now, although it's unlikely to go through for another couple of months, and the couple at Lawn Farm have let us drop the price by a couple of thousand, so things are not too tight. In fact, things aren't quite so disastrous as usual which means I could – I just could – nip into Oxford on Saturday and have a little peep into the shops. What I really need are a couple of floaty dresses which will do for work and the evening. But what shoes do I have to go with them? And in the evenings I'll need a cardigan, possibly, or a couple of light jackets . . . I sense a mega-shop coming on. Sod Mike. I need some FUN.

Saturday 25 July
'Mike?' I said, as we sat amongst the turmoil of Saturday morning breakfast. Tom was happily discovering how far he could send bits of wheat and milk by banging his spoon down heavily into his Weetabix, and Rebecca was carefully stripping her chocolate croissant of all the chocolate and strewing the pastry bits all over the table. 'Could you have the children this morning while I nip into town? I need to get a few things, and you know how hard it is to shop with Tom . . .'

'Fine,' said Mike, not lifting his eyes from his newspaper. He is actually being very helpful with the children. Maybe he's preparing his case for a custody battle. *Every weekend she left her children to go off and fuel her shopping addiction whilst I was left to care for these helpless mites* . . . I am getting very tired indeed of living in a Greek tragedy. But I am determined to go, and I'm *not* taking Tom and Rebecca with me. Rebecca does a great line in hiding in shops, so I end up crawling under racks of sales clothes while she darts out the other end, laughing hysterically. Tom now hates being strapped into his pushchair, preferring instead to walk with me holding on to his hands. This means we proceed around the shops rather slower than a tortoise wearing orthopaedic shoes. Honestly, shopping for clothes with children is like being stapled to a drunken geriatric, only more embarrassing. When Rebecca was about four she did an excellent line in waiting for me to bend down to heave my trousers off, before whipping back the changing-room curtain to reveal my rhinoid posterior to the aghast public.

I need to shop. If ever I feel depressed, or upset, or totally stressed, then shopping is the one thing which makes me feel better. You can spend all the money you like on Jungian therapists, but retail therapy works for me every time. Call me a shallow person, but thumbing through a rack of clothes has the same soothing, hypnotic effect as a deep massage. I can block everything else out as I chat animatedly to myself: that a navy blue velvet frock coat is *just the thing* I will need this autumn. Of course there is no real reason why buying things should make you feel better or happier. But it does. And I can spend *hours* trying things on. Entering a changing room for me is like entering Dr Who's tardis. Whole *years* can disappear before I emerge. Of course, once I've bought one item, the whole thing snowballs. I then need lots of other things to go with it, and begin the shopping equivalent of a shark's feeding frenzy, rushing around snatching clothes off the hangers and biting people if they get in my way.

Today I excelled myself. I bought two pairs of palazzo pants, and desperately wanted to buy a pair of boot-cut trousers but they were far too snug on my thighs. I hate it when your thighs bulge against the material. They obviously weren't very well cut. I also had to reject a gorgeous little yellow shift dress (rather like the one Harriet had on for dinner) because my chubby knees emerged from it like a wrestler's. But undeterred I went on to buy several crop-top T-shirts, a new pair of hipster jeans and a pair of clumpy-heeled sandals. I am going to change my image dramatically and Mike will not recognize me. Goodbye helpless wifey in print dresses, hello fierce nineties chick in platforms and wide trousers. But when I got to the till I had a nasty reality flash. How did I get to be standing here with my arms full of clothes about to hand my credit card over to be debited with money I didn't have? But I had been possessed by Retail Therapy Madness and there was no turning back. I paid up, and ran to the door. As I walked through the packed city centre, swinging my bags, I felt that life was looking up. This is the beginning of a new me. I am not going to go down without a fight, and I am going to be so gorgeous and thin for France that Mike will be on his knees, begging for forgiveness. And sex. Quite possibly, lots of hot, sweaty, French sex.

Wednesday 9 July
Rebecca's Sports Day. A Very Important Day which has been pencilled into my diary for at least a month. For the past week she has been on and on at me to remember, and has been frantically practising her long jump and skipping in the back garden. Last night I made a special effort to wash her shorts and T-shirt to make them brilliantly white and even stuck her pumps into the washing machine; they clonked about alarmingly but came out pristine. I just hope they haven't shrunk.

I have a meeting this morning but I'm sure it will be finished by two when the races start. At breakfast I tried to stop Mike before he left. He was looking immaculate in his navy blue suit and the yellow shirt I bought him a couple of months ago, and I longed and longed for him to touch me. 'It's Rebecca's sports day at school. Could you come?' I said, as calmly as I could.

'Please, Daddy,' Rebecca said, running out from the kitchen and hanging off his arm.

'I can't, sweetheart,' he said, bending down to kiss her. 'I have to be at work.' I put my hand on his arm, but he shrugged it away. Rebecca paused, sensing with the acute perception of a child the space between us. She looked up at me, and I had to fight hard not to cry. She reached up and held my hand, glancing quickly between Mike and me. 'See you tonight,' he said, to Rebecca, and shut the door behind him.

I am slowly learning that the only way to stem the agony is not to try to reach him. If I don't try, then I can't get hurt. I'm sure I can be just as tough as him. But it must be hurting him too.

The meeting was about the Boston trip, and there are masses of logistics of camera crews, flights and access to sort out. We've booked ourselves into what seems to be a very posh hotel in the centre, near to Harvard University, called The Charles. If you're going to travel on the BBC's money, you may as well travel in style! With phone calls about visas flying backwards and for-wards, I kept glancing at the clock to make sure I wasn't late. Quite safe, it was only one o'clock. Then Nick stuck his head round the door and asked if I could run through the schedule with him. By the time I'd done that, I looked up and saw with horror that it was half past one. 'Look, I have to go,' I said.

'Why the rush?' said Nick.

'Dentist,' I yelled over my shoulder. 'Agonizing pain.'

I drove like a bat out of hell towards Rebecca's school, willing the minutes on the clock not to click forward. It normally takes about half an hour, but in Studley, the nearest town to her school, I suddenly hit a tail-back. What the hell was going on? Oh Christ, temporary road-works. A rickety old traffic light had been plonked in the middle of the road, and there was an old bloke with a cigarette stuck in his mouth leaning on a shovel next to it. There didn't seem to be any cars coming the other way. Eventually, when I could bear the tension no more, I pulled out and inched past the lights, to honks from the line of waiting cars. The bloke didn't even look up when I drove past him, and when I got to the other end, the light was on red there too. Bloody marvellous.

It was half past two when I screeched down the driveway, having narrowly missed a lorry coming the other way as I turned into the gates. A long line of cars were parked on the grass, and in the distance I could see small white-shorted figures darting about. I panted over the grass, my high-heeled shoes sinking into the turf. As I got nearer I could see the parents: embarrassed fathers in suits ostentatiously clutching mobile phones as if only temporarily wrenched away from the office and awaiting Very Important Calls from America, mums in cool cream linen dresses, looking exactly the part of Private School Mother. I looked desperately around for Rebecca or Claire. There was Claire, standing on the other side of the tape. Tom was in his pushchair at her side and she was hugging Rebecca. Hurdling the tape at the side of the tracks, I ran across to them, narrowly avoiding a small child clutching an egg and spoon. As I ran towards Rebecca, calling her name, she turned furiously. Tears were running down her face.

'I won!' she shouted. 'I won the two hundred metres out of everybody and you *missed* it. Where *were* you?' Claire stood back and I pulled Rebecca into my arms, feeling her body racked with sobs against me.

'I'm so sorry, I'm so sorry,' I said, feeling tears running down my face. 'I was held up, the road—'

'I wanted you to see me,' she said, looking up at me, her face red and blotchy. 'I ran really fast and you didn't *see* me.'

Her teacher, Mrs Lewis, was marching towards us and I hastily wiped away signs of my tears. Her hockey-sticks voice boomed, 'Well done, Rebecca! You must be very proud of her – she beat the boys as well!'

'I am,' I said, holding on to her fiercely. 'I am.'

The other mothers were standing in small groups, chatting happily away, their friendships formed after endless days of dropping off and collecting, laughing about the drudgery of it all to each other, arranging teas and sleep-overs for their children. Claire and I stood alone to watch the rest of the races, until a few other nannies came over to chat to Claire. Tom hung onto a balloon in his pushchair, then Claire lifted him up to sit on her shoulders so he could see better and he pushed his hands into her hair to hang on.

'I'll take them home,' I said, as we walked back to the car after the last race, Rebecca clutching her little cup. She'd cheered up later on, and took me off to introduce me to some of her friends. A few I knew, because I'd made the effort to find out their parents' phone numbers and invite them over to play at the weekends, but many I didn't seem to have met before.

'Are you sure?' said Claire.

'No, really, I don't have to go back to work,' I said, reaching down into my bag for my mobile phone. Rats. Four missed calls. I fought back the urge to ring for my messages there and then, and thought, Sod it.

Whatever they are can wait. But when I went to lift Tom off Claire's shoulders and strap him into the seat in my car, he struggled and cried.

'Tommy,' Claire said. 'Stop being silly! You're going home with Mummy!'

'Ice-cream,' I said, which usually works wonders.

'No, no,' shouted Tom, hanging on to Claire's sleeve as she bent over to strap him in.

'Hush,' she said, bending over to kiss him, and said something to him I couldn't hear. He quietened slightly, but all the way home he let little sobs squeak out around his ice-cream while Rebecca chanted, 'Ice-cream, ice-cream, we all scream for ice-cream,' until I wanted to brain her.

8

AUGUST

Saturday 3 August

'Tell me honestly,' I said to Jill, twirling about the kitchen this morning in my new crop-top and jeans, 'am I too old for this?' The jeans did feel very snug indeed and there was a little roll of fat above the waistband, which made me want to heave down the bottom of the T-shirt.

Rebecca, Susie and Daisy were splashing about outside in the paddling pool I'd spent several hours this morning putting together, having rescued it from the spidery hell at the back of the shed, and then had to scrub off all the green slime from last year. The girls had promised to look after Tom, who was crawling about, starkers, but were paying no attention to him whatsoever and he was currently digging up a flowerbed while eating a begonia. I'd left the hosepipe on to fill the pool earlier, and there were hysterical shrieks and yells as they sprayed each other. It is the first really hot day we've had all summer, and close contact with the back garden this morning tells me that things are wildly out of control. Not my problem. The new buyers will have to deal with the triffids. We don't have fairies living at the bottom of our garden – we probably have several tramps instead, selling *The Big Issue.*

Mike went out in his car this morning quite early. I've honestly given up thoughts of any kind of rapprochement until after I get back from America, because it's pretty clear he's furious about the fact I've decided to go at all, and sees it as a deliberate act of independence. I think he wants me to throw myself to the floor at his feet, sobbing that this row must end and that I need him desperately. What a pity. No chance of that. But where *is* he going? He looked very *clean.* Perhaps I should hire a private detective. Or perhaps I could just ask him, but then that would betray the fact that I am interested in his movements, which of course I am not. Absolutely not.

'You look fabulous,' said Jill. Bless her. She always tells me I look great, but then I always tell her she looks great, even when we both know we look more like Les Dawson than Claudia Schiffer.

'Does it make my bum look big?'

'Not all all,' said Jill, firmly. 'Helena Christiansen would be proud of a bum like that. Who's this Gary person who's going with you?'

'Presenter,' I said. 'Full of himself, lots of wavy dark hair, tan, tight trousers, big head – you *know,* the one you've seen on the programme. You said he had no neck.'

'Oh yes,' she said, nodding sagely, the beginnings of a glint in her eye. 'Mr Sexy No Neck. And how does Mike feel about you going away for a week with a man who throbs with sex appeal?'

'He doesn't know who I'm going with,' I said.

'Cold war continues?' said Jill, raising her eyebrows and spooning chocolate froth off the top of her cappuccino.

'Yup,' I said.

'Much more peaceful,' she said. 'At least you don't

have to talk to him. I need a big row with Pete. That new Jane Austen adaptation starts tomorrow and he'll sit next to me, sighing and reading the paper until I have to kill him.'

Monday 3 August

Packed and ready to go. I had my hair cut on Saturday afternoon in the short flicky-out style, in a bid to tame the wild Bohemian curls and to complete the new image. It took a hell of a lot of courage to sit there while my pre-Raphaelite locks hit the deck, and Tom bounced up and down on my knee. The hairdresser had to use lots of hot rollers to straighten out the top bit of my hair, which made me feel extremely concerned that when I wash it (and I know I will fail to put it in rollers because there is never time and anyway, I can never be arsed) it will spring out from my head in the style of the early Jackson Five. Rebecca hung onto the back of my chair, tripping up the hairdresser and refusing all blandishments to go and watch a video. 'Do you like it?' I asked as I peered at myself hesitantly in the mirror, turning my head this way and that to see if it looked any less dramatic from another angle.

'*Awful*. Your hair was like Rapunzel Barbie before. Now you look like *Ken*,' she said, making her 'yucky' face.

'Thanks, darling,' I said, handing over my credit card to be debited for yet more vast sums of money. Why do hairdressers charge so much these days? Honestly, hairdressing is being treated now as if it's some kind of art form.

Outside I pushed Tom towards the car, with Rebecca hanging off my hand dragging her toes along the ground – thereby scuffing her new shoes – and I caught sight of myself in a shop window. I started, like a pig seeing its reflection for the first time. Ye gods. Is that me? I've always had long, wavy hair, and this short, snappy me is going to take some getting used to. I look like everyone else now, I thought, sadly. Then: No, I don't. I look young, trendy and *different* from before. Different is good.

When I got home at teatime on Saturday (more shopping – in fact I loaded so many bags onto the back of Tom's pushchair that when I let go for a moment by the lifts in the department store he flipped over backwards. He let out an astonished yell as his world went vertical and I hastily righted him before anyone could see what a bad mother I was) I could see Mike standing by the sink as I pulled up the drive. I whipped round to get Rebecca out of the car but it gave him time to see me. Even from the drive I could see his look of horror. He loved my hair. When we made love (we did used to make love, didn't we? I'm sure we did) he would plunge his hands into it, curling the thick hair round and round his fingers. He liked nothing better than pressing his face into my hair as he sat behind me, running his hands up underneath its heavy weight. Now it had all gone.

Rebecca ran into the kitchen. 'Daddy, Daddy, Mummy's had all her hair cut off! I hate it! Isn't it horrid!'

'Becca,' I said, trying to laugh in a weak sort of fashion, 'it doesn't matter, come and help me with the bags.'

'Mummy looks like a boy, doesn't she, Daddy?' Mike looked up, and for the first time in weeks, our eyes met and held. We stared at each other for what felt like minutes, and all I could think was, I love you, I love you, come back. We know each other so well, that look told each other more than we could ever say about how hurt we were, how much pain the lack of contact was causing. I would have given anything for him to have walked forward and held me, held me so close I could feel the warmth of his body, his heart beating, been able to put my hands up into his hair and pull his face down to mine. For several moments there was that look of searing honesty – I know you, I *know* you, stop hurting me – then the shutters came down. He looked away.

'Very trendy,' he said. 'I'm sure it will go down well in America.'

There was a bit of a scene with Rebecca last night as I packed – it was the first week of her school holidays and I had said I would try to get an extra week off before we all went away. 'It's work,' I said, as she sat, a disconsolate Buddha, in the middle of my bed, 'I have to go.'

'Let me come with you,' she said. 'I'd be very good and I could carry things.'

'I can't,' I said, laughing. 'You'll be here with Daddy and Claire, then we'll all go off together. It'll be lovely. Just let Mummy get her work done now and then I'll have lots of time for you later.'

'You always say that,' she said. 'And you never do.'

The flight was due to leave at seven from Heathrow, and as usual I was horrendously late setting off. I'd forgotten how awful the motorway was at that time of night, and I sat in a traffic jam for what felt like hours, feeling my blood pressure creeping up like mercury in a thermometer. Calm down, I thought. You'll have a stroke. So I put my favourite Eric Clapton tape on and sang very loudly indeed, banging on the steering wheel. 'Lay-la,' I yelled. Thump, thump. I threw back my head and let rip. The man in the next car looked at me curiously and then away very quickly, but not

178

before I'd caught his eye. I tried to rearrange my face instantly from madwoman to perfectly sane night-time commuter. I was very glad when he edged forward and I couldn't see him any more. 'Come on, come on,' I said, gripping the steering wheel with white knuckles. 'I'm going to be really late.'

It was quarter past six when I hurtled into the departure lounge, having found the only luggage trolley in the whole of Heathrow which only moves sideways. Gary and the crew were standing about impatiently, looking at their watches. All their luggage had already gone through. I am supposed to be the responsible producer-person in charge who will arrange costs of excess baggage etc. but I can't even get to the airport on time. I flew forward to check in my luggage, and then ran back, apologizing profusely. I could feel sweat trickling down my nose, and my flicky-out bits had wilted in the heat. 'That's OK,' said Gary. 'We didn't want to go to Duty Free anyway, did we, boys?' They all shook their heads, grinning. Goodness, I was the only girl.

'Where's Sammy?' I said. She was the researcher who'd been assigned to the trip.

'Her boyfriend didn't want her to go,' Gary said. 'Isn't that pathetic? Nick sent Mark instead.'

'Hi, Mark,' I said, smiling reassuringly at the nervous young lad, straight off his media studies course and completely over-awed at being in the company of the famous Gary. And then I sensed that everyone was looking at me a bit oddly. I was wearing a new button-through linen dress, and when I glanced down, I saw to my horror that all the running about had popped open the bottom six buttons of my dress, which meant that I'd run towards them with my black knickers flashing. I turned hastily and tried to fumble the buttons together. Turning back, Gary caught my eye. We burst out laughing. 'Come on,' I said. 'We'll miss the plane.'

I'm not great on planes. I like the *idea* of them, and the speed of getting places, but the actual up-in-the-air stuff worries me a lot. I can't quite believe that you *can* stay up there, and I'm sure that it's only a matter of time before I become a statistic. As the plane began to taxi down the runway, I pulled my seatbelt – totally inadequate: how could that help you when you plunge to earth at a million miles an hour? – even tighter, and braced my feet against the chair in front. This is my mother's rule of passenger-seat driving, whenever we go round a corner she leans and when I slow down, her foot brakes for me as well. The cabin crew were still doing their what-to-do-if-we-crash which as usual no-one was taking a blind bit of notice of, and clearly the captain was in a hurry to take off. The steward nearest to me was in the middle of the finger-pointing-forward bit to show you where the emergency exits were and he staggered slightly as the plane picked up speed. 'You can see we have Stirling Moss for our captain today,' he said, to much nervous laughter. We were all going to die. On take-off, I closed my eyes and awaited the inevitable crunch. There was one of those sickening lurches as we went up when your stomach rises to meet your throat, then the plane levelled off.

'You can relax now,' said Gary, who'd sat himself down next to me. 'Fancy a drink?'

'I never drink and eat on aeroplanes,' I said firmly.

Tuesday 4 August
By the time we landed at Boston this morning I was rolling. Gary had insisted I have a double gin to steady my nerves and after that there seemed no point resisting. One of those mini bottles of champagne,

several small bottles of red wine and the entire tray of plastic-looking aeroplane food later, I was well away. I sorted out Gary's entire love life (which is extremely complicated and involves several women in this country and quite a number abroad), told Mark the researcher how to succeed in journalism and become a big star, and lectured Mick the cameraman about the benefits of independent education for his children. Then I fell asleep. When I woke I couldn't remember where I was, and I had a mouth like cat litter. Gary was asleep too, leaning heavily on my right arm. I prised it out from under him, crawled past him, Mark and Nick and staggered in the darkness to the loo. Inside its dim metallic interior I thought, what a laugh. Then I threw up all the coronation chicken and red wine, making a noise like a small frog.

Filming today passed in a blur of hangover and jet lag, but it should make a really great story. Most of the children are taught at the school using interactive CD-ROMs, and their progress seems remarkable. My biggest success today was not actually being sick on anybody.

The hotel is great. Really luxurious, with a marble reception area full of very rich-looking people in cashmere and plaid trousers. There is a swimming pool, and I am determined to swim twenty lengths every morning, as part of my pre-France fitness regime. I am not going to be shamed next to Harriet. We've also hired an American crew, and the cameraman is a dream. Chuck, he's called; his white hair is pulled back in a pony-tail and he has the most incredibly laid-back attitude to life. Tonight he took us out to eat at an amazing seafood restaurant down by the docks, a vast place full of shouting waiters and charging lobsters. The menu was eight pages long. 'Buckets of beer!' Gary yelled as soon as we sat down, which pretty well set the tone for the evening. The BBC are paying such generous expenses we all felt compelled to splash out. I was wearing my new white halter-neck silk top with the black palazzo pants. I'd caught the sun a bit filming the exteriors this afternoon, and for once my hair obeyed me. It is such joy to be able to run a bath, CNN blaring from the hotel-room TV, and lie there with no-one to disturb me. Peering at myself as I put on my lipstick, I had to admit I looked pretty good. Gary clearly thought so too. At the meal, he scooted round the table so he could sit next to me. Mick raised his eyebrows, and I shook my head at him. I really don't want any gossip – our world is such a small one it would fly back to Mike. But it was very flattering to have someone as good-looking as Gary catching my eye, filling my glass and laughing at my jokes.

We all ordered the seafood platter, and when it came it was like an entire Sea Life Centre had dropped on the table. There was a vast central dish groaning with lobsters, crayfish, mussels, squid, prawns – you name it, if it was fishy, it was there. 'I really can't do this,' I said, trying to drag the meat out of my lobster with those long hooky things they give you.

'Let me,' said Gary, leaning across. It's no wonder he has so many women. He's very good at it: flicking his eyes at you, smiling, leaning his head close to you whenever you say anything. By the end of the meal my foot accidentally brushed against his leg.

'Sorry,' I said.

'Don't be,' he said. His dark eyes held mine. A shiver ran through me, and for the first time in years I remembered what it was like to really fancy someone, to feel faint when they were close. During one of our long discussions over a bottle or two of chardonnay Jill had admitted that the thing she really missed about dating was that first kiss. The first kiss when a whole evening

182

– or a series of evenings – have been leading up to it, and then he leans forward and . . . wow. You don't get that when you're married. A kiss is – just a kiss. The same as the last one, and very likely the same as the ones for ever more into infinity. I thought that feeling had gone, but now, as Gary smiled wickedly into my eyes, it came back, as powerfully as before. It still happens. But I'm not really sure I am equipped to deal with it. I must not get pissed.

'I'm too old for you,' I said quietly, smacking him on the hand with a lobster claw. Most of his girlfriends seem to be about nineteen. 'Anyway, your love life's complicated enough. Chuck,' I said much more loudly, leaning forward across the table. 'Tell us about your shark-fishing exploits.'

But can I resist drink? I cannot. Just a couple of glasses of wine and my resolve dissolves. By two o'clock we were on the cocktails in the very smart bar in the hotel. Gary had commandeered the piano and was playing Simon and Garfunkel extremely badly, while Chuck and Mick sang along. I blew happily down my straw into my slow comfortable screw, which was the nearest I was going to get to it, I thought, giggling helplessly. I hadn't had such a good time in ages. I felt like me again: reckless, independent, *free*. 'Boys, boys!' I yelled. 'I want "Kathy's Song"!'

Thursday 6 August
After the cocktail binge we had a rather more civilized meal last night, in the restaurant at the hotel. Even in a big group, Gary made you feel that you were the only person he wanted to talk to. I was knackered and said I was going to bed at ten. As I walked down the corridor I heard his footsteps behind me. 'You tired too?' I said as he drew near.

183

'Not really,' he said, his eyes narrowing sexily. 'I've got a great mini-bar in my room.'

'Snap,' I said, 'so have I. But I had too much last night, and now I'm going to bed.' As I put my hand out to swipe the computer card in the lock, he reached forward and touched my hand.

'Carrie,' he said, and I could feel his breath against my cheek as he moved closer, 'can I come in?' I raised my eyes to look at him and he smiled, putting his head on one side and raising his eyebrows in an expression which clearly said, I know I'm a naughty boy but I'm a brilliant fuck. I had to laugh.

'*No* thank you,' I said, convincing myself as much as him. 'I've got quite enough problems in my life without you!'

'Go on,' he said, running his fingers down my face and stopping at my lips. 'No-one would know.'

'Surprising as this may seem,' giving him a determined shove – 'I don't fancy you,' I lied, and then I fell into my room and slammed the door, my heart thumping. Liar, liar, knickers on fire, I thought, repeating Rebecca's current favourite playground chant. How singularly appropriate.

Thank God I hadn't been as drunk as the first night. I'd probably have given in, and then how would I feel? Just being close to Gary, feeling his long muscular thigh pressed against me and knowing that under his shirt was a broad back which would be smooth to the touch, made me feel extremely faint. Get a grip, I thought. You are a married woman, not a teenager. But I need to be loved. I need to be held. I need to feel that I'm worth something and Mike at the moment makes me feel that I am worth nothing. I ran a bath and then lay sweating in the hot hotel room, fed up with the strangeness of it all and wanting to be at home. When I did sleep, I had a restless, erotic dream about making love in a dark, shady corridor. I couldn't make out the man's face, but he smelt like Mike. I thought, Thank God it's over, but when I woke to reach out for him, the bed was empty.

Saturday 8 August
Trying to pack my suitcase I ended up having to bounce heavily up and down on top of it. It was rather fuller than when I arrived because I had done some Very Serious Shopping. Being out filming all day, I was terrified that the shops would be closed by the time we got back to the hotel at night. Not a bit of it. The lights of the shop interiors winked invitingly well into the night, and I for one took full advantage. While the boys headed straight for the bar, I hurtled upstairs and put on my training shoes. I aimed to cover a lot of ground. Best of all by far was Gap Kids. It was vast, a veritable cornucopia of splendid spending opportunities. And it was all so *cheap*. I bought enough clothes to kit Rebecca and Tom out for an entire year – in half an hour. I could have won prizes for spending that particular evening, and it was very close to the best night of my life. What really made me happy was that the BBC's daily allowance was far more than I was spending at the hotel so these clothes were virtually for free! Perfect! I also bought myself armfuls of stuff – well, it was so reasonable it would have been criminal to resist. The only problem with trying things on was that my waist had expanded ever so slightly. It felt like I had been eating and drinking virtually from the moment I stepped off the plane. Every type of sandwich under the sun! You really cannot expect to lose weight on a holiday, oops, business trip, when you are eating chocolate muffins – for breakfast.

I also could not get over the fact that everyone was

so *nice*. On Tuesday night I had had problems placing a call home. I dialled everything the phone book told me to but I got a continuous whining tone. I rang the operator. 'That's no problem at all,' she said. 'I'll dial it for you. No charge.' And she did, and it worked. At home I would have got some bored Sharon, or even worse, one of those sodding BT answerphones which gives you eight lists of options demanding you push lots of square and star keys without ever speaking to a human being and you end up at the same electronic message you started with. Then you shoot the phone.

Mike had picked up the call. 'Hallo,' he said, managing to sound both bored and irritated. He hates answering the phone.

'It's me,' I said. Silence. 'How are you?'

'I'll get Rebecca,' he said.

Rebecca exploded onto the phone. 'Mummy!' she yelled. 'What's it like? Have you been to Disneyland? Have you seen Mickey Mouse? Will you get me some real American sweets?'

'Of course I will,' I said, laughing. 'How's Daddy? Is he there? Could I have a quick word?'

'Daddy!' Rebecca yelled into the handset. My ear vibrated. 'He says he's busy,' she said. 'When are you coming home?'

On the homeward-bound plane Gary and I were sitting next to each other again, but this time there were no flirtatious looks, no egging on to drink more wine. When I'd jokingly turned him down that night he'd looked at me quizzically, as if he couldn't believe what I was doing. He was so used to women giving in to him, he couldn't believe I meant it. So the next day he'd been very cool with me, which made me snort quite a bit. I don't think he could get over the fact that I wasn't gagging for him, but I think that has only made me more attractive to him. That's OK. I can cope with being fancied by Gary. In fact, it will make work just that bit more interesting, and with Mike's lack of interest at the moment I need *someone* to get dressed for in the morning.

Mike. Just thinking about him makes my stomach clench, as if I'm in for a bad bout of diarrhoea. Being here I feel so irresponsible, so confident about myself. Not sure I can face the drama of home.

Friday 14 August

The ferry leaves at five this evening from Dover. I had hoped that Mike would let us fly to Bordeaux and hire a car from there, but his puritanical regime is being upheld. We've now got a date to exchange contracts on the house – in six weeks' time – and, as my father would say, the Purse is Closed. I've hardly seen him all week as I've been plunged into the Stygian gloom of the editing room to try and get all the on-line work on the documentary done before we go away. It's meant leaving the house at seven in the morning and not coming back until late, certainly after the children are in bed and Mike has been staying out until around eleven every night. Rebecca has now of course noticed what's going on and asked me in a very loud voice in the supermarket on Sunday morning why Daddy and I aren't sleeping in the same bed. 'Daddy snores,' I said. 'Keep your voice down.' God knows where Mike is eating – presumably he's going into the office canteen and then on to the pub. I just hope he doesn't get done for drink driving. I bought several shirts and some Levi 501s for Mike in America. After all the kerfuffle of giving the children their presents and fending off leaps from Turtle and Angus I turned shyly to Mike and said, 'These are for you.' He didn't open them while I was there. But when I got back from putting the children to bed the bags were gone, and, peering into his wardrobe upstairs, I found he'd hung them up neatly. It made me want to cry. Why can't he at least give me a sign he wants this row to end?

I leapt out of bed shortly after seven this morning, resolved to get on with the packing. All week I have been frantically washing to try to get everything ready, but as usual last night I was hauling shorts and T-shirts out of the washing machine at midnight and draping them over the radiators, which I left full on, with the result we all woke up pink-faced and sweaty. It was also rather unfortunate that a navy blue sock had stowed away in a white pillow-slip, with the result that my whites wash came out gun-metal grey. Bollocks, bollocks.

I was determined to employ minimalist packing, and only take the things we really needed for two weeks in the sun. Swimming costumes, shorts, T-shirts, *one* jumper each and only a couple of smart outfits. Surely it won't be very dressy if it's just us? Harriet, who rang me every night this week and made us have a get-together to discuss where we should stop on the way – does she have nothing else to think about? – says the farmhouse is in the middle of the countryside but near the *sweetest* little town which has a *darling* little market. She and Martin took the boys last year and had a *fabulous* time. Nothing to do but sunbathe and drink wine, *so relaxing*, darling. But then Arnold and Sidney are seven and nine, old enough to play on their own and swim in the pool without immediate threat of drowning. Rebecca should be OK – she can swim without armbands now but Tom – oh Tom. I would have to keep an eye on him every second of the day. I just hoped Mike was prepared to be helpful. But then who knew with the Incredible Non-Speaking Man?

I managed to fit all of Mike's and my clothes into one suitcase. There seemed to be an awful lot of my clothes and not very many of Mike's. Oh dear. Mike had taken the children out for the morning, so I had the house to myself. I normally feel very happy packing to go away on holiday, but ever since I'd got up I'd had a feeling of dread. Surely Mike and I can make it up on holiday? I thought. I wish – I really wish that we *were* going on our own because I know that both Harriet and Martin will drive me round the bend and I want Mike all to myself.

By eleven, I'd piled all Tom's paraphernalia up by the door: pushchair, travel cot, sunshade, nappy sacks, high chair, car seat. Honestly, it was like a small travelling circus. The dogs had gone to sit disconsolately by the pile, their ears flat to their heads and their tails drooping. They hate any signs of change and the sight of suitcases gives them terminal depression. Turtle has been known physically to lie in open suitcases in an attempt to make you stop packing. They were due to go to kennels at lunch-time. Mike was taking them because I cry when I drop them off, which is rather embarrassing. Must find their vaccination certificates.

You would need to have a brain like a computer to remember everything a family needs to go on holiday. It is simply not possible, no matter how many lists you make. Inevitably our journey is punctuated by U-turns as, yelling 'Oh God!' I remember I've forgotten the camera, or to lock the back door. One year I was so determined to switch everything off I switched off the freezer so we returned to ice-cream all over the floor and a chicken the size of a beach ball.

Mike brought the children back at twelve, Rebecca on the ceiling with excitement. Tom, bless him, has no idea what's going on, although Rebecca kept grabbing his hands and saying, 'Tom, Tom, we're going on holiday!' and dancing around with him.

'All packed?' said Mike, tersely. Looking at him closely, I saw his face was lined and strained. He didn't look like himself at all.

'Mike,' I said, my hand hesitantly reaching out to touch his face. Rebecca had taken Tom through to the garden and we were alone in the hall. 'Mike, *please.*' I could feel my eyes filling with tears and I was fighting to stop my voice breaking. I physically turned his face to mine, and *made* him look at me. 'Tell me what's wrong. We can't go on like this, it's nuts. I love you,' I said. His face seemed to crumple and he put his arms round me, hugging me so hard it hurt. Just to feel his body, his hair, his face against mine – it was like coming home after a long, long journey.

'I'm sorry,' he breathed into my hair. 'I'm *so sorry.*'

'It's OK,' I said. 'We've both been stupid. Can it stop now? I can't stand not talking to you. I need you.'

'Yes,' said Mike, very quietly. 'It's over now.' He pulled away from me, and rubbed his hand over his eyes as if in pain. Then he turned away.

Rebecca came running down the corridor. 'Mummy!' she said, stopping short. 'Why are you crying?'

'Because I'm happy,' I said, bending down to hug her.

'I'll get Tom,' Mike said, and, turning his back on me, walked away.

Packing up the car I reflected it was ironic that the smallest person in the family took up about two-thirds of the space. At this rate we'd need an articulated lorry to get us to France. I'd also told Rebecca to choose a teddy to take with her. Coming out of the kitchen, I saw she had constructed a teddy-mountain. 'Rebecca,' I said. 'We won't have *room.*'

'But I can't *choose,*' she wailed.

'Does Tom really need this?' said Mike, trying to ram the high chair into the boot.

'Where's he going to eat?' I said. 'On our knees?'

'In his car seat – in the car,' said Mike, grimly.

Eventually, the only place left was the space between the front seats, which meant Rebecca had to climb underneath it to get to her seat. 'Ow, ow,' she said, trying to find some room for her feet amongst Tom's nappy sacks and the travel cot bag, which was far too big to go in the boot. We had to take towels and linen with us, and the only place for that was in the well by my feet, so it meant I had to spend the entire journey with my feet stuck straight out in front of me. The only people who looked remotely comfortable were Mike and Tom.

'Shall I drive?' I said.

'Sod off,' said Mike, seeing me gingerly try to arrange my legs to avoid paralysis.

As we set off my brain was working feverishly. Everything locked; bins emptied; fridge cleaned out; milk and papers cancelled; answerphone on; passports, tickets, money with us; camera. Camera. Oh fuck. It was sitting in the middle of the kitchen table alongside . . . Mike's GSN mobile phone and charger he'd put out to be placed securely in my handbag in case of emergency office problems. 'Mike . . .' I said.

Departure number two. Rebecca then decided she needed the loo which meant we had to de-scramble part of the car. Tom by now had sensed the tension and began to yell. 'Give him some paper and crayons,' said Mike.

'They're in the . . . boot,' I said. We drove most of the way to the sound of Tom's lusty wailing. I didn't care, I was so euphoric about Mike's capitulation I felt like singing, but glancing over at him, his face was a mask of tension. After a couple of hours Tom suddenly stopped crying and a deeply thoughtful look came over his face. An unmistakable smell filled the air of the car.

'Mummy,' Rebecca said helpfully. 'Tom's done a poo.'

'Mike,' I said, 'we'll have to pull over at the next turn-off.' Changing a baby in the back of a car is not easy at the best of times, and Tom made it even worse by squirming and yelling as I tried to get a new nappy on. Then what to do with the old one? 'We'll have to take it with us,' I said.

'Put it in the boot,' said Mike, looking green.

Put a man and two small children in a car for a long journey and you have a reliable recipe for disaster. By the time we arrived at the ferry terminal you could have twanged the atmosphere. Jill and I have always said that it would be far easier to go away with each other, because women just get on with things and don't get so wound up over minor child incidents like spilt drinks and sudden loud shouting. But men seem to operate on a much shorter fuse, which can make life very difficult indeed. The only answer, I think, is to drug the man, tie him up and put him in the boot, to be brought out only when you have arrived, the children are out of the unpacked car and you can press a bottle of cold beer into his hand. Then you run your holiday along completely separate lines, meeting only in the evenings when the children are asleep and you can begin drinking. A rota system of caring for the children is best, on a male/male, female/female basis. This is the only way you will achieve a successful holiday.

We are meeting Harriet and Martin at the house, because they, like sensible (rich) people, have decided to do a far more expensive fly-drive. At this moment they are probably sipping champagne at two thousand feet and thumbing through the in-flight magazine. We, meanwhile, are desperately trying to find the overnight bag I'd packed, and remove Tom's essential things without unpacking the entire car on the ferry. Mike is not good with lots of people at the best of times, and a crowded ferry is clearly his idea of hell. We have paid extra for our own cabin, so at least we should get some sleep. 'I hope the cabin's nice,' I said hopefully to Rebecca, hoicking Tom up the narrow metal staircase and trying to keep Mike in sight amongst ten thousand other people.

Saturday 15 August
The cabin was not nice. It was like an iron lung. To close the door, we all had to stand at the far end and not breathe. 'Christ,' Mike said.

'Oh, stop fussing,' I said. 'It's only for one night.'

Mike sighed, took out his book and climbed up onto the top bunk. Rebecca dug into the red plastic bag she'd packed herself (Barbies, felt tips, books, small teddies, skipping rope and lots of loose beads), hauled out Roald Dahl and climbed up to lie beside Mike. They were settled. Tom needed something to eat, so I set off in search of the restaurant. Up and down various staircases we went, with me carrying an increasingly heavy Tom, and trying to follow the immensely complicated maps full of red squares and arrows saying 'You are here'. We ended up popping out on deck next to the lifeboats. I tried not to think about *Titanic*.

After a rather gross meal of chips and beans in a café full of screaming small children who all seemed to be called Leanne or Ryan – you don't get *quite* the same class of people on ferries as you do on aeroplanes, do you? – it was still an hour until Tom's bedtime and I couldn't face returning to the iron lung. We went and looked at perfumes. When we got back to the cabin – which took half an hour, back up and down a hundred staircases – Mike and Rebecca were fast asleep. I tried my best to undress Tom silently but he squeaked and chatted, yelling when I tried to wash him in the tiny metal sink which admittedly must have been very cold on his bottom. Eventually I force-fed him into clean pyjamas and gave him a bottle of milk, rocking him as I whispered his story. Then I lay him down in the cot provided, and tiptoed over to my bunk. Maybe I could get some sleep. As soon as I lay down, two large eyes peered at me over the side of the cot. 'Tom,' I hissed. 'Lie down! Sleep time!' There was a pause while he took in the fact that I, his mummy, was within sight but *not holding him*. This was unthinkable. I turned my back on him and pretended to sleep. There was a pause, a small intake of breath and then – a huge wail. I bounded over to pick him up.

'What? What's going on?' said Mike, rising mussily from the bunk. 'Ow, Rebecca, get off. My arm's gone to sleep.' At this point, the ferry revved its huge turbine engines several feet below us. The cabin became a loud, *vibrating* iron lung. We slept the night in very short shifts. All except Tom, of course, who spent all night crawling around the floor of the tiny cabin, refusing point-blank to go back in his cot. By six o'clock this morning we were all sitting nauseous and grubby in the otherwise empty restaurant. Only Tom looked remarkably bushy-tailed.

Wednesday 19 August
'How *was* the journey,' said Harriet solicitously as we pulled the car up thankfully on the deep shingle in front of the farmhouse. The house is gorgeous, but then I knew it would be because Harriet has such good taste and would not tolerate anything remotely down-market. Made of the golden stone of the Dordogne, it sits in the middle of lush fields at the end of a long, winding drive, and from the road we could see the deep azure

swimming pool glittering next to it, like a jewel.

By the time we arrived we were all in much better spirits. As we drove off the ferry, exhausted, sweaty, dirty and hungry, Rebecca said, 'I *loved* the ferry. Can we do that again?'

Mike and I looked at each other and started to laugh helplessly. 'Never again,' said Mike. 'Never, never again.'

'Until we go home,' I said. 'Maybe we could ask for a cabin directly *inside* the engine on the way home.'

'And perhaps it could be a bit *smaller*,' said Mike.

'And *hotter*,' I said, weak with lack of sleep and mirth.

Already, even in the early morning, the sun is beating down strongly. Just feeling its warmth when we stopped for coffee made me feel better. We are in *France*. Everyone speaks a different language. Rebecca was amazed. 'What is she saying?' she said as the woman in the café reached down to stroke her lovely blond hair, exclaiming, *'Comme elle est mignonne, si mignonne.'*

'She says you are very pretty,' I said.

'Oh,' said Rebecca happily, and smiled at the woman coquettishly while the woman cupped Rebecca's chin in her hand. The French are so tactile and friendly with children.

I love all the differences here. The different bread, the different coffee. It is all wonderfully exciting. Even Mike looked like he was beginning to relax as we sat outside the café, the lines of tiredness falling away as he turned his face up to the sun. I'd packed him a pair of linen shorts in the overnight bag, and his legs are already quite brown. Mine resemble bottles of milk. I will have to work seriously on my tan.

Last night we stopped at a romantic little *auberge* to break the journey. The children went off to bed quite happily, thrilled with the novelty of sleeping in a different room. Even though it was only a tiny place, the food was fabulous. '*Pâté de foie gras*!' I exclaimed. 'Look, it's only twenty francs! That's about two pounds.'

'Two *hundred* francs,' said Mike, smiling. 'Choose again.'

Over the meal we talked – and what bliss it was. I told him all about Boston (no mention of Gary) and Mike told me he'd been going through an awful time at work. His immediate boss had been sacked. I would have heard about it if I hadn't been away – news in the media spreads like wildfire. The new guy, poached from the BBC just as Mike had been, was determined to make his mark and was interfering in everything. 'I'm worried he might want to bring his own team in,' said Mike. God. I'd never thought of Mike's job as insecure, he was so good at it. 'Being effective doesn't come into it,' Mike said.

After the meal we sat out on the terrace, sipping brandy in the balmy evening air. I stretched out my toes and sighed. Thank God I now had a *reason* for his weirdness. Later, we tiptoed into the room, trying not to wake the children. They were both flat out. After I'd undressed, I lay in bed, waiting for Mike to slide in next to me. Surely we could make love, if we were quiet? But Mike reached over to me, kissed me on the cheek and whispered, 'Goodnight.' I lay restlessly. It was hot even though the windows were open. A mosquito's high-pitched wine buzzed above me. We'd made it up, hadn't we, so why didn't he want to make love to me?

It was midday today as we pulled up outside the house, and Harriet, emerging from its dark interior, was wearing only a tiny stinging-yellow bikini. Her skin is already a dark tan, and she is as slim as a supermodel. Does she never eat? As she bent to kiss me she smelt of Ambre Solaire and sun. 'Darling!' she exclaimed. 'How was it?'

'Don't ask,' I laughed, and heaved a hysterically shouting Tom out of the car. 'This is wonderful,' I said as we wandered into the cool, dark entrance.

'Isn't it? Now, I've made us a salad for lunch, with a little cheese and bread. Is that all right?' she asked, her head cutely on one side.

'Chaps!' boomed Martin, strolling in from the pool. 'Thought you were never coming!' He smacked Mike on the back, and gave me a side-crunching hug. Rebecca hid behind my legs. 'The boys are in the pool. Why don't you go and join them?' he said to her.

'Can I, Mummy?' she said, her eyes shining with excitement.

'I'll just try to find your swimmers,' I said. Out by the pool, Harriet had laid out a feast with masses of different cheeses and hams. 'You shouldn't have bothered!' I said.

Harriet looked hurt. 'Is it too much?'

'No, it's perfect,' I said hastily, seeing her expression.

Saturday 22 August
Lying prone in the sun this morning, basting blissfully while Mike plays with Tom in the pool, I mused that you should only ever go away on holiday with other couples you loathe already and will be happy never to see again in your whole life, or with couples like Jill and Pete, whom you know so well you can say, 'Stop being such a lazy arsehole and help in the kitchen,' or, 'Your children are being vile and I'm going to smack them.' Harriet and Martin, unfortunately, are falling into neither camp. Martin I could cheerfully pitchfork over a cliff – he seems to think that just because he's rich everyone should put up with his domineering

behaviour – but Harriet *is* a nice person underneath all the wafting about and, as the days go on, I am coming to feel increasingly sorry for her. I thought she had the perfect life, but she clearly does not. OK, she has far longer than me to spend lying by the pool, topping up her already perfect tan, but she is far more often to be found in the kitchen, cleaning, cooking, wiping down the surfaces. What is she trying to prove? I clean, therefore I am?

She is obssessed with creating a perfect environment and making Martin's and the children's lives totally hassle-free. She *waits* on them. If Mike says, 'Carrie, go and get me a drink,' I am far more likely to say, 'Sod off, go and get it yourself.' Harriet wouldn't *dream* of saying that. As soon as a glass is emptied, a plate wiped clean with bread, Harriet has grabbed it and is heading off for the kitchen. 'Harriet,' I say, 'please let me help.' 'You've got your hands full with Tom,' she says. 'I really don't mind.' No wonder she's so thin – she's constantly rushing around after her family. 'Mum,' Sidney or Arnold yell from the pool, 'get me a drink!' 'Of course, darling,' she says, hopping up immediately.

'Why don't you make them get it?' I asked yesterday, appalled by their constant demands, my hands itching to give them a good smack.

'Why?' she said, turning headlamp eyes on me. 'I like to look after them.'

I have also discovered another reason why she is so thin. She never *eats* anything. Going out for meals, I am groaning with joy over the lovely thin French chips and *bifteck* while she pushes a couple of lettuce leaves around a plate. 'Let *go*,' I feel like saying. 'Have a big pudding and *please* get drunk.' But she never does. She has to be up bright and early to make the boys' and Martin's breakfast.

It has become a battle as to who can get down to the kitchen first. I am up first with Tom, of course, but once I've given him his early bottle, I try to make him have another hour's sleep. Usually I just let him play about on the floor of our room with the door closed, while I doze. So, inevitably, by the time we emerge, Harriet has been to the baker's to get the bread, laid out the table and set the coffee pot bubbling. She makes me feel deeply inadequate. She is such a *home-maker.*

Mike is spending most of the time in the pool with Rebecca. Even though we've made things up, he still hasn't made love to me. It must be because I'm going to bed before him, I told myself firmly, applying another layer of suncream, and he is drinking an awful lot. He and Martin have sat up every night so far drinking brandy into the early hours, but I am mindful of Tom's early start, and by eleven my head is nodding. While it is lovely to be in such a beautiful place, I can't say I am having the most relaxing holiday of my life. I can't take my eyes off Tom for a moment because of the pool, and as soon as I pick up my book he sets off at a determined crawl towards the glittering water. I am really worried about him burning, so I keep trying to make him wear a hat, but he takes it off immediately. He has also, extremely annoyingly, dropped his morning sleep – probably because there is so much going on and he doesn't want to miss out on any of it.

Rebecca has fallen headlong in love with Arnold and Sidney, who just about permit her to trail after them as they play cricket in the garden or leap onto lilos in the pool. Martin, as I suspected, is an Organizer. While I am happy just to doze by the pool, Martin wants us to Do Things. 'Come on, chaps!' he bellows. 'French cricket!' 'Oh Christ,' I mutter. 'Eff off!' But Mike willingly joins in. Anything, it seems, rather than being left alone with me.

Thursday 27 August

Last night we managed to persuade the housekeeper who came in to clean (rather pointless after Harriet's obsessive ministrations) to baby-sit the children so we can all go out. About five miles from the house is a gorgeous little *moulin* restaurant. We booked a table on the terrace, and set off in high spirits. I am revelling in being so brown, and can even bear the fact that Harriet's red silk halter-neck dress makes her look absolutely stunning. Mike by now is as dark as an Arab and his pale blue shirt sets off his tan to perfection. He looks wonderful. He and Harriet would make a stunning couple, I thought, sadly.

Martin, rather than going brown, has gone bright red. His bald spot has really been hit by the sun and glows like a beacon. We ordered copious quantities of wine and plumped for the *menu gastronomique*. Harriet would probably eat a snail. As the evening wore on, the conversation turned to politics. Martin, a staunch Tory, roared about the state of the economy. Mike wickedly wound him up, and I chipped in. Harriet remained silent. Eventually, in response to one of Martin's completely outrageous statements about the unemployed, she said, 'But surely it isn't because they're *unemployable*. It has more to do with lack of training, doesn't it?'

'Harriet,' boomed Martin 'do shut up. You have no idea what you're talking about. Now, Mike,' he said, turning his back on her, 'what do you think about interest rates now? Up or down? You know, what you really need are some shares. I know a really good chap . . .'

I looked over at Harriet and was amazed to see her eyes had filled with tears. She hastily put down her napkin and, clumsily getting up, ran off into the loo. Mike looked up, surprised. Martin ranted on, oblivious. I made a shruggy face at Mike, and then followed her into the toilet. She was bending over the sink, her shoulders heaving. 'Harriet,' I said. 'Are you OK?'

She lifted her face and her eyes met mine in the mirror. 'He's such a *bastard*,' she hissed. 'I hate him. I'm sick of this. I'm really sick of being treated like an idiot.'

'But I thought you two were . . . happy,' I said. I felt like I'd been hit over the head with a shovel. She *seemed* to worship the ground he walked on.

'He's been having an affair,' she said.

'*No*,' I said, profoundly shocked. Who would want him?

'I found this number on his mobile phone bill and when I rang it, a woman answered. And then when I checked his credit card bill there were payments to an account I'd never heard of and a hotel in Jersey when he said he was in London on business,' she sobbed. 'He treats me as if I'm worthless and my opinions aren't worth having.'

But she was so gorgeous. How could he take her for granted? 'What are you going to do?' I said, hesitantly. 'Are you going to leave him?'

She looked at me pityingly. 'How could I leave him?' she said. 'I'd have nothing. I haven't got a job, like you, I haven't got anything. No money, nothing. What about the house? I couldn't bring the boys up, and what about their school?' She straightened up, wiped the mascara from under her eyes with a tissue, and, with only a slightly shaking hand, carefully put on some more lipstick. 'There,' she said. 'That's fine.' She smiled into the mirror, not a trace of misery on her beautiful face. 'Let's go back. The men will be wondering where we are.'

Sunday 30 August

So much mail has arrived while we've been away we could hardly get the door open. The answerphone cheerfully told us we had fifteen messages and the post contained two bank statements, two credit card bills, the telephone, electricity and gas bill and a cross letter from the local council about non-payment of a parking fine (mine, I'd forgotten all about it). 'Lovely,' I said to Mike, drifting into the kitchen clutching a wedge of brown envelopes. 'The perfect home-coming.' The weather on arriving home was grey and cloudy, and as soon as we set foot on English soil I longed and longed for the sharp, bright sunlight of France. I always find holidays terribly unsettling. Coming home is *awful*. No wonder so many people decide to pack it all in on their return and rush off to buy a guest-house in the Outer Hebrides. I felt like a huge weight of responsibility was descending on me which had been temporarily lifted, and the house seemed lifeless and dusty – not like our home at all. Work tomorrow is a prospect which doesn't bear thinking about. So many things to *do*. And leaving Tom . . . Our umbilical cords have been reconnected and they are both *my* children again. Rebecca hasn't mentioned Claire once all holiday and Tom feels totally *mine*, the touch and smell of his skin against me as we lay dozing together on the sun-lounger, his laughter as he bobbed against me in the pool, splashing and kicking. It has been wonderful, if exhausting, to have so much time to devote to him.

All the way back home yesterday Mike seemed preoccupied. When I spoke to him, he started, as if he were miles away. He's probably worried about his job. We had been perfectly civil to each other all holiday – not a cross word, after the trip to the ferry – and I felt we were paddling into calmer waters. But physical contact all holiday has been practically nil. I was so thrilled to have ended the row I kept going up and hugging him, and although he didn't pull away, he didn't hug me back, either. We haven't made love, but I *suppose* that's understandable – our room was very close to Harriet and Martin's and I was usually asleep when he came in . . . but when we were asleep he wasn't curling himself round me, and when I put my arms round him, he turned over away from me. Now we're home things will surely go back to normal. And, unusually for me, I am *desperate* for the reassurance of love-making.

After we had dragged all the bags in from the car, Mike glanced at his watch. 'Look, I might just pop into work, if you don't mind. I can get a couple of hours done when it's quiet – you know what chaos it is Monday morning. I'll grab a sandwich at the garage, don't worry about dinner.' He leapt into his car and roared off. Oh. Alone again, naturally.

9

SEPTEMBER

Monday 7 September

Rebecca back to school today. She had a huge fit about this yesterday, sobbing as I laid out her school clothes on her bed. A depressing number of her shirts had buttons missing, or the collar coming away from the seam. This means sewing, and braving the sewing basket. The mass inside it is now so bad I am terrified to lift the lid in case it hurtles out and gets me by the throat. I'd meant to go shopping for new clothes on Saturday, but we were really behind on the documentary editing and Nick was having a fit, insisting we all work overtime, so I had to go into the office. The details had been sent off to the television guide, so I suppose it had to get finished, didn't it? Very satisfying to see my name after *Executive Producer*. I am a Famous Person. Mum will buy ten copies and spread them around the hairdresser.

Both Tom and Rebecca cried when I tried to leave the first Monday morning after the holiday. Claire burst in at eight, tanned and beautiful from her holiday in the sun. I saw she had a small gold chain around her ankle. 'Tom!' she cried, swooping down on him.

He looked at her doubtfully. Who was this? Then the memory clicked and he clung to her. She'd bought presents for both of them – sweets and more sweets – and they rooted about in her bag for them. But when I picked up my briefcase, Rebecca turned and ran to me. Clinging onto my skirt, she said, 'Don't go. Don't go to work today, Mummy.'

I gently prised her fingers away from my tights. 'I have to. Look what Claire's bought you! Claire, Susie's coming over to play this afternoon, if that's all right. Rebecca, you'll have Susie this afternoon, and Claire's here now.' I had to go. I was going to be late.

'I don't want Claire,' said Rebecca fiercely. 'I want *you*.'

'Don't be silly, darling,' I said, seeing Claire's hurt expression. 'I'll be home soon.'

Tom, too, snug in Claire's arms, suddenly realized I was leaving. 'No!' he shouted, his arms out to me.

I shouldn't have gone back to hold him, but I couldn't resist. I rested my head on his, and breathed in his smell. 'I love you,' I said quietly to him, and then gently handed him back to Claire.

'Come on!' said Claire, 'let's go and see if the tadpoles have turned into frogs!'

'Yes, yes!' said Rebecca, letting go.

Claire turned and smiled. 'See you later,' she said. 'Is there anything you want me to buy? I'll do the ironing. Don't worry, they'll be fine. 'Bye!' She raised Tom's hand to wave goodbye to me and then led them away down the corridor. But before they went out of the door Tom turned to look at me. It was a look which plainly said, 'Don't leave me.'

Friday 11 September
Red Letter Day in that Nick is going to watch the first screening of our documentary, *Dyslexia Rules KO*. No, of course it isn't really called that, it's just a vile

journalist's joke. We've had them all during editing: –
'Heard about the dyslexic who didn't believe in Dog?'
etc. I think really it's just a way of coping with the
depths of emotion we come across; I guess policemen
and doctors are the same. At the time of Princess
Diana's death it became unbearable: 'What was
Princess Di's driver drinking before the crash? Harvey
Wallbanger and seven chasers'; 'What's the difference
between a Mercedes and a mini? Princess Di wouldn't
have been seen dead in a mini'; and so on. Awful. But
that kind of gallows humour does keep you going.

It has been deeply stressful trying to get all the final
cuts done but Gary has done a brilliant job of the voice-
over and his pieces to camera work really well. He
looks extremely handsome, and every time I've seen
him since the week in Boston I've felt panicky and
breathless. Gary is easing off in his attentions, because,
like all womanizers, he is only interested in success,
and if he feels there is no hope, moves swiftly on to the
next challenge. So there I am. I had my chance, and I
blew it. Still, it has made me realize both what a shallow person he is and that for me to give it all up for a
night of hot, sweaty sex with a stranger would be
totally counter-productive – even if sensationally
alluring. I feel like I have been doing nothing else but
edit for weeks, and am also twanging with nerves
because completion date on the house is next week
and I have not started to pack up the house. I keep
opening cupboards, surveying the hoard of junk, and
closing them very quickly again. I have even been
tempted to hire those removers who come in and pack
everything up for you, but that would be just too
embarrassing – they'd see the state of my knickers.

How are we going to move the fish? I put this to
Mike and he suggested we post them, which made
Rebecca burst into tears. She is very wound up at the

thought of leaving her bedroom and is leaving lots of yellow sticky notes all over the place saying, 'I love you, house.' Barmy. But I suppose most of her life has been spent in the cottage and she's bound to feel attached to it. I can't wait to see the back of it, and tomorrow I'm going in to Lawn Farm to measure up for curtains and such like. I cannot *wait.* If we move next Saturday I'm going to take the following week off. Mike says he can't, he is too busy. I'm busy at work too, but it's funny, my 'busy at work' still seems to leave enough time to deal with many other things whereas for Mike it means he can do nothing else save sleep on the sofa.

Nick, Gary, Mick, Mark, me and the video editor Sue crowded into the tiny editing room. I was feeling quietly confident – we'd put appropriately tasteful music round some of the most moving shots of the kids, the interviews were great, the writing sharp and to the point. When it started though, I felt I couldn't bear to watch, and kept glancing at Nick's face. It was impassive. After the half-hour – which felt like several hours – Sue flicked on the lights. 'What do you think?' I said, turning to Nick. He was quiet for a moment and then he shook his head. What?

'I found it disjointed. I couldn't follow the storyline and at the end I just wasn't convinced you'd made the point you set out to make – that it was worth the money and actually made a real difference to the children. I'm sorry, but I'm really disappointed.'

There was a stunned silence in the room, then Gary said, 'I don't really think that's fair, Nick.'

'Well, I'm pulling it,' he said. 'You'll really need to convince me it's worth re-editing. Carrie, can I see you for a moment?'

I followed him into his office, waiting to feel awful about this. I didn't. I just felt, Well, bugger off then.

Why didn't I care? A year ago this would have been the end of the world.

'It's just not strong enough,' said Nick after I'd closed the door. 'All the regions are in danger of losing this slot and I can't afford to put docs out which aren't potential award-winners. It's too sentimental. You're focusing far too much on the emotion of the parents and children and not getting the facts across. I didn't check the script because I trusted you, but now we've got a hole to fill. Thank God we've got the documentary Gary made earlier in the year about that blind mountaineer — that can go out. We were waiting for publication of his book, but we'll have to jack that. Carrie, it doesn't get any worse than this. I can't understand it. Your performance review comes up next month, doesn't it? So you've got a month to pull things together. You should be able to get a salary review because the rest of your work has been excellent,'

'Yes,' I said, not really listening. I was just longing and longing to get out of his office. Nick adopted a more conciliatory tone. He liked me, and he was finding this very hard, I knew.

'How's Mike? How's things going down the road? I hear some changes have been happening . . .'

'I really don't know,' I said shortly. 'Mike hasn't told me anything about it.' I wasn't going to pass gossip on to him, and anyway, Mike really hadn't told me anything about it. He hadn't told me anything about anything.

Sunday 13 September
Mike refused to come to the new house with me yesterday. He said he needed to go into the office, and that I hardly needed him to measure up for curtains. Actually, I did. Who else would hold the end of the

tape measure? I took Rebecca, and made Mike take Tom to the office with him. He was extremely boot-faced about this but *tough*. Tom was very excited to be going off alone in Daddy's car.

Driving up to the front gate – the house fronts on to the main road through the village, with the garden, orchard and paddock at the back – I stopped the engine and just stared at it for a while. Honey-stoned, with its twin gables, it looks far too grown-up a house for us to own. It's a proper person's house. Just pushing open the front door – it made a satisfying *creeeak* noise – made me thrilled. Soon to be *our* front door, with its big old metal ring and latch. I quietly reached out and touched the old wood. This had stood here, letting people in and out, for over two hundred years. The sense of history – real history – was overwhelming. How many children had run down the stone-flagged passage, shouting, laughing, calling to their mothers? It was so exciting to think that my children would grow up here, that this would be their memory of home. It was well worth the financial sacrifice, to let them live their early years in the peace and security of these old walls. The kitchen even had a panel of tiny bells, where the mistress would have rung down to the kitchen maid for more tea. Sounds a damn good idea to me. But there was more to do inside than I'd remem-bered – bits of plaster are falling off all over the place, and all the electricity sockets are the old type, which means we are going to have to re-wire as the survey suggested. Gulp. My mental geography of the house was also completely out, and entire rooms seemed to have moved.

The Gowers are being fiendishly organized and everything is already being packed into boxes. Most of it seems to be books and pictures. How strange, at their age, to be packing away their life. The rugs have been rolled back to reveal much darker flagstones, and the sunlight reflects the patches on the walls where their pictures have hung for so many years. Where the house had seemed so calm, so *complete* when we looked round, now it seems bare, a shell awaiting new life. Would it like us? I felt somehow that we wouldn't be worthy of it, the children too noisy, Mike and I too quarrelsome. Maybe we were much too common to live here. But surely this house would have a calming influence on us. I could lead the kind of life I wanted to – I would sit and read in the evenings, in the still air of the library, rather than slumping on the sofa watching television, and I *would* cook delicious home-made food on the old Aga, rather than bunging ready-made cartons into the microwave. This house would give all our lives added value. It just needs some fresh air and some brighter colours to make it feel like home. Mrs Gower glided in, with a cup of tea for me, orange for Rebecca and home-made fruit cake. She looked about her, at the half-filled boxes and the empty walls. 'It'll be lovely to have young ones living here,' she said. 'It needs new life, this old house.' Then she leaned towards me. 'You'll be very happy here. You look at home already.' I felt a surge of overpowering emotion. It will be perfect for Mike and me, it's what we've both always wanted. Surely we *will* be happy here?

Wednesday 16 September
Got home from work, and couldn't find Claire and Tom. Rebecca was slumped in front of the TV, her head on Angus, who was snoring loudly. All around her were cardboard boxes full of random items. I was trying to be really organized in my packing but it was so difficult to be enthusiastic after a hard day at work. I'd said firmly to myself that this was the ideal

opportunity to clear out loads of stuff. When it came to it, however, the mental effort of deciding what was essential and what was simply disposable family debris was simply too much. Books were going in with ornaments (not neatly rolled up in tissue but bunged in amongst towels), insurance documents with toys. Unpacking was going to be a bit of a revelation. In fact I will be very surprised if we don't lose an entire child.

'Where's Claire?' I said.

'Upstairs,' said Rebecca, her eyes glued to the TV.

Sure enough, there was Claire, bending over Mike's chest of drawers. 'Claire?' I said. 'What are you doing?'

She started guiltily. 'Just . . . sorting a few things out,' she said.

'Whatever for?' I said, astonished.

'It was just I heard Mike going on about his – well, socks, this morning, and I thought you had enough on your plate at the moment. I'm sorry. I thought it would be helpful.'

Mike had got up a bit later this morning, and Claire was already here while he got dressed. I simply cannot cope with washing as well as packing, so the laundry situation has deteriorated totally. I was in the bathroom, and heard him opening a drawer. 'No fucking socks!' he yelled. 'They're on the rack downstairs,' I'd yelled back, coldly. I could cheerfully have shot him. I really hadn't realized Claire could hear. God. It's come to something when your nanny begins to take responsibility for your husband's sock drawer.

Friday 18 September
Completed on the house today. We both had to belt over to the solicitor's at lunch-time to sign the documents. The mortgage offer has come through, thank

God, and now all we have to do is meet the repayments, which seem about the size of the national debt of a small West African state. Even our solicitor looked twice at the amount. 'By heck,' he said. 'You're pushing the boat out.' Hmm. But I was as high as a kite and, clutching Mike's arm on the way out, said, 'Let's go and have a drink to celebrate. Sod work.' I was in no hurry to return and face Nick anyway.

'I can't,' said Mike. 'I've got too much on. We'll celebrate later.' He kissed me on the forehead and turned and walked quickly away.

I was losing him. Why did I suddenly feel that? As I ran forward to hail a taxi, I thought, I'm losing him, I'm losing him and I don't know why. Since the holiday we have made love several times, but it has seemed mechanical, orchestrated in a way our love-making never has before. Mike has always been desperate for sex, and I've been the one beating him off with a stick. Now I practically have to force him to make love to me. Last night I'd even made the effort to put on stockings and suspenders – killingly uncomfortable but normally one hundred per cent guaranteed to turn him on. As he brushed his teeth, leaning over the sink, I slid into the bathroom and gently pressed up against him, taking his hand and rubbing it under my skirt. Only a few short months ago this would have been the signal for him to throw me to the floor and give me a good seeing to on the bathmat. But as he looked up and our eyes met, I registered only . . . what? Embarrassment? Fear? 'Come on,' I said, trying to make a joke out of it, 'you normally have to beg for such a treat.'

He turned and put his arms round me, but there was no wild abandon on the carpet, rather we sedately moved to the bed and he made love to me in a perfunctory, detached way. As he came, his eyes staring rather wildly at a distance inches above my head I tapped him on the shoulder. 'Excuse me,' I said. 'I'm here too.'

Saturday 19 September
The removal men are Barry and Trevor. They took one look at the numbers of small boxes I'd amassed and said 'Jesus!' Then they went out for a calming cigarette. They'd brought with them huge packing cases and I began to pile things into them randomly when they wandered back in and said, 'Better let us do that, missus.'

Rebecca looked up at me. 'What are we going to do about the fish, Mummy?'

'Fish?' they said, as one. 'We don't do fish.'

'Or dogs,' said Barry, who was looking with some alarm at Turtle and Angus. Both had worked themselves up into a state of canine dementia. Take their suitcase paranoia, and times it by ten. Their entire world was being packed away around them. The kitchen table – the table that Turtle spends most of his life lying beneath – was currently lying upside down in the hall. In a sad and futile gesture he had gone and sat in the middle of it, whining gently. Angus was lying across the front door, which meant you had to hurdle him as you went in and out. He knows I'm so vague I might easily forget him, so I think he's placed himself in the most obvious spot just in case he does get left behind and is forced to thumb a lift to our new home.

Moving the furniture revealed all kinds of horrors: sockets hanging off, peeling plaster and large stains on the carpet. Thank God we'll have gone before the new people arrive. Mike was little in evidence all morning, having set off early to collect the keys from the estate agent. It's only five miles away, but he'd been gone for over two hours. Where the hell was he? I really needed him to come and take Rebecca and Tom off my hands so I could have a final trot around the house and make sure we hadn't left anything important, like beds. 'Mrs Adams!' shouted Barry from the garden. 'What do you want us to do with this lot?' Oh bugger, blast and damn. I'd forgotten about the garden shed.

Eventually, after lunch, Mike returned. 'Where the hell have you been?' I asked furiously, trying not to let Trevor and Barry hear. 'I've been trying to cope with these madmen all on my own – they've already smashed two pictures – and we lost Tom in a packing crate. I really needed you.'

'I went on to the house to open it up,' he hissed back at me equally furiously, 'and they're still there! Mrs Gower was pottering about with teacups. I told them we were arriving after lunch, and she said not to worry, they'd be out by then. She made me stay and have a cup of tea.'

'It'll be your last for ages,' I said, starting to laugh. 'Come on, you can help the dynamic duo pack.'

We decided I would follow the lorry, and Mike went on ahead to make sure the Gowers really had gone, and hadn't perhaps invited a few friends round for bridge. I had to drive very slowly anyway, because Rebecca had the fish tank between her knees. Turtle and Angus were perched on duvets and towels in the back, leaning perilously as we went round corners. The fish looked extremely traumatized, as their normally sedentary tank became a surging ocean. Their little fins went like the clappers to keep themselves upright, and their mouths were open in a wide 'O' of astonishment. Do them good. Not enough challenge in their lives by far.

When we arrived Rebecca carefully placed the much-relieved fish on to the solid earth of the pavement, and, lifting Tom out of his car seat, ran up the path with him, panting slightly. She wanted to show him the house, and she'd already chosen her room. I marshalled the men this way and that, contradicting Mike's instructions since he clearly had no idea where things were supposed to go. Eventually he retired to the kitchen in a huff. It felt rather cold. I had presumed they'd leave the central heating on, and although Mr Gower had given me a long and detailed lecture last weekend about the workings of the rather ancient boiler, I have to confess I had glazed. That's why I'd wanted Mike to come with me. Show me a dial with lots of arrows and buttons, and I'll show you someone who wants to lie down and die.

By tea-time, everything was in, and Barry and Trevor had taken their leave. In the middle of the afternoon I'd said, 'Would you like a cup of tea?' and then looked about rather wildly at the fifty packing cases.

'It's all right, missus,' said Trevor kindly. 'We've got a Thermos.'

'Can I have some?' I said.

We went out for fish and chips for dinner, and ate them sitting on boxes in the rather chilly air of the living room. The sofa has disappeared under assorted sheets and blankets and I cannot face sorting everything out now. It can wait until the morning. Tom and Rebecca were packed off to bed unwashed and wearing jumpers over their pyjamas. The whereabouts of their toothbrushes remains a mystery. Rebecca lay in bed with her duvet pulled up tight to her chin. As I bent to kiss her, she said, dreamily, 'Is this our house for ever?'

'I hope so,' I said.

Friday 25 September
Mike has fixed up a rope swing to the biggest apple tree in the orchard, and this afternoon I went out

collecting apples while Rebecca pushed Tom backwards and forwards, backwards and forwards. They look so right here. After the nightmare of the first evening, when Mike and I had opened the boiler cupboard to peer in horror at the vast, clunking machine, things have steadily improved. 'If it's clunking,' I'd whispered, trying not to alert it to our presence, 'then it must be working.'

'But the radiators are freezing,' hissed back Mike.

'Press that button,' I said.

'Which one?'

'That red one.'

Mike leant hesitantly forward and pressed his finger against it. There was a loud sighing noise, the entire metal weight shook violently and small particles of rust shot off. Then the clunking stopped. 'I think,' said Mike, turning back to me, 'we'd better get a man in.'

Trying to cook with an Aga has also been a steep learning curve – it's one of the four-oven variety, and I keep forgetting where I've put things. Into its grimy depths goes a casserole, and there is an orchestration of door-opening while I try to find it again. 'It must be here somewhere,' I say rather desperately to two hungry children and two dogs sitting patiently next to me with their ears raised enquiringly.

I'd given Claire the week off, which was very brave of me, but I couldn't face her bustling about, organizing things and taking the children off me. Unpacking with them milling about my feet has been a bit of a trial, for everything I put in a cupboard, Tom firmly takes out again, but it's been so lovely to feel like a real family in this cosy – if temporarily shambolic – environment. There's so much more space for them to play: gates to run in and out of, real trees for Rebecca to climb, long meadow grass in the paddock to breach chest-high. We're going to have to buy lots more furniture – our stuff looks very lost in the much bigger rooms and not antique enough by a long chalk – but already it feels like home. Not just home, but Home. Tearing myself away to go to work on Monday is going to be a nightmare. I shall drop the portcullis and start heating up the extra-virgin olive oil.

10

OCTOBER

Sunday 4 October
'So what's it like being the lady of the manor?' Jill said this morning, wandering around the downstairs rooms of the house, coffee mug in hand, taking in the mullioned windows (mine) and stone-flagged floors (mine), and opening and closing the old pine doors with their satisfyingly solid brass handles (mine).

'Wonderful,' I said. 'The children love it – Rebecca's like a different child. You know how stroppy she was about moving? Well, now I have the perfect child. The perfect child in that I never *see* her.'

'Ideal,' said Jill nodding in agreement, as she peered out of the window at Susie, who was pulling Daisy along the grass by her hair.

Since we moved in Rebecca has spent every moment she can playing rapturously outside despite the chilly autumn air, hanging off the branches of the orchard trees like a spider monkey with Tom toddling happily beneath her. Her Disney videos remain in one of the packing cases; she hasn't asked for *The Little Mermaid* once. In fact the television hasn't been on at all. I really would feel that I have died and gone to heaven were it not for the distance that remains between Mike and me.

I expected him to be as thrilled about the house as I am, but he unpacked with all the enthusiasm of a prisoner on death row. After work last Monday I rushed home, heaved all the curtains out of their boxes, and made a stab at putting them up on the heavy old oak poles. Even that was exciting, and I hate hanging curtains. 'Mike!' I yelled, my voice muffled under the heavy folds of dark green velvet as I balanced precariously on a chair, my arms up above my head and already going numb. 'What about these for in here?' I heard him walk into the room, and I turned to get his reaction.

'Fine,' he said, walking out. 'Fine.'

'Do try to curb your natural enthusiasm,' I said icily, and fell off the chair.

'Just leave it,' he said to me firmly on Wednesday, after I'd asked him for the millionth time if he was OK while he sat at the kitchen table after work, his head bent over a newspaper. Our rows before always seemed to revolve around the fact that I didn't spend enough time with him, that I didn't make enough time for *us* and I was too preoccupied with the children. Now I desperately *want* to be with him, but every time I reach out for him, he rejects me. I have always taken our love for granted, it's just there, no question about it, like the inevitability that one or both children will immediately need to talk to me about something vitally important as soon as the phone rings.

'How *are* things with Mike?' asked Jill cautiously, as we peered out at the children through the attic window. It is very dark and grimy up here, with soup-plate-sized spiders which lurk, breathing heavily, in dark corners. Switch on the light and they scuttle forward, egg-sized bodies raised, great hairy legs outstretched. Never mind a cobweb brush, you would need a *mallet* to get rid of these fellas. Gargantuan

spiders not withstanding, I am determined to turn it
into a sixth bedroom and playroom for the children.
It's so great to have a house you can make plans about.
I haven't talked to Jill about the Mike *détente* situation
for weeks – it is becoming almost too painful to mention.

'Awful,' I said gloomily. 'It's like living with a total
stranger.'

'Well, talk to him about it,' said Jill reasonably,
before squeaking and leaping sideways as a bionic
spider made a run for her feet. 'Can we get down from
here?' she said in a high-pitched voice.

'I *can't* talk to him,' I said as we tip-toed carefully
down the ladder, to emerge into the sunlight of the
landing, shaking cobwebs from our hair. 'Every time I
ask him what's wrong and can we talk he snaps my
head off and says that everything would be fine if I
stopped going on and on at him, and that things are
just very tense at work. I can't *reach* him. It's as if he's
built a barrier around himself and every time I try to
get close, I bump off. I can't even imagine sleeping
with him any more – I can't imagine being so *intimate*.'
My voice tailed off a bit and I looked up at Jill.
'Honestly, if I didn't know him better, I'd say he was
having an affair.'

'Which he isn't?' said Jill, hesitantly.

'Of course not,' I said, totally shocked. 'Don't be
ridiculous. We're far too important to him. And anyway, I'd know. I'd just know.'

Friday 9 October
Tonight Mike and I had a screaming row. It all started,
believe it or not, over a bin bag in the kitchen. Marriage
rows are so noble in intent, aren't they? I gently asked
Mike if he could empty the bin and take it outside,

because we'd been cramming things in for several days and the swing bit at the top hasn't swung for ages. He went to lift the bag out – and it fell apart. In the rush of sorting out the house I haven't had time to buy decent bin bags from the supermarket, so I bought cheap ones from the village shop instead. Chicken bones, wine bottles, carrot peelings, tea leaves, old newspapers, all manner of domestic debris spilled out all over the floor. I clapped my hand over my mouth as I had an awful urge to laugh, and a gurgle escaped me. Mike just stood there for a moment, his hands full of shredded black plastic, then he threw the rest of the rubbish onto the floor – including a broken milk bottle I'd meant to wrap in newspaper but, naturally, hadn't. 'I'll get another one,' I said. 'Help me clear it up.'

'Your fucking problem,' he said, stepping delicately forward over the debris and heading for the door. 'You bought the crappy bags. I'm going to bed.'

I wasn't having this. As he moved to walk past me I grabbed him, and we silently grappled. I mean, Laurel and Hardy wasn't in it, but at the time it didn't feel funny. 'You help me!' I shouted, clinging onto his arm. 'I'm so tired I can hardly stand up. Just think about me for a change!'

'That's always your excuse,' Mike said, removing my hand from his arm as if it were contagious. 'You're too tired for everything. You think your job is so stressful – well, you ought to try mine. You've no idea about stress. You're just so happy to potter about this house making cakes like Mrs Fucking Beeton and all you want to talk about is what colour we're going to paint Rebecca's bedroom. I have far more on my plate than that. Like paying this bloody mortgage. You have no idea what could happen if the interest rates go up, just so long as you can boast about your orchard and impress all your friends with the fact that Rebecca's going to get a pony.'

'That is so unfair!' I yelled back. 'I'm paying half this mortgage and we couldn't have got it without my salary! I work just as hard as you – it isn't a piece of cake doing my job either, but you never ask me about how *I* feel. You're so wrapped up in your own problems. So what if you lose your job? We've still got my salary. We could manage.' At that, he gave me a furious look and stormed out of the kitchen. I slumped down, in tears. I can't bear this any longer. It's like living with Attila the Hun.

Saturday 10 October
Mum rang this morning. 'How are you all?' she said anxiously. If she hasn't heard from me for more than a day she assumes we've all been killed by a frenzied axe murderer.

'Fine,' I said, carefully. I hadn't slept at all last night and I felt brittle, as if someone breathed too hard on me I might break. Mike had disappeared this morning, and the house felt empty and cold.

'How is the house?' said Mum.

'Lovely,' I said. 'It's lovely, we all love it.'

'Are you *warm* enough?' she said. 'Those old houses are fearfully difficult to heat. Your gas bill's going to be a fortune,' she added, with some relish. 'Has it got bats?'

'Bats?' I said, rather wildly.

'*Bats*, darling,' she said slowly, as if to a small child. 'All old houses have bats and they flit about in the roof. You can't get rid of them because they're protected. Droppings everywhere. Have you had the damp done?'

'Yes, Mum,' I said wearily. 'The man's been here all week injecting the walls.'

222

'That's no good,' she said. 'When we had our damp done it was all the plaster off the walls downstairs. Sounds like you're only having half a job done. Anyway, I have to go. I want your father to go and look at a new garden centre. Honestly, it's a job to keep him occupied.'

''Bye, Mum,' I said.

''Bye, darling.' She rang off happily after shedding just a little more sunshine into the world.

I just wish I could talk to her about Mike and me, but she'd be so horrified she'd probably have a heart attack. Marriage is for life and, if in doubt, her motto with Daddy has always been 'give in'. But with Mike there's nothing to 'give in' to. How can I give in to a man who doesn't seem to want what I have to give? But I can't just let our marriage go. Jill? I can always have a good moan to Jill but she'll tell me to leave him and that it isn't worth making myself miserable and I'm worth more than that. But I do love him – I've tried indifference and it doesn't work – and he is Rebecca and Tom's father. How can I take them away from him? I can hardly deprive them of a father just because *we* can't get on. It's not *their* fault. And, horrors, he might want to take the children away from me. That would be unthinkable. Harriet? Harriet would just laugh and say that all men are bastards, darling, that you just have to play the game and get as much out of them as you can, and I should just grin and bear it, like she's doing with Martin. Kate? Now, Kate. Kate is an independent, free-thinking career woman who has a very clear view of life. She doesn't understand all the ups and downs of marriage, but she does know Mike and me pretty well. I haven't had a chance to see her much since our health farm weekend, and we have been working in separate offices since my promotion. But I will give her a ring, I thought thankfully. It'll

223

be lovely to tell someone who's *neutral*.

The phone rang for a long time, and I'd almost given up, thinking she was out. When she answered the phone she sounded slightly breathless. 'Are you OK?' I said. 'I haven't caught you at a bad time?'

'Carrie! No, not at all,' she said, her voice dropping and sounding calmer. 'I was just in the bath.'

'Christ. I dream of having baths on Saturday mornings. How are you? I've hardly seen you at work for weeks.'

There was a long pause. 'I'm leaving,' she said.

'What! Why didn't you tell me?'

'I'm going to Midlands as a presenter,' she said.

Why hadn't Mike told me she'd been given a job? 'Did you go and see Mike?' I said.

'Yes,' she said. 'Months ago.'

'What does Oliver think?'

'Oliver's not here,' she said. 'He's left. He left two weeks ago.'

'Oh God, Kate, I'm sorry. Why didn't you tell me?' I said again, anxiously.

'You've been so busy with the house and America and things, I haven't been able to catch you.'

Humph. Some friend I am, so wrapped up in my own problems I haven't even noticed that Kate has been going through hell. I must admit she has seemed very pale whenever I've seen her in the office, and every time I've gone looking for her to have coffee she seems to have disappeared.

'But that's great news for you, isn't it? About the job? You've always wanted to present,' I said.

'Yes,' she said. 'Look, Carrie, I have to go, I've promised to meet a friend for lunch. Give me a ring next week, we'll talk then. Are you OK?' she added as an afterthought.

I could hardly dump all my problems on her now.

'Fine,' I said. 'It would be lovely to have lunch next week—' But she'd rung off.

Sunday 11 October
'Are you and Daddy going to get divorced?' We were driving frantically towards Rebecca's swimming lesson, late as usual, and she'd been unusually quiet and thoughtful all morning. I had to concentrate hard not to swerve the car into the kerb, and swivelled my eyes sideways to catch her expression. 'You haven't talked to each other for ages and I heard you crying last night. You thought I was asleep but I wasn't. I heard you.'

'Of course not,' I said, furiously concentrating on keeping the car in a straight line. 'We're fine, don't be silly. We're just very tired with moving house and everything, and work is hard for both of us at the moment.'

Rebecca thought about this and said, as if she'd been considering the matter very deeply, 'I talked to Katie at school about you being sad and she said her mummy cried a lot and then her mummy and daddy got divorced. Now she's got two different beds and four cats but she doesn't like her daddy's girlfriend. She smells of perfume and she kisses too hard. Her mummy still cries too.' Rebecca carefully arranged her furry toy cat more comfortably on her knee and then looked at me very intently. 'Are you sure you're not going to get a divorce from Daddy?'

I turned to look at her properly and saw her eyes were full of tears. 'Of course not.' I stopped the car at the side of the road and, switching off the engine, I pulled her into my arms. 'We love you too much,' I said, but even as I spoke I found my eyes were filling with tears too. This is crazy. Even Rebecca can see what's going on. We can't live like this.

Tuesday 13 October

The only laugh I had this week, if you can believe it, was the smear test I had today. Nick said I could have the morning off – I just told him I needed to go to the doctor's: if I'd said 'smear test' he probably would have gone green and fainted. I hate having smear tests. Jill has recommended a doctor at the new practice in the village, because she says he has sexy eyes and warm hands. Apparently all the village women are flocking there in droves. I'd hoped I could take Rebecca to school, but the appointment was for nine and I wouldn't have time to get back. I rushed in, and met the usual death's-head spinster on reception. 'You'll need to fill in a new patient form,' she said.

'We're a whole family,' I said.

She raised her eyebrows. 'Then you'll need to fill in one for all of them – but your husband must sign his. And ideally we do like new patients to come in for a brief medical. Could you ask your husband to make an appointment?'

'Of course,' I said, knowing full well Mike would never turn up in a month of Sundays as he never goes to the doctor and would have to lie heavily about the amount he drinks every day.

I filled in the form and when it got to the bit about 'How many units of alcohol do you have every day' I crossed my fingers behind my back and put two. A dozen, more like. Unfortunately it turns out smears here are done by the nurse, not the doctor. Rats. Although it might not be the best way of introducing myself to young Dr Kildare. Not exactly my best side. In the surgery the nurse went through my pregnancy record and asked if I was on the pill. Yes, I said (although God knows why, it would take an immaculate conception at the moment). 'Has your husband thought of having the op if you don't want any more children?' she said.

I imagined Mike's face at the thought of having his testicles mangled. 'I don't think it's a possibility,' I said. 'At the moment.'

'Well, pop behind the screen and remove your lower garments,' she said. Oh Gawd. I made a neat bundle on the floor, and then hopped up onto the couch and hastily pulled the towel over me. 'Lovely,' she said, appearing waving that nasty iron thing which looks like curling tongs. 'Just open your knees . . . a little wider . . . just relax.' How can I relax when a complete stranger is about to insert a pair of curling tongs into my fanny? 'You might just feel a little scraping,' she said. Too bloody right. It felt like I was being reamed out. I tried my best to think of something entirely different which didn't involve lying flat on my back with my knees spread. 'You've just moved into Lawn Farm, haven't you?' she said, scraping away.

'That's right,' I squeaked.

'It's a lovely house. You've got lots of land. Are you going to get a pony?'

'We're hoping to,' I said.

'We've got some land too,' she said. 'At Steeple Aston, just up the road.'

'Lovely,' I said.

'We breed alpacas,' she said. What? 'In my spare time – I only do this part time. Alpacas are my *passion*.'

'How interesting,' I said.

'I don't suppose you'd like one, would you?' she said. 'They make lovely pets for children, they're ever so gentle.'

'I think we've got enough on our plate at the moment,' I said, 'but thanks for the offer.'

'No problem. You get dressed now. That's lovely,'

she said, carrying my cells carefully over to her desk.

It's not every day you go in for a smear test and nearly come out with an alpaca.

Thursday 15 October
Performance review day. Nick has been bustling about importantly all morning while I tried in vain to catch his eye. I'd rather get it over with, it's hardly a priority for me at the moment. There has been much shock and debate about Kate's departure, because the gossip from Midlands is that she's been given the main presenter's role, the plum job occupied for what seems like a hundred years by a waxy-faced harridan called Monica, who regards herself as *the* face of Midlands TV. She is apparently spitting blood and threatening the company with all kinds of law suits for breach of contract. I would have thought Mike would have been bursting with all this news, especially as he knows how close Kate and I are. I'd thought Kate would be slipped in as a junior presenter and do the daytime bulletins, not the main programme. Well, good for her, it's a major career leap. It would be some consolation at least for Oliver's departure. She still hasn't told me why he's left as she hasn't rung me, but I would guess it was because she'd taken my advice and tried to pin him down about marriage. Oops. What's the opposite of match-maker?

It was after lunch when my phone buzzed signalling an internal call. 'Carrie, could you pop into my office for a minute?' Nick.

'Sure,' I said. Normally I'd be on tenterhooks about a meeting like this – potentially more money, a pat on the back, hints about my glittering future, general confirmation that I am the best thing since sliced bread – but today I feel incredibly flat about the whole thing.

I'm too worried about Mike, and ever since the week-end Rebecca has been preoccupied and tearful. She's taken to following me everywhere, waiting patiently when I'm on the loo and howling if she can't see me. I had to prise her off like a barnacle to get to work this morning.

'Well, Carrie,' said Nick, settling his stomach behind his large oak desk and pushing the performance review sheaf of papers towards me. 'Have a look at that.' Silently, I read it through. Apart from the balls-up of the dyslexia documentary, praise has been heaped upon me. Efficient, calm in a crisis, an excellent manager, well liked, sociable, a great team-leader. Is this me? It's the sort of report I'd have given my eye teeth for even just last year, but today I cannot work up any feelings of enthusiasm. All I can think about is the way Rebecca bit her lip as I was leaving the house. I told her to be brave, that everything is fine, but she isn't buying into this particular fantasy. And Claire had been rather brusque with her, pushing her back towards the kitchen as I opened the front door. What right does Claire have to dictate how my children behave? Every right, I suppose.

'What do you think?' said Nick, smiling happily. 'Pretty good, isn't it? And I've got even better news for you. Tom Warner, the head of forward planning at TV Centre, rang me last week. He wants a recommendation for an attachment as an assistant editor in his department. I suggested you. I think you're ready for it, and it would be a big step forward, wouldn't it? Network TV?' I looked at him wildly. Television Centre? How the hell could I work there? Who would look after the children? Nick didn't notice my confusion; instead, standing up to open the door for me, he said, 'Have a think about it. Chew it over with Mike. It would only be for six months initially, and commuting

229

from your neck of the woods wouldn't be too much of a problem, would it? I'd be sorry to let you go, but within these four walls, I think I'll be off there myself soon. It's the place to be.'

I went back to sit at my desk. My head felt thick and befuddled like I was going to faint. It would be a wonderful job, lots more money and where I've always wanted to work. The culmination of all my ambitions. I should be over the moon, making plans, working out the logistics of how I could get there and back, the child-care I would need. Pegs to be slotted into the appropriate holes. But I could not make myself care. It seemed unimportant. Where once I would have been on the phone to Tom Warner like a shot, charming the pants off him down the phone and making arrangements to meet, now I felt only panic and despair. *More* work. *More* separation. *More* dizzying arrangements which would spiral and spiral, until one small disaster like an ill child would make them collapse. Mike would never move, and after the six-month attachment it would be crazy to think I could commute every day. We'd have to move permanently. That would mean uprooting the children again, finding another house, finding a new nanny . . . Or I could move. I could move on my own with the children. With a London salary I could manage a mortgage on my own and TV Centre has an excellent crèche and after-school club . . . No. Not more separation. I really needed to think. I have to go home, I thought, and rang Nick to say I needed this afternoon off, if that was OK.

As I drove home I realized that it was nearly time for Rebecca to be picked up. I drove round by the school, thinking I could get there before Claire arrived, intercept her and then kidnap my own children. I could make a proper meal with *cooked* food and spend some time just playing with them. I'd light a fire in the snug and Rebecca and I could play cards . . . the comforting tableau took shape in my mind. Rebecca had ballet later as well so it would mean I could take her. For the first time today I began to feel happy. But the traffic was heavy, and I pulled up at the school as all the children were streaming out. I stopped the car and ran up the road, looking for Claire. There she was, on the opposite side of the road. Tom was happily waving a balloon from his pushchair and, as I stood there, Rebecca ran out of the gates with two of her friends. She saw Claire, and even from the distance of where I was standing, I saw her face light up. She ran towards Claire and they hugged, hard. Then Claire turned to walk to her car, pushing Tom, her arm round Rebecca, and I could see Rebecca chatting excitedly away, before turning to wave at her friends. It was a moment caught in time, a snapshot of my children's lives which happened every day. Not an extraordinary moment, just a minute out of the thousands of minutes which were a closed book to me. I felt like I had finally opened the pages and seen what I was missing. To all intents and purposes, Claire *was* their mum.

I didn't call out. I turned back, taking care they did not see me, and climbed into my car. I was neither needed nor wanted. A mother surplus to her children's requirements.

Saturday 17 October
The whirlwind of the day's activities over - washing, shopping, dog-walking, cleaning (we still haven't got a cleaner and it took me over five hours to clean the house, towing Tom around behind me like a small boat) – and I was ready to collapse by eight. But I can't. I have to talk to Mike this evening. Earlier this afternoon he'd been sweeping up leaves in the back garden

with Rebecca jumping in and out of the piles, kicking about in her new Barbie wellington boots. I walked up to them, hands deep in the pocket of my poacher's jacket, Tom toddling along behind in outsize wellies (a Rebecca hand-me-down). I'd heard their laughter from inside the house, but as soon as Mike saw me approaching it was as if a bucket of cold water had been poured over their joy. How can it be that my own husband can make me feel awkward and embarrassed?

'Mike,' I said, 'are you in tonight?'

'Yes,' he said. 'Why?'

'I just wondered, that's all. I've bought some steak for dinner, so I just wanted to check you hadn't made any plans.'

'No,' he said, turning away from me. 'No plans.'

'Great,' I said, managing a smile. As I turned away, swinging down to pick up Tom, the laughter resumed.

While I lay in the bath I felt ridiculously nervous. This is my own husband, I kept telling myself, someone I've lived with for over seven years. So why do I feel like a teenager on a date? If he approves of my plan, it could mean the beginning of a big change for all of us. A really, really big change. Quite possibly, it *could* save our marriage. Or it could break it completely. Our future lives could go one way or another as a result of this evening, and it feels quite bizarre to think that such a momentous decision could be made tonight. I was getting dressed when the phone rang. 'Mrs Adams?' said an unknown voice. 'I wonder if I could have a moment of your time. We're doing a survey about loft insulation in your area and I wondered if . . .' I stared at the phone for a moment. My whole future was about to be decided and a man was asking me about *loft insulation*? 'No thank you,' I said politely, and put the phone down. Then I cried.

Surely we should have opera playing, with vast

Italian women wailing their guts out as we faced each other across the big pine table in the kitchen? Surely we deserved more of an audience than a politely interested Labrador and a soporific golden retriever? I considered going over and giving him a shove with my foot. Your future could be decided tonight, I thought. You could become an urban dog in a single-parent family. He opened one eye and peered at me blearily. No respecter of crisis, he closed his eye, sighed, and let out a loud snore.

Mike came in carrying Rebecca's special night-time cup. 'She wants cocoa,' he said, opening one of the top cupboards.

'It's bad for her teeth,' I said before I could stop myself. He wanted to give her a treat. They'd had a lovely day together, setting fire to the leaves and throwing all the rotten brown apples into a big wicker basket while I hid inside with Tom.

'OK,' he said calmly. 'Milk it is.' He went off to read her story, while I fumbled about putting sour cream into the jacket potatoes and dropping baby carrots on the floor. I can't cook when I'm nervous, and the hefty slugs of red wine I was taking were not helping. I hadn't eaten all day and I already felt quite heady, as if I might suddenly pitch forward into the bubbling carrots.

'OK,' said Mike, sitting down at the table as I put his plate in front of him. 'What's all this about?' I had rehearsed what I was going to say endlessly, putting my case one way and then the other, remaining completely calm and rational. As soon as he looked at me my bottom lip wobbled and I burst into tears. Brilliant. A brilliant start. 'What the hell's the matter?' said Mike, hastily moving his plate away so I didn't drip into his food. He hadn't eaten this well in weeks.

'What the bloody hell do you think is the matter?' I

sobbed. 'We haven't spoken to each other properly for months and living with you is like living with the incredible disappearing man. You don't talk to me, you don't want to make love to me, you don't seem to want me at all. How do you think I feel? How do you think I feel when you shrink away from me in bed, when I touch you and you move away? You haven't told me anything about work, anything about how you're feeling in weeks and weeks. I can't *touch* you. I feel like I don't know you any more and our marriage is just being – lost.' I leapt up and grabbed a piece of kitchen roll. I meant to be so calm and beautiful and in control, and here I was, with a face like raspberry ripple. Angus snored on.

'You haven't told me about Kate, or anything, or asked about my work,' I went on.

'What about Kate?' he said, his voice dangerously quiet.

'About her *job*,' I said. 'I feel like I'm being shut out of your life, as if I'm not important any more.'

'Carrie, Carrie,' said Mike, and for the first time in weeks he reached out to touch me. 'That's not true. None of this is true. You turned away from me, remember? You told me I was *useless*, that you didn't need me, that you could run the house better on your own. How do you think that made me feel? Great? I've had to virtually tie you to the bed to make love to you since Tom's birth and now you're telling me *I* don't want to make love to *you*? That's rubbish. You've made it perfectly clear that you don't need me at all, and that I'm just in the way in your and the children's lives. You've got the house you want, the job you want, the children you want, the lifestyle you want. You just want to fit me into the package when you need me but it's not *fucking enough*.' He'd been so calm up to now, but on the last words he completely lost it, and his fist hit the

234

table. The plates bounced, and Angus woke with a start. He sneezed, looked at us inquiringly and then settled back down with a sigh. Do you mind keeping the noise down? There's a dog trying to sleep here. Mike made a visible effort to calm himself. 'I've tried to plough myself into work, but it isn't enough. You don't want me. You certainly haven't shown me that you do.'

'But I have!' I argued, making deep grooves in the old pine of the table with my fork, my hand shaking. 'I've shown you all the time, hugging you, trying to touch you – you've been avoiding me!'

'Only because I thought you didn't want me, that I *repulsed* you,' Mike said.

'Christ,' I said. 'What a bloody mess.'

'It certainly is. And is this the very important thing you wanted to tell me? That we're useless at being married? That you want to – end it?'

'*No*,' I said, looking at him in horror. 'Obviously we need to talk, but there's something else. I've been offered a job at TV Centre.'

Mike looked at me, long and hard. 'And?' he said, his voice trembling slightly.

'And,' I said, 'I've decided not to take it.'

The hand which had been clenching his fork until the knuckles went white, relaxed. 'Thank God,' he said.

'In fact,' I said. 'Not only am I not going to take the job in London, I'm giving up my job here. For good.'

The atmosphere in the kitchen went very still and quiet. The only sound was the clock and Angus's snoring as Mike took this in. 'You mean you intend to stop work and just – stay at home?'

'Yes,' I said, trying to dredge up the confidence I was definitely not feeling. Why was he making this so hard? I took a deep breath. 'I've had enough of handing

235

the children over to Claire. It isn't working for me any more. I want them back.'

'But,' said Mike, 'how are we going to pay the mortgage?'

'We'll have to work that one out,' I said. 'I don't mean to be selfish. I just feel . . . I just feel that if I carry on like I'm doing now I'll go mad. I don't want things at work any more, I'm not heading anywhere I want to go. I don't care about promotion, I don't care what Nick thinks, I just want each day to end so I can go home. I'm so tired of rushing backwards and forwards, never having any proper time with the children, never having time to get anything done in the house. Tom's so lovely and I'm going to miss all his baby years and Rebecca really needs me. I don't want to turn round in ten years' time and say to them, "So, did you have a good childhood?" Please,' I said, 'say it's OK.'

'You seem to have already decided,' said Mike, reaching forward and taking a big gulp of wine. He looked at his glass, and then down at Turtle, who was pressing his nose against his leg, eager for steak fat. 'Quite a decision to take on your own.' Then he got up from the table without another word, and walked up the stairs to bed.

Saturday 24 October
'You must be mad,' said Jill. 'You must be stark, staring, bloody mad. How are you going to pay for the house? How are you going to keep Rebecca at school? How are you going to run a car? How are you going to *live*?'

'You only work part-time,' I protested feebly.

'Yes, but I don't live in bloody Hampton Court and send my children to private school, do I?' said Jill. She'd been on at me ever since I rang her on Monday

236

to tell her the big news. I'd expected support, but she was outraged. 'How can I tell my girls that if you work hard and go to university you'll get a wonderful job like Aunty Carrie and not have to rely on a man if *you* go and give it all up? You're the only decent role model I have for them. What's happened to equality and all the valid reasons for working full-time that you used to spout at me?'

'I'm not happy,' I said.

'Who's happy?' said Jill. 'Are you really going to be happy relying entirely on Mike?'

'It'll bring us together,' I said. 'It'll stop him feeling emasculated.'

'Carrie,' said Jill, 'if you think having to ask your husband for money every week is a recipe for marital harmony you must be fucking bonkers.'

'I think it's *marvellous*,' purred Harriet down the phone. 'It'll be so lovely to have you available for coffee mornings. And you can help out with the summer fête this year. Oh, and I could even persuade you to do a morning or two at the charity shop. The best thing is,' she said, her voice becoming even more excited, 'we'll be able to go *shopping* together.'

'Shopping,' said Mike just before dinner, 'is totally out. No more little trips into Oxford to stock up on even more clothes to fit into your bulging wardrobe. The children don't need any more clothes, their drawers are full to bursting as well. And I'm not sure we'll be able to run two cars.' He was sitting at the kitchen table with all our bank statements and credit card bills spread out in front of him. On Wednesday night, after two days of withdrawal and silence until I was ready to *explode*, I was bending over the kitchen sink after work, rinsing out one of Tom's bottles. I heard the door bang, but didn't turn round. I'd been ignored quite enough, thank you. But a minute later I

237

heard footsteps behind me. I stiffened, and began rinsing like crazy. Then I felt his arms round my waist. 'I think it's a great idea,' he said, into my ear. 'The more I think about it the more sense it makes.' I laid my head back against his with relief. Oh thank God, thank God. Perhaps now we can *all* come home.

What is now worrying me is that Mike has slipped into the role of breadwinner with ease. Alarming ease. Sitting there, with his hands placed firmly on our bank statements at the head of the table, I thought, Who does he remind me of? The answer that came back was like having cold water poured over me. *My father.* If I start apologizing for buying a magazine, I know the worst thing in the world will have happened. I will have become my mother.

I meanwhile have been having all kinds of awful doubts. It seemed at the time to be such a brave, such an *obvious* decision, that there could be no doubts about its validity. But now reality has begun to creep in. My car is a company car. That will have to go. What about my pension scheme? That will have to be either cashed in or transferred into a private scheme, and I will lose all my employer's contributions. Thank God I've been back at work more than six months, or I would have to pay back my maternity leave payments as well. Then there's the small matter of actually telling Nick I am leaving. At least five times this week I've been on the cusp of telling him, but then I thought he'd have to talk to me about the attachment anyway, and I could tell him then. He didn't mention it. And – oh God – Claire. How can I tell Claire she doesn't have a job any more?

Friday 30 October
'Nick,' I said this morning, sticking my head round his door. 'Do you have a second?'

'Sure,' he said, smiling happily at me. 'Come in. Thought about the attachment? I had Tom on the phone this morning and I said I'd put the idea to you. He seems pretty keen. Did you know he used to work with Mike? He's very interested to meet you . . .'

'I'm not going to take it,' I said, very quickly.

'What?'

'I'm not going to take it and there's something else I have to tell you . . .' I paused here and forced myself to look directly into his genial face. 'I'm resigning.'

'You are *joking*,' he said, the bluster all gone. He looked genuinely shocked. 'Why? Look, I know I came down hard on you about the documentary, but that was a one-off, for God's sake, Carrie. Where are you moving to?' he said, his eyes narrowing angrily. 'Joining Mike's team?'

'Christ, no, Nick,' I said. 'I wouldn't leave the BBC, you know I wouldn't.'

'So where *are* you going?' he said.

'Nowhere,' I said. 'I'm going to give up work completely and look after the children. At home.'

Nick looked at me as if I had two heads. '*You* are going to give up work and be a *housewife*?' He started to laugh. 'Carrie, that's priceless. You, of all people! You'll *hate* it, stuck at home with the children all day. When I look at my wife – well, she hasn't got a life, just looking after me and the children. I've always admired you for the way you've coped. You wouldn't know you *have* children.' I winced. 'You've got such a good job here, such a bright future. You really can't throw it all away. It would be madness. All the training you've had, all the courses, all that experience . . .' His mind was now whirring like a computer, clocking up all the money the region had spent on me. I began to feel appallingly guilty. Maybe it was the wrong decision, maybe I hadn't really thought it through . . . Oh shit. If

239

I resign now they'll never let me back. I'll be stuck in mummyland for ever. No. This lady is not for turning. Can't anyway, I'd look a right prat. Giving up work because I wanted to see more of my children, returning with my tail between my legs, presumably because I wanted to see *less* of them?

'I'm sorry, Nick,' I said. 'I really am. But I'm not going to change my mind. This feels right for me, and you'll have no end of applications for my job, and if I'd taken the attachment I'd have been leaving anyway.'

'Well,' he said, 'if you're absolutely sure. It's your decision. But if you ever want to come back, just give me a ring. I'm really sorry to lose you. I suppose another five thousand wouldn't make a difference, would it?'

'Nick!' I said. 'Stop bribing me!'

He laughed, holding his hands up in front of him. 'OK, OK, you win. But I'll miss you, we all will.'

'Thanks,' I said, feeling tears rising behind my eyes. Oh Jesus, I really must not cry. I pushed open the door and wandered back towards my office. My ex-office. I looked down the length of the newsroom. Pete was talking animatedly into the phone, pen in hand, his feet up on the desk. Ranks and ranks of humming computers, piles of newspapers spilling onto the floor, shouts of laughter, phones constantly ringing, the bang of the doors as people ran in and out, the printers churning out bulletins and scripts. My world. This was the place which energized me, which lifted my spirits every morning by its sheer vibrancy and noise, the sense of urgency that working in news brings. It was all so familiar, as familiar as my own home; in a way it *was* my home. I've spent far more time here than I have at home. And all these people, my friends, people I'd laughed with, panicked with, been furious with – I was going to walk away and never see them again.

Who would I be? My identity, my vision of myself, would cease to exist. Everything in my life, in a way, has led up to this. Working hard at school, getting my exams, going on to university, taking a degree, getting into newspapers, breaking into radio and then television – everything has been calculated, a career path, a progress of achievement. Work is my way of being proud of myself, of making other people respect me. I am who I am because of the job I do. Take that away, and what am I? Just another face in the crowd, going nowhere. Struggling to push a pushchair around the shops, worrying about the price of food, waking up each morning to a day the same as the last.

What would I look forward to? Mike coming home? Holidays? All the stay-at-home mothers I know spend their lives planning the next holiday, as a means of escape. I don't have to do that, I have my work, always different, always exciting. I meet new people every day, I go to new places. It matters where I am. I matter. I have a function in the real world. Perhaps now I'll start putting on lipstick to go down to the shops. Oh God. I might be coerced into joining the coffee-morning set, twittering about my children, nothing else in my life. I will suffer Death by Housework. My brain will be lobotomized. Jesus! I might even start liking the clothes in Marks & Spencer's. I want giving up work to be a noble, challenging, stimulating, fulfilling prospect. But all I can think about is becoming Harriet, dressed up to the nines to take the children to school, nowhere else to go. Having to ask my husband before I buy a dress. Fucking hell. Am I really going to do this?

I sat down in my office and logged on. I'd lose this, my password. Adamsc, password Rebecca. Not Carrie Adams any more. Mrs Adams. Housewife, mother-of-two. Nobody special.

Immediately *message* flashed up on the right-hand

corner of the screen. *You're not serious? You're not really going home to make cakes and wipe snotty noses?* It was Pete. *There's more to life than this place. Time to move on.* I typed back. *We'll miss you,* flashed back. Then, *When are you going?*

Little swine. He's after my job already. But he has a point. I should really give a month's notice, but that would take me almost until Christmas. Having made such a momentous decision I want to sweep out now, not limp on for another month. I messaged Nick: *Would it be possible just to give two weeks' notice?* The message flashed back: *I should think so. Why the hurry?* Because I might just change my mind, I thought.

11

NOVEMBER

Sunday 1 November

I am desperate to tell the children but can't until I tell
Claire, because of course Rebecca would blurt it out
immediately to her. Half of me is ecstatic, so ecstatic I
keep hugging the children and twirling Tom round –
mine, mine, all mine – and making elaborate and ill-
conceived plans about what I am going to do with the
house. Paint Rebecca's bedroom, sort out the drawers
in every room in the house, clear out the garage, get rid
of all the packing cases, clean the Aga, start on the
garden – the list is joyously endless. All this *time*. All
this lovely, lovely *time*. And I can buy some new
curtains for Rebecca's room . . . Oh. Maybe I can't. This
is the other half of my worries. As well as being terrified that I will effectively cease to exist as an
intelligent, thinking person and will lose all confidence in expressing my views at dinner parties – after
all, what would I know? I won't be part of that great
thinking, doing mass out there, I'll just be fluffing
about in the house listening to *Woman's Hour* on
the radio – money is going to be very tight. Mike
has worked out that after we have paid the mortgage
and assorted bills we will have roughly half the
amount we have now to live on. That's perfectly

feasible. There's no reason why I have to do a mega-shop every week, spending a king's ransom in the supermarket. Now I will have time to buy fresh food every day from the village. I might even buy a *wicker basket*. No. Maybe that's going too far.

Mike has decided he will commute to work, and I will drive him to the station every morning, meaning I have the car to take Rebecca to school and pick her up. Our petrol bill will be halved by only having one car, and last night I sat down and worked out how much money I actually spend on work. Most of the clothes I buy are to look good at work. All the petrol money getting to the office and back every day, lunches, drinks in the bar. Eating out will have to go by the board, and saving for holidays will have to be a far more organized affair. Christ, bring on the hair shirt. I cannot imagine being this *careful*. My whole life has been a series of mad splurges, followed by appalling guilt, followed by more mad splurges. I *hate* couples who budget, with their fussy little building society accounts and their careful lists of what they've spent each month and *denying themselves* things. Working out how much the baby-sitter will cost before they go out. Adding up what they've eaten in restaurants when they go out with other couples – 'No, I didn't have a pudding and I didn't have much of the wine because I'm driving' – rather than just halving the bill. I cannot *bear* to think we might become like that. But thank God Mike put the lump sum of his profit-related pay into the school–fees scheme last summer, so we're covered for at least another year. I hate the thought that we're going to have to think about money, which always brings out the Hitler in Mike.

Friday 6 November

Nick, bless him, says that I can leave at the end of next week. That means I have to tell Claire tonight, because I'll only need her for another week. But I must pay her until the end of the month, that's only fair. This is all becoming frighteningly real.

When I got home, Claire was ironing in front of the television. Rebecca was splayed out on the sofa, Tom was happily building a Lego tower. 'Claire,' I said hesitantly. 'Could I have a quick word?'

In the kitchen I poured water into the spout of the Aga kettle (getting the lid off is a nightmare) and rattled around in the cupboard looking for coffee cups. I couldn't look at her.

'What is it?' she said, nervously.

I took a deep breath. 'Claire, look, this is really difficult, but I've decided to – give up my job.' The words came out far more sharply than I'd intended. 'So I'm afraid I won't need you any more. But of course we'll pay you until the end of the month and we really appreciate everything you've done for the children and I'm sure I can help you find another job, perhaps if we put a notice up at Rebecca's school . . .' The words rushed out, tumbling over each other. Claire looked as if she'd been smacked in the face.

'No,' she said. 'No, no, no . . .' Her voice rose and she put her hands up to her face as if she'd been hit.

'Claire,' I said, moving towards her, clumsily putting my hand on her arm, 'I'm really sorry, but I've been thinking about it for ages and Tom will be at nursery next year anyway . . .' My voice tailed off as she rocked backwards and forwards, sobbing. 'Look, of course you can come and see the children any time you want.' (Could she? What am I saying?)

'You can't do this.' Her voice came out suddenly, clear as a bell and quite calm.

'What?'

'You have to give me a proper month's notice.'

'But I've said I'll pay you for a month.'

'Two months,' she said. 'I should get two months' pay because I haven't been given proper notice.'

'OK,' I said wearily. I didn't want a row. I didn't want it to end like this.

'I'll just go and see the children,' she said, quietly.

'Of course,' I said.

Monday 9 November

Last week at work. The air of unreality pervades. Every thing is a last. Last Monday morning at work. Last Monday afternoon conference where everyone sits about like a lemon and is too scared to come up with ideas in case they are shot down by John, terrifying old reporter who has a whiplash tongue and appalling halitosis. There is always a clear space around him at conference because if he breathes near you you will go green and faint. Last Monday night programme – and all the captions (names at the bottom of the screen to say who people are) came on in the wrong order so the (male, pompous old buffer) leader of the city council was undoubtedly surprised to see himself referred to as 'Ms Dorothy Harwell, resident'. After the programme I ran out of the office as quickly as possible because this is when the complaint calls come and today I would be very tempted to say, 'That's extremely interesting but I'm awfully sorry, I don't give a shit. Goodbye,' which would undoubtedly get back to Nick and mean I would leave under *something* of a cloud.

Pete messaged me this morning saying that drinks were being arranged for me in the bar on Friday after the programme. Yuck. I hate leaving dos. Either they take off and everyone gets completely rat-arsed, go on to some seedy night-club and snog each other with appalling repercussions (but very interesting gossip for the rest of us) or people stand about sipping warm gin and tonic and trying not to talk shop. No-one ever talks to Nick for fear of appearing an arse-licker so he is forced to keep breaking into other people's conversations who are then very embarrassed because they have been discussing career moves and how pissed off they are working for him. But I don't suppose I'll be able to avoid it. You can't really not turn up for your *own* leaving do, no matter how strong the temptation.

Saturday 14 November
Two a.m. I am sitting huddled on the downstairs sofa, Turtle is lying at my feet and the remains of a fire glows feebly in the grate. Mike is in bed, but not, I would imagine, asleep.

I thought, I really thought, that my life was coming together at last. That I could shake off the awful guilt of leaving the children to Claire, that I could finally have some time to myself to be at home, to bring up the children how *I* want them to be brought up, not just parcelled off to a hired hand, the most pressing need to get rid of them and leave for work. We have bought the house I have always longed for, and for once we seem to be – albeit temporarily – on an even financial keel. Then, last night.

The leaving do started off pretty well. Everyone turned up in the bar, including Kate looking stunning in black Prada, who is due to leave herself next week, and Nick made a speech about how much I'd be missed, and then gave me a huge bunch of flowers and some presents, including an apron, ha ha. I *had* planned just to stay for a couple of hours, as Claire had agreed to baby-sit, and Mike had said he'd join us later, and then maybe we could go off for a meal together. But by nine o'clock he still hadn't turned up, and everyone started nagging me to come on to the Chinese with them. If Mike can't be bothered to turn up then I may as well go, I thought. I left a note with the barman to say where we'd gone.

In the restaurant, the usual mass of orders, and bottles and bottles of sake. 'Don't worry about driving,' Pete said. 'I'll give you a lift home. You need to leave the car here, anyway, don't you?' True. I'd already given it a fond goodbye pat. You're too shiny and new for me, anyway, I thought. I can't afford you.

With fears about driving removed, I got stuck into the sake. Everyone was on really good form, although I was worried about Mike. Where was he? I nipped out and rang him on the mobile phone. 'Carrie, I'm sorry,' he said over the crackling, distorted line, 'I'm really tied up. There's a bit of a crisis here. I'll see you at home.'

'No sign of Mike?' said Nick, as I walked back in, concentrating very hard on not cannoning off other tables. 'Stuck at work,' I said. 'Boring bugger.'

At about eleven I stood up very unsteadily to go to the loo. 'Jesus, look at me,' I thought, peering into the mirror. My mascara had run under my eyes and my lipstick was smudged. My eyes looked baggy and my face shone with sweat. Funny how we imagine we're so gorgeous when we're pissed, when one glance in the mirror reveals the awful truth that we've been flirting outrageously with a large white-headed spot just beneath our noses. I staggered into the loo and plumped myself down, missing the toilet seat slightly, which was one of those slidey plastic ones which gives your bum a sharp nip. 'Ouch,' I squeaked, trying not to pee on the floor, giggling to myself.

The door thumped, and I heard the sound of

laughter and shrieks as Georgia – yes, it was her Barbie-doll voice – and someone else came in. 'I'm surprised Kate came along this evening,' Georgia said.

Another voice – Carole's, the newsroom secretary. 'She's got a brass neck, hasn't she? Swanning off to join lover boy and then having the nerve to come to his wife's leaving party.'

'And they're supposed to be friends,' said Georgia. 'Some friend! I'm amazed nobody's told her – everyone at Midlands knows as well as here.'

'He's a shit, isn't he?' said Carole's voice.

'They all are,' said Georgia. 'They all are.' Lipstick reapplied, the door banged and there was silence.

I sat very still. Then, very quietly, I stood up, pulled up my tights, and put my hand to slide the knob back. As I leant forward, my head started to bang, bang so violently that I thought I would faint. I rested it against the cold Formica door. I wanted to lie down, to physically lie down on the floor and not move at all. I'd read about the weight of grief, but I'd never felt that weight before, as if I could no longer move, no longer function as a person, that I was just a shell, with no life. Slowly, I pushed open the door, praying that no-one else would come in. I moved hesitantly over to the sink, holding onto it with both hands, rocking, forcing myself not to faint. Then I slowly raised my eyes to the mirror. Into my eyes, deep into my eyes I looked, seeing for the first time what had been so blindingly obvious, so *exactly* the reason for everything that had happened. As I stared at myself I saw not my face, but our lives, running like cine film through my head. Rebecca's birth. Tom's birth: Mike bending over me, holding my hand, making me laugh as the contractions hit – 'At least you get to lie down' – holding Tom to him, the tears streaming down his face, 'Look, our *child*.' Rebecca and him, playing in the leaves, kicking the amber shapes up into the air, seeing them spiral down amidst the smoke of the fire, around their laughing figures. His face above mine as we made love, tender, caring, his whispered 'I love you' as we lay close afterwards, his face pressed into my hair, his legs entwined with mine. Lies. All lies. All *nothing*. Not any more.

Somehow I got myself out of the toilet, dried the tears under my eyes, blew my nose, splashed cold water on my face. Walked very calmly back to the table, noting Georgia's appalled face as she realized I'd been in there and must have heard. Left money on the table, thanked Nick, found my coat, walked out. Couldn't look at Kate. I don't think I can ever bear to be near her again. In the cold night air, I realized I was about to drive my car very pissed. What the hell. Nothing else in my life felt significant any more. Normal rules need not apply.

It was only in the car that the tears really came. Tears – and rage. Bloody, murderous, head-splitting rage. And jealousy. Jealousy so painful it bent me double. The thought of Mike and Kate making love. Her blond hair on his face, his hands stroking her; what did they say, what did they say to each other? Were they in love? Was it just sex? What did they do, what had they done every minute, every second of their time together? I didn't know, I couldn't get that information, it was a part of his life, it had been a part of his life for months, months that part of him hadn't been with me, had been far away. Had been with her, talking, making love, touching, laughing, all this time and I didn't know. I didn't know.

I drove very slowly home, pushed open the door, praying the children were asleep. Claire came towards me. 'The children are fine, sleeping like tops – what's the matter?' she said, seeing my stricken face, eyes red and swollen.

'Nothing, nothing,' I said. 'I'm fine. I just had too much to drink, shouldn't have driven home. Mike isn't back?'

'No,' she said. I made a determined effort and pulled myself together. 'Can I come on Monday to say goodbye to the children properly, and give them some presents I've got?'

'Of course,' I said, mechanically. 'Thanks, thanks so much.' I gave her the cheque I'd written earlier for her last wages and thankfully closed the door. Then I went into the sitting room to wait.

It was after one when I heard his key in the door, heard him calling the dogs, walking into the room, whistling. I'd only put a small lamp on, so at first he couldn't see me. 'Christ, Carrie!' he said. 'You made me jump! Why are you sitting here in the dark?'

'I have found out about you,' I said quietly. 'I heard about you, I heard about you in the most awful way. I know what's been happening.'

Mike looked at me, horrified. 'No,' he said. 'It's over. It's been over for weeks.'

'Do you love her?'

'No,' he said, forcefully, holding my hands, pulling me close to him, trying to hold me tight. 'I was just – desperate. You didn't want me, everything I did was wrong, she came to see me about the job, we had a drink, too much drink and—'

'Don't tell me,' I said. 'I don't want to know where, how many times, anything. Could you let go of me?' I pulled back, and moved to the other end of the sofa. 'I can't live with you any more,' I said.

'NO!' Mike shouted. 'Not after all this, the children—'

'The children will stay here with me. Could you leave now?' I said.

'Not tonight,' he said. 'Let me stay tonight.'

'Tonight,' I said. 'Just tonight.'

'Please, Carrie,' he said, kneeling in front of me, 'I'm sorry, I'm so bloody sorry but what can I do? It's done, I can't undo it, we can go forward from this.'

'No,' I said, pulling away my hands from his, warm, beseeching, familiar, beloved. 'I can't speak to you now.'

He stood up slowly, and I heard him walk out, softly call the dogs, shut them in the kitchen. Then he went upstairs. I sat here, still and cold for a long time. Broken. Vows, real vows, 'as long as you both shall live,' broken. Torn asunder.

Eight a.m. Mike is packing. I have told the children he has to go away on business for a while. Rebecca cried that she didn't want her daddy to go. I heard Mike too, in the night, crying. I slept in the spare room, woke to its unfamiliar wallpaper, hit immediately by the knowledge. I can't look at him, can't bear to be near him, am worried that if I do get close to him I will hit him, smack his face, tear at his clothes. Sorrow this morning has become anger, anger at his weakness. That sex, just sex, could spoil all this. Not love; he'd said very firmly it wasn't love. Just someone who wanted him and made him feel good. Skin on skin, touch, simple sex could break the years we had, the children, this house, our life. Why? If I could understand why I might be able to accept it. But I can't.

'I'm going now,' he says, opening the front door, putting his foot out to stop Turtle escaping. His face now is cold and hard. He won't forgive me for this. But forgiveness should surely be mine.

Tonight I sit in the kitchen, nursing a glass of red wine, and the house feels desolate. I cannot even think about the future, what my life will mean, how I will cope. I desperately want to know where Mike has gone, where he will be staying, but I could hear only a murmured conversation he had on the phone before he left. Has he gone to her? Oliver has left. Of course Oliver has left. He found out before, long before me.

How *could* Kate do this? How could she talk to me, be my friend, smile at me, chat in the corridor, message me on the computer, *be normal* while all the time she was betraying me in the worst possible way? And not just me, Tom and Rebecca – for Christ's sake, she is Rebecca's *godmother*. Did she think of me at all, as she slipped into bed with my husband? What did she want from the relationship? Was she in love with him? I couldn't work it out. I knew she fancied him, of course, but then lots of my friends fancied him – it was a joke between Mike and me that there were so many women waiting in the wings for him. I coped by never being jealous, never thought I had to be. But now – now I was wrong. He could be tempted, had been, and for how long?

Having told him I didn't want to know anything, now I was burning for information. I wanted to know when it had started, what had happened, when it ended – if indeed, it *had* ended. Did Kate think he would leave me? Did she aim to take my husband away from me, or was she just testing her claws? Halfway through the evening I picked up the phone to ring her, then dropped it again. What would I say? I couldn't trust myself to be rational, all I would be able to do would be to howl down the phone, 'Why?'

In bed, I long for him. Can't sleep, can't find a comfortable place in the bed. I wake in the early hours, reaching out to feel his warm skin and turn, comforted, to sleep some more. I reach out and find – nothing. Cold, empty sheets, a person gone.

Friday 20 November

My first week of freedom, my first week as a real wife – without a husband. The days have felt very long indeed, without the anticipation of seeing Mike. It has made me realize just how much I depend on him to be happy, how I need to see him at the end of the day, need to tell him everything, rely on him for advice. The house feels very big, too big for us, and I am already beginning to panic about how I'm going to cope. I have two months' wages in the bank, and the anticipation of my pension fund, which I can cash in. But it seems very lean. Every time I've been to the cashpoint this week I've been terrified it won't give me any money, that Mike has closed our account. Nick has said I can keep the car for the moment, he knows what's happened, everybody knows what's happened.

Jill came straight round on Saturday after I'd rung. She sent the children to play happily outside, and she held me as I rocked backwards and forwards in her arms, sobbing hysterically. It all seemed too real, too awful, like a nightmare that couldn't be real. Surely suddenly someone would say, 'April Fool,' and the world would tilt back on its axis? But nobody did, and every morning I woke to a few seconds of normality, and then hell came back. This was hell, hell in my familiar room. 'What will you do?' she said. 'Are you going to ask for your job back?'

'I can't,' I said. 'And anyway, I can't face seeing people day after day who know exactly what's happened. At least here I'm anonymous, none of the parents at school know.'

'But have you heard from him?' she asked anxiously.

'Not a word. Nothing. He's disappeared off the planet. I just hope to God he hasn't rushed off to Kate.'

'I think we need to know,' said Jill, looking thoughtful. 'Who can you ring who knows him well? Where else could he stay? Bill's?'

'Quite possibly,' I said. 'But I can't ring Bill. He's on Mike's side, and I threw him out. It would look like I want him back if I start ringing up.'

'We could find out where he is,' said Jill grimly. 'And then we can kill him.'

'We can't do that,' I said, starting to laugh weakly, for the first time since he left. 'You're talking about the father of my children.'

'Can't I just *harm* him a bit?' she said.

'No!' I said, outraged but giggling. 'Thank God,' I said, 'for you.'

Claire turned up on Monday afternoon to say goodbye to the children. In all the drama I'd completely forgotten, and so when she rang the doorbell I stared at her rather blankly for a moment. I don't seem very capable of dealing with real life at the moment. 'Come in,' I said. 'The children have been talking about you all the time. They really want to see you.' Which was a total lie, they hadn't asked about her once. But as soon as they saw her, they came running towards her and Rebecca flung herself at her so hard Claire nearly fell over.

'Hang on!' she laughed. When she picked Tom up, he clung to her, twining his hands into her hair and making little crooning noises. 'My little man,' she said, and I didn't even want to hit her.

'Have you found another job?' I said, as the children excitedly tore at their presents.

'I'm going to college,' she said. 'I'm going to train to be a nurse.'

'That's brilliant!' I said. 'I'm really happy for you.'

'How are you?' she said. 'You looked so – upset – on Friday night.'

'I'm fine,' I said, and then, horrors, the tears came back. 'Come into the kitchen.'

'Mike's left,' I said, as she closed the door. Her face registered total astonishment.

'Why?' she said.

'I found out – oh God, Claire, I'm sorry this is so awful – he'd been sleeping with one of my friends. Rebecca doesn't know,' I added quickly. 'She just thinks he's away on business.'

Claire turned to look at me and her eyes were fearful. 'I think I knew,' she said.

'What?'

'One night when you weren't here he was on the phone, talking very quietly, and he didn't see I'd come into the room. I wanted to say I was going, so I just hung back, waiting for him to finish. I thought it was business, then he said – I think this is right – "I'll see if I can get away. 'Bye, Kate. Of course I do. Don't worry." There was something about his voice, it was as if he was whispering even though he didn't know there was anyone else in the room. I coughed, and when he saw me I thought he was going to faint. He didn't say anything, just walked past me. He never talked to me much anyway, so I just left it. The next day he tried to imply to me it was a colleague from work, worried about a story. It sounded wrong at the time, but I didn't think any more about it. Should I have told you?' she said, sounding desperately worried.

'No,' I said. 'How could you have known? It's all right, we'll manage. We'll be fine. Anyway – good luck.' She walked forward and gave me a hug. 'Thank you,' I said. 'Thank you for everything.' Tom didn't want her to go, and Rebecca hugged her legs, crying. Claire was crying too.

'I'll come and see you soon,' she said. Her handbag fell off her shoulder as Rebecca clung to her, and her purse fell out. It was open, and when I picked it up, I saw that she had two small photographs of Tom and Rebecca under the clear laminated plastic. Just as if they were her own children.

Friday 27 November
Mike rang for the first time today. Two weeks of silence. Two weeks of jumping every time the phone rang, two weeks of dashing out frantically whenever a car pulled into the drive, two weeks of scanning the post every morning for a letter. It is perfect revenge, this silence. He must know Rebecca has been asking for him, how she runs into my bedroom every morning, saying, 'Is Daddy back?', scanning the humped duvet as if somehow it might be concealing her absent father. Every morning I have had to say to her, 'No, he's still very busy, but I'm sure he'll be back this weekend. He sends his love, I spoke to him on the phone.'

'Hello?' I said. There was a pause, then Mike's voice, very calm, very controlled. My hand holding the phone became sweaty, I had to grip it to make sure I didn't let it fall.

'Could I see the children this weekend? When would suit you?'

'Tomorrow,' I whispered.

'I'll take them out,' he said.

'No,' I said quickly. 'Don't do that. They'll . . .' I paused, and my voice stumbled slightly. 'They'll know something is wrong. I haven't told Rebecca. Stay with them here – just come and be here with them.'

'How are you?' he said, his voice almost unfamiliar.

'Fine,' I said. 'Absolutely fine.' Then the receiver went dead.

How can you hate and love one person so much at the same time? Kate is easy. I can hate her, oh boy, can

I hate her. If I met her now I wouldn't trust myself not to attack her, desperate to make her see how much damage she has done. I want to *wound* her. I never thought I could feel so – so *primeval* about this, as if I really could kill her. But Mike? I cannot understand how someone I know so well, love so well, thought I knew *everything* about, can have had this secret life, this part of him which has been detached from me, from the family, as if we were totally unimportant. In a way I can't believe it was just sex. No-one in their right mind would risk their family just for sex. Surely.

Saturday 28 November
'Daddy's coming home today,' I said to Rebecca as we snuggled in bed together this morning. Quite how I was going to explain the fact that he didn't have a suit-case with him, that he wouldn't stay, would have to be sorted out later. She leapt excitedly on the bed.

'Daddy!' Then she looked at me beadily. 'Will he have bought me another Barbie?'

'I wouldn't ask for it straight away,' I said.

I spent all morning trying not to look out of the window, and put on about six changes of clothing to achieve the I'm-not-bothered-you're-here look required whilst also communicating the facts that a) I am gorgeous and b) I have lost weight. I settled on a pair of black ski pants. Rebecca positioned herself like a small sentinel by the door, and ran up and down the path, peering over the gate, looking for his car. I washed things frantically. I cleaned out the kitchen cupboards, mopped the stone flags in the kitchen, emptied the hoover bag, loaded the washing machine, even brushed the dogs – extremely useful displacement activity.

It was after twelve when his car drew up outside. I

bent my head furiously over the pan I was scrubbing in the sink. I didn't want to, couldn't bear to catch his eye. I heard Rebecca yell 'Daddy!', and Tom, who'd been sitting on the kitchen floor aimlessly banging pans with a wooden spoon, looked up. Hearing Rebecca's voice, he heaved himself to his feet and toddled off rapidly towards the door, falling over Turtle's paw with a hefty thump. I was just righting him when I felt, rather than saw, Mike. He was standing by the entrance to the kitchen, and as I slowly looked up I could see Rebecca clinging onto him, her legs round his waist, her face pressed against his. Our eyes met. The way he looked at me said far more than words ever could – pain, regret, hurt, exhaustion. Satisfyingly, he looked awful. His face, normally tanned all year round, handsome, confident, was lined and pale, with deep bags etched under his eyes. He'd lost weight, and he was wearing a jumper I knew he hated, which had shrunk and lost its shape in the wash. He must have thrown it into his suitcase that night in desperation, because I knew for a fact none of his other ones were clean. In the worst moments of last week I'd touched his clothes, pressed them to my face, smelled his smell, revelled in the masculinity of his clothes. He could only have packed what was in his drawers at the time. Quite how he'd survived two weeks with four shirts, including one which needed cuff-links (and Tom had lost his last pair down the back of the radiator at the old house), was a mystery. How extremely satisfying that he had been forced to leave with only two good pairs of socks – the others were the thin, holey variety. I knew he didn't have his best coat because that was buried under acres of junk under the stairs, so he must have been cold, too.

'How are you?' I said. 'Rebecca, could you run and get your spelling book so you can show Daddy how well you did in that test?' She leapt down happily and ran off upstairs to her room.

'Awful,' he said. 'I've been staying at Bill's and I've had to sleep in the spare room with all the early Christmas presents. I can't even leave my toothbrush in the bathroom because I'm so scared of getting in the way and Sue had a big fight last night with Bill because we've been going to the pub every night. Oh, and their cat has adopted me and you know I hate cats. I keep waking up with its arse in my face. Carrie – let me come home.'

I had started to laugh, laugh at the thought of Mike perched in Bill and Sue's fussy spare room, with everything neatly in its place, expressly not designed for an adulterous ex-husband with a large battered suitcase and heaps of dirty clothes. I am glad his 'revenge' has proved so uncomfortable. No wonder Sue was pissed off; she hadn't just gained a lodger, she'd lost a husband. The role models for men and their friends are Fred Flintstone and Barney Rubble. They lie endlessly for each other, support each other through thick and thin and enjoy each other's company far more than they do that of women.

'How have you washed your clothes?' I said. The most bizarre thoughts were occurring to me. 'Laundrette,' he said, gloomily. Excellent. The thought of smart, successful Mike sitting in a gaudily lit Formica hell for sad people seemed a tiny but fitting part of the overall punishment.

'And how's – Kate?' I could hardly bear to say her name. Pete from the office had rung to say she'd left last week, no-one had heard any more from her. Apparently she was taking a week's holiday before she started at Midlands.

'No idea,' he said shortly. 'I told you it was finished, finished weeks ago . . . it was *nothing*.'

Rebecca came running back, clutching her blue exercise book. 'Look Daddy! Ten out of ten!'

'Brilliant,' he said, hugging her hard. His eyes were full of tears.

Tom hadn't let go of his legs since he'd walked in. Now he was crowing to be picked up, arms outstretched. 'Up, Daddy, up.'

Mike picked them both up and held them close to him, closing his eyes, pressing them shut. 'I'll take them out for a walk,' he said. I did a double take. This was a first. I am the one who does walks, pressing reluctant arms into anorak sleeves, forcing woolly hats onto recalcitrant heads, scrabbling about under the stairs for lost dog-leads and then being hurtled forward by an over-excited Turtle as soon as Tom is strapped into his pushchair. 'Where are the leads?' said Mike.

'No idea,' I said, walking off into the snug.

Time to think. Turtle, overjoyed to see Mike, weaved backwards and forwards against his legs, and instead of giving him the normal boot up the bum for getting in the way, Mike bent down to hug him. 'Hello, old boy. How have you been? Eaten any good cats lately?'

As soon as the door banged shut after the ten minutes of coat-hell, I sat down on the old sofa in the snug and pulled my knees up to my chest. Come home. He wants to come home. He hadn't gone to Kate, that was over, she had lost him, lost whatever small part she ever had of him. How much *did* it matter that he'd slept with her, taken his clothes off, indulged in the most intimate of seconds, minutes, hours? That she had seen him naked, that she had felt him? *Was* it important what he had said to her, how he felt with her? Nope, I've had enough of this, the pain, the mental torture which had been playing through my head for the past two weeks, worst at night, with no other distractions, no caring for the children. How to

261

weigh this, this *betrayal*, this loss of trust, the most important pact made between man and woman, with the security of my family? Trust had gone. Trust would take a hell of a long time to come back. Mike had broken Trust, might he not do it again? Does a man, once a sinner, continue sinning?

But he looks so broken, so defeated, so lost without us. Should have thought of that before, I thought to myself angrily. At least now he knows, now he really knows what it *is* like to live without his family, to be alone, to have all that freedom he's often said he craved, to stay out when he wants, to drink as much as he wants, to be responsible only for himself and to get rid of all the constant, exhausting, messy responsibilities of small children? He had tasted that forbidden fruit, and its taste was bitter. Up to him now, up to him to prove himself, I thought, smoothing my hand on the old maroon brocade fabric. Or rather, up to me to judge him. For the first time in our entire marriage, I held the reins of power. Only I didn't know, I didn't know which way to head. My most important thought was: I need a *drink*.

When they came back, their faces reddened and glowing from the wind, Mike came into the snug and said, 'Would you like a coffee? I'll make the children lunch.'

'Thanks,' I said. 'Can I have a bacon sandwich?' I yelled after he'd gone.

'Don't push it,' he said, sticking his head back round the door with the beginnings of his old smile. 'This is as nice as it gets.'

When it came for him to leave, he went reluctantly. He stayed and bathed both children, and put them to bed. I sat in the kitchen, reading the papers. 'I'm going now,' he said.

''Bye,' I said, turning the page.

12

DECEMBER

Tuesday 1 December

'So what *did* you say?' said Jill this morning as we trudged up the hill at the back of our house, with Tom strapped into the back-pack and the dogs charging on ahead, churning up mud and scattering dead leaves.

'I told him I would think about it,' I said. 'For a week.'

'And what do you think?' she said.

'God knows,' I said unhappily. 'I can't decide. I long and long to see him but when I do I just want to hit him, very hard. I don't know if I can live with him again. We feel like two strangers tip-toeing around each other, as if we have to get to know each other all over again. I'm not sure I've got the *energy* to try to trust him again.'

'Try,' said Jill, astonishingly. I stopped and turned to look at her, making Tom swing round as if he was on the waltzers. He let out a small yell and clung to my hair.

'What? You were the one telling me we should kill him and have done with it!'

'Yes,' she said, looking down and scuffing the earth with the toe of her wellington. 'But who else are you going to get?'

'Oh thanks a lot!' I said, laughing. 'Brilliant reason. Take Mike back because I might not be able to find anyone else! Excellent! Very nineties feminist reasoning!'

'No,' she said. 'But the children . . . I just keep thinking how Susie and Daisy would feel if I left Pete . . . I mean he's useless in most directions but he is their father and they seem to like him . . . Is it worth setting off on your own, disrupting their lives so much?'

'What about my life?' I said. 'What about turning my life upside down and betraying everything we had? What about screwing somebody else?'

'Somebody thin,' said Jill, nodding her head in commiseration.

'You are not helping,' I said, marching angrily off down the hill. 'You are not helping *at all*.'

The only consolation is being at home. It is so bizarre to wake up each morning and think, I don't have to rush off to work. But ye gods, how exhausting it is looking after two small children *all the time* – especially on my own. Just getting Rebecca off to school is a ritual form of torture. I don't know how Claire has managed to avoid killing her for the past year. Being with them at weekends just isn't the same, it's the *every day-ness* of it that grinds you down. This morning, for example. 'Rebecca, get up.' No answer from the inert form under the duvet. 'Get up or we'll be late for school.' I am very conscious of presenting the perfect-mummy front at school, and lateness is out. So are dirty fingernails, unbrushed hair and lost recorders. I am becoming a bit obsessive about getting this right. I leave Rebecca to go and get Tom out of his cot. He immediately makes a dash for the kitchen, wet night-nappy making his pyjama bottoms bulge. I catch him, squawking, by the collar and decide to get him dressed. Half an hour until we need to leave the house. Ten minutes later, having pinned Tom to the bed to get his clothes on, he is relatively ready. The nappy was a bad one. 'Rebecca,' I shout from outside her room, 'I hope you are dressed.' There is a loud scurrying noise, and when I open the door Rebecca is caught red-handed (so to speak) with one leg in her tights. 'Hurry *up*!' I say. 'I'm going to start breakfast.' Fifteen minutes to go. In the kitchen I boot the dogs out: they will have to be fed when I get back from school. No time for coffee for me. Plonk Tom in his high chair, Weetabix, cup of orange juice. I haven't put the top on properly and he pours it down his front. He is not wearing a bib. He starts to cry. I heave him out and run down the corridor to his room, shouting, 'If you're not dressed, Rebecca . . .' As I pass the door I see Rebecca lying on the floor of her room, wearing just a pair of tights, her arms round Angus who has his paw on her arm. 'Christ, Rebecca,' I hiss through her door. Ten minutes to go. Heave Tom into clean dry top, run back to the kitchen. Two minutes later Rebecca appears. 'I can't find my tie.' 'Watch Tom!' I yell, charging back down the corridor and up the stairs. Her room is in complete chaos. No sign of tie. Run back downstairs. 'Can't find it,' I pant. 'We'll just have to apologize. What do you want for breakfast? Now,' I say, as she puts on her thoughtful expression. 'I need the toilet,' she says, heading for the door. 'You're having Weetabix too,' I say. Five minutes to go. 'I don't like that mat,' she says on her return from the loo. 'Tom's got the mat with the dog on it.' She swipes the mat from under Tom's bowl. He grabs it and there is a brief tussle. 'For crying out loud,' I yell, 'it's just a mat.' Both burst noisily into tears. 'I hate Tom!' yells Rebecca. 'Toast?' 'Yes please,' she says. 'And tea.' 'No time for tea,' I say. 'Tom's making faces at me.' 'No he isn't.' 'He *is*. I have to move.' Takes her bowl to sit on the other side of the table. We are now officially late. I try to brush her hair and put it in a pony-tail as she eats her cereal. Her hair is so knotty I have to jerk her head backwards. 'Not that brush!' she yells. 'I want the soft brush.' 'Can't find it,' I say through teeth gritted around the hairband. Tom's hair looks like a pan scrub. Tough. 'Teeth,' I say. 'My toothbrush's got soap on it,' she says. And so it has. She used it to clean her Barbie in the bath last night. 'Use mine,' I shout down the corridor. Coat, recorder, book bag, spelling book, form about tickets for Christmas carol concert. Tom tucked firmly under one arm (no coat), I push her through the door. 'Mum,' she says. 'I haven't got any *shoes* on.' 'Nobody speak,' I say, as we hurtle down the country lanes. After ten minutes Rebecca says carefully, 'It's ballet today.' 'I'll bring your stuff in at lunch-time,' I say. At least it'll be something to do. At school there are only three cars left. 'Run,' I say hastily. Rebecca runs off – and then comes back. 'I haven't had a kiss,' she says. She presses her little face against mine. 'I love you.' 'I love you too. *Go.*' Getting home I find her tie – down the back of the car seat. 'Well, Tom,' I say, 'it's you and me,' as I push the door open on the chaotic house. 'Wonder if it's time for your sleep yet?'

Wednesday 9 December
Mike remains at Bill's, no doubt facing a cat's bottom every morning (good) but has taken to driving round by the house every night on his way home from work, to see the children and show me what a wonderful, caring father he can be. Useless shit as a faithful husband, but father – brilliant. Rebecca is beside herself at the joy of lying in front of the fire playing cards with him, Tom is ecstatic that his father now baths him most evenings. I hang around, spitting blood that it has taken a nasty dose of adultery to make him realize just

how wonderful his children are. Fucking MEN. I've even lost Jill's support in my exile campaign because Rebecca burst into tears at her house this week and asked Jill why her daddy wasn't at home. Jill, the most unnecessarily savage person in the world when it comes to her own husband, says I am being unnecessarily savage to mine. But how do I know Mike and Kate are over? He *says* so, but then he went weeks and weeks *not* saying that he was sleeping with her. How can I trust a word he says when he has lied, and lied, and lied? What *are* his words to me? And what pisses me off, what *really* pisses me off is the fact that he was shagging her after tearing off the shirts *I'd ironed*. That really *is* injustice.

Friday 11 December

What am I going to do for money? Soon I can see myself sitting on the steps of Rebecca's school, Tom in my arms, Turtle lying at my feet, cap in front of us with me holding a big placard saying: *Abandoned wife, child at private school to support. Please give generously.* That will go down well with Harriet.

She rang me last night, full of concern for the poor abandoned wife, enjoying herself tremendously. Friends just love a lipsmacking dose of tragedy. 'How *are* you?' she said, her voice oozing sympathy and barely suppressed desperation for me to spill the beans. Maybe I could suggest we form the Shat-On Wives Club, but I don't somehow think she'll agree. She is the perfect example of how to live without love and divert all need for deep emotional passion into shopping.

'Fine,' I said. 'Totally fine. It's much easier without him.'

'Oh Carrie,' she said, shocked. 'You don't mean that.'

No, I don't mean it, I just want you to get off the phone so I can go and have a drink, I thought.

It is also becoming increasingly difficult to avoid the parents' coffee-morning rota. There is a list up in Rebecca's classroom, and you have to sign your name which commits you to a Friday morning every week sipping coffee and talking about – what? Private education? Agas? The price of knickers? God knows. It also means you then have to have them back to your house, which makes me break out in a cold sweat because I don't own more than three matching cups and saucers and absolutely no biscuits and cakes. (If I do buy biscuits Rebecca scoffs them in one go and then refuses all normal food for the rest of the day.)

What I am enjoying hugely, though, is the *freedom* of being at home. The freedom of not having to be in one particular place at a particular time, constantly chasing the clock, someone waiting anxiously for me to arrive wherever I'm going. Four weeks ago, it mattered where I was every moment of the day. Now it doesn't. I could disappear off the face of the earth and only the children would know or care. If Tom and I want to spend an hour wandering by the lake after we've taken Rebecca to school, we do. If I want to go shopping *in the middle of the morning*, I can. I keep expecting the Career Police to march up to me in department stores and say, 'Excuse me, madam, shouldn't you be at work?' I am now one of the great army of women who wander round the shops during the day, pushing a pushchair with my handbag hanging off the back, deliberating over nappies; anonymous, unimportant. But I don't feel unimportant. I feel powerful, in control of my own destiny, *free*. God, I pity working women. Where once I looked down on any woman who didn't work, now my instinctive reaction when I hear some career woman wittering on about the lack of decent child-care on the radio, as if child-care is the panacea, I want to scream, 'You are so *wrong.*' Child-care isn't the answer, it's finding a way of working, if you must or want to, in a way which doesn't mean your children are farmed out to strangers. My generation of women has been led down a blind alley which has made many of us deeply unhappy. We have, quite frankly, been sold a dream which mutated into a nightmare.

I also feel . . . dreamy, and not very real. As if I will wake up suddenly and Mike will be back, and I will be leaving for work, as usual. But it already seems inconceivable that anyone could boss me about, that I could be *told off* for doing something wrong. I can't imagine having that fear of anyone any more. Or being made to care about what happens in an office. Speaking to Pete on the phone today, he filled me in on all the latest office gossip, and it seems so petty and irrelevant. So what? Who cares? Who cares if Nick blew a fuse over a late story and Gary might be off to London as a presenter and the rotas have been changed? It's only *work.* The trouble with work is that you get so wrapped up in it you lose sight of everything else and start believing *it* is real life. It isn't. It's just work. Nobody dies. This, out here, is the real world. I'm off for a walk in the crisp winter air now and then I might just make some buns. So there.

Sunday 13 December

Rebecca came and snuggled down in bed with me this morning. Since Mike went, she has made determined efforts to sleep in my bed every night, but I have been resisting this, because if I set the precedent, then I'll never get her out when Mike comes back. *If* Mike comes back. 'Mummy,' she said, nudging up the bed to be next to me. 'Tickle my back.' She sighed, lulled into a soporific trance. 'When is Daddy coming home? Why is he living at Bill's? Can I see their cat? Daddy says it's horrible but I don't believe him.'

'Mummy and Daddy had a bit of an argument,' I said. 'Anyway, you see him more now than when he was here.'

'It's not the same,' she said. 'I want him home properly. Is he coming to see my play?'

'I think you could put money on it,' I said.

Monday 14 December

This play is giving me some very nasty moments. Mrs Lewis buttonholed me this morning as I steered Rebecca into her classroom. 'Mrs Adams!' she exclaimed. 'We need someone to help backstage with the costumes. You know Rebecca is an angel' – really? – 'and they're all going to need a lot of help with their wings. Or perhaps you might like to help with the make-up?'

'No,' I said hastily. 'I'll do wings.' I can't paint a child's face to save my life. I once tried with Rebecca and instead of turning her into a cute little cat she looked like a hideous gargoyle. Tom screamed in terror and I had to scrub it off immediately.

The thought of making the costume is worrying me considerably. All the other professional mothers seem to have been at it for weeks, sewing tiny sequins onto acres of cream silk or nipping off to London to spend fifty pounds on a fancy dress costume their child will only wear once. I had a bit of a go last night with some gauze and pipe cleaners, and looked rather helplessly at some white silkish material I'd bought in Oxford. Must be simple enough, I thought, holding the material up against Rebecca and making some measurements with pins. 'Ow, ow,' said Rebecca, as I accidentally jabbed her. 'What are those?' she said, looking pity-ingly at the bumpy heap of gauze and gold tinsel which I was trying to fashion into wing-shapes.

'Your wings, you twit,' I said.

'Katie's got white swan feathers,' said Rebecca.

'You can have these,' I said, angrily pinning them onto her back, 'and you can lump it.'

Rebecca has now totally taken for granted the fact that I take her to school every day and pick her up. At first she came running towards me at the end of each day, thrilled that here I was, her mummy, standing with all the other mummies. She would swing on my hand, desperate to show me off, saying to all her friends, 'This is my mummy. She's taking me home now,' holding on to me as if she would never let me go. And how proud I am of her, how gorgeous she is, so grown-up, putting her books importantly away in her drawer, towing me round the classroom to show me her story about the dogs (*Turtle was sik on the flore and mummy kiked him*, oh God) and her paintings. She is so pleased that I can see all this, every day. Little things, such little things but they are her world. We read together before school starts, cramming my knees under the little table, as she labours over the long words, fingers pointing at the letters. But she's getting much more fluent now – she's started to read to herself at night, although she still reads aloud. I have dis-covered that I like teaching her, and I can do it. 'Read it in your head,' I said to her, 'like Mummy does.' We've started to plough our way happily through the books I had as a child, reliving forgotten pleasures. It's wonderful to read a story at bedtime without feeling that I'm going to fall off the bed with exhaustion.

My life is, however, lacking in . . . how shall I put this? *Glamour.* Glamour has gone. The temptation I have every morning is to pull on an old pair of jeans, disreputable jumper and old pair of flatties. After all, I'm only going to spend the day walking the dog, playing with Tom and cleaning. No point getting dressed up for that. The only people who see me now are the man in the fish van (on a Thursday), and, if I'm extremely fortunate, the postman. I am already having trouble with normal conversation. I keep having to ring Jill to check I have not lost the power of articulation *completely*. When you only have a one-and-a-half-year-old, a nearly-seven-year-old and two rather dim dogs who have definitely not kissed the blarney stone to talk to all day, you do begin to *stagnate* a little. I am now beginning to understand why my mother always talked to people in shops a lot, and frenziedly organized coffee mornings and bridge dos. It was to check, on a regular basis, that she could string more than two or three words together. If I do not get out soon the extent of my conversation will dwindle to: 'Put that down!' 'Stop that!' 'Out of your mouth' and 'Mind the—', yelled fortissimo. Maybe this is what coffee mornings are actually for. They are for stay-at-home mums to practise their vocabulary.

Friday 18 December
The piano plays 'God Rest Ye, Merry Gentleman' tinnily, and Tom is bouncing up and down on my knee, trying to grab the immaculately coiffed hair of the mother in front. I have left a seat next to me free for Mike, because he promised last night he would definitely be coming. Rebecca made him promise. Cross your heart and hope to die. I firmly put a programme down, and have had to repel several large-bottomed grandmothers in cashmere who obviously feel that saving places in the packed hall for the junior nativity play is *not on.*

The angels have already fluttered on stage by the time that Mike comes in, crashing through the door into the darkened hall. I turn to catch sight of him – thick blond hair, dark Crombie coat, handsome, mine and yet not mine – and wave. Getting to the seat he stumbles over plaid-skirted knees before throwing himself thankfully down. 'Sorry,' he hisses.

'OK,' I hiss back, and Tom leaps onto his knee. Rebecca, who has been craning her neck for a sight of us, now waves frantically from the stage. I mouth, 'Stop it,' at her, smiling, but not before she crashes into the angel on her left. Mike sighs and puts his head in his hands, his shoulders shaking with laughter.

By the time the boy playing the smallest donkey has wet himself, and been ushered hastily off-stage by a mortified Mrs Lewis – such a shame he is wearing crêpe trousers – Mike is silently hysterical. I am biting my lip and praying for the end because I can feel huge snorts coming. All the other parents are sighing and ah-ing over the cuteness of their children, whispering, 'Aren't they doing well,' at each other, whilst Mike and I are helpless with restrained laughter. Eventually they are all gathered around the crib – Mary dropped the baby on its head and Joseph lobbed it back into the manger where it bounced twice – ready to sing the final song. Rebecca is standing, arms crossed in front of her, her face beatific with joy, and Tom has gone to sleep against me like a drowsy duckling in his yellow fleecy coat. Mike reaches out and, silently, takes my hand. I turn to look at him, his face just inches from mine. 'I love you,' Mike says, softly, so no-one else can hear.

Saturday 19 December
Outside the school yesterday Rebecca hung from both of our hands, taking the praise, thrilled with herself.

'Did you see Mark?' she whispered to me. 'He wet himself – lots. It went all in his *shoes*,' she added, happily. 'Was I brilliant?'

'Brilliant,' said Mike. 'An excellent shepherd.'

'I was an *angel*,' said Rebecca witheringly.

'Then why did you have a dead sheep on your back?' asked Mike.

'They were *wings*,' we both said, as one.

'Come on,' Mike said. 'Let's go out for tea.' And we did. Almost like a real family.

After the tea we hung about outside the hotel. I still had the company car which *must* go back next week, they'll think I've kidnapped it, and Mike had his car too. 'I have to work this weekend,' he said, 'but can I come home tomorrow evening?' I cursed the fact that I'd arranged to go out with Jill. I couldn't let her down. 'Sorry,' I said. 'I'm going out.' He looked crest-fallen.

'It's the office do on Tuesday night,' he said next. 'Would you like to come?'

'Yes,' I said quickly.

'I'll get tickets. It's at a new restaurant in the city. Should be OK,' he said carefully, carelessly. Remarkable, I thought. How remarkable *that* was going to be.

Over linguine with pesto and parmesan in an Oxford bistro with Jill this evening, followed by chocolate fudge cake, all washed down with *two* bottles of Sauvignon, I tried to sort out my feelings. He's making all the right noises, but how can I *trust* him? 'Are you going to have him back?' she said.

'I want to,' I admitted. 'But I can't just give in and pretend everything's rosy.'

'The bastard has to be made to suffer,' agreed Jill.

'But what can I demand? He's promised that he and Kate are over, that he will never, never do anything like this again. He has turned into the perfect father and spends every moment he can with the children, he is extremely handsome and half of me is desperate to have him back. The other half thinks he should burn in hell for ever.'

'Perhaps you should withhold conjugal rights,' says Jill.

'Withholding conjugal rights,' I said, 'is partly what caused all this bloody mess in the first place. And I'm at his mercy now, because I don't have any money.'

'You could go back to work,' she said, hesitantly.

'I don't want to,' I said, realizing in that moment that I really *don't* want to. The thought of having to be in an office by nine every morning made me panic-stricken. Even in this short space of time I couldn't *imagine* handing Tom over to someone else.

'The problem is,' said Jill, twirling linguine around her fork and sucking it off like a bird eating a worm, 'how can you have the freedom of bringing up your own children and keep any power in your relationship?'

'The problem our mothers faced,' I agreed. 'My mother was terrified of taking any decision on her own and was completely beaten down by Dad. I don't see,' I said, gathering speed, 'why we can't be honoured and respected for our decision to stay at home with our children – after all, just think of the benefits to the children! Half the kids bunged into nursery at four months who emerge as adults without much more than a passing glance at their parents are bound to be pyschologically scarred in some way, aren't they? We're probably raising a generation of pyschopaths.'

'Depends who the parents are,' said Jill. 'A lot of children I know would be better off away from their parents. Think of Martin.'

'True,' I said, taking a slug of wine. 'But I don't see why I should become my mother just because I haven't got a label any more.'

'As long as you're proud of yourself,' said Jill, 'who gives a fuck?'

Wednesday 23 December
Waking this morning, I gently reach up to feel my head. It is still there. Something is different. Something is different about me. I have a hangover. Yes, that's certainly true, I think, as I try to raise my head from the pillow. Something is also different. A stirring, a movement beside me. The bed is warm. I am not alone.

I took a lot of time and effort getting ready for Mike's party yesterday. Dresses flew in and out of the wardrobe; Rebecca sat there, minute fashion expert, head on one side, saying 'Yup, that one', and 'No – awful', while Tom tried on shoes. (Potential transvestite.) Eventually the three of us mutually decided on a long red linen halter-neck. If you are going into battle to face the enemy, you do not want to slink in the side door wearing black like a hesitant crow. Nope. I was going to stride into that restaurant looking like a Sexy Hot Chick who can have Any Man She Wants. Thank God, the misery of the past month has had one good effect – I have shed pounds and pounds. Nothing like a bit of tragedy to make you lose weight. Never mind the Hay Diet, just encourage your husband to go off and shag someone else. Works a treat, although I can't see the clucky daytime women's programmes recommending it wholeheartedly. My hair has now grown and the curls are coming back, so I just put my head forward and dried my hair upside-down, so that when I threw my head back my face was surrounded by huge pre-Raphaelite curls. Lots of this, I thought, as I smoothed bright red lipstick on, and lots of *this*, as I pencilled bold dark lines under my eyes. Spraying perfume liberally onto my wrists, behind my ears and into my cleavage – plumped up under the neckline, thanks to the wonderness of Wonderbra, and I was ready to face the world.

Squeezing my feet into kitten-heeled, peep-toed black velvet high heels I surveyed the effect in the long bedroom mirror. 'Wow,' said Jill, baby-sitter deluxe, walking into the room. 'He'll be gagging for it.'

'That,' I said frostily, 'is not the point. This is for *me*.'

'Of course it is,' she said soothingly.

Mike and I had arranged to meet at the restaurant, as he was coming straight from work. I pulled my car into the BBC car park, where I was going to leave it for good. I hobbled out – long dresses look great, can't walk in them – and hailed a taxi. In the taxi I took lots of deep breaths and sprayed on some more perfume. The taxi driver coughed and pulled the little slidy window across. Even as I got out I could hear loud music; the warm orange light of the restaurant spilled out into the black of the night.

Walking in, I concentrated very hard on not falling over. Lurching down the steps was not the image of a cool, calm, sexy woman I wanted to project. Was I sweating? I had a nervous glance at the material under my armpit. Nope, fine.

There was a definite hush as I walked down the stairs. The party had taken over one half of the restaurant, and there seemed to be hundreds of faces I knew, all looking up at me, all knowing, all feeling for me. Mike surged forward immediately. 'Carrie,' he said, holding tightly onto my arm. 'You look great!'

'Thank you,' I said regally, trying not to appear to be scanning the room for the one face I feared to find: Kate.

There she was, at that far table, dressed all in black, her head on one side as she listened to the man talking animatedly next to her. Then she looked up, and for the first time since that night, our eyes met. Her look was horrified, fearful – did she think I'd storm over and scratch her eyes out? Compared to her former self, she looked pale, and much *too* thin, I noted with some pleasure. Half of me wanted to speak to her – there were so many questions I wanted answered – but now wasn't the time. My greatest weapon against her was to pretend I didn't care, that she was *nothing* and that *I would win*. Mike wanted me, not her. I had what she longed for – a family. Mike's family. No-one could take that away from me, and what had she had from him? A few moments of intimacy, the excitement of an illicit affair? Hardly a lifetime's achievement. So I looked away dismissively.

I didn't feel dismissive. I felt as if my insides were churning and I might throw up. But then Mike was immediately by my side, turning me away. 'Champagne?' he said.

'Why not?' I said.

I had buckets of the stuff. Picked at the food – not hungry at all – slurped champagne, danced wildly. Kate didn't dance.

Mike's colleague Steve came up to me as I was standing at the bar. 'You look terrific,' he said, his eyes sliding over my exposed shoulders and down to my cleavage.

'Thanks,' I said. 'Fancy a drink?' From across the room, I could see Mike watching us with alarm. Maybe he thought I was going to pull Steve into my arms and snog him to get my revenge.

'Did you know,' said Steve cautiously, 'that Kate's leaving?'

'No,' I said. 'Why?'

'Hasn't worked out,' he said. 'I think she's going to another station.'

278

'I see,' I said calmly. 'Come and dance.'

'You're pissed,' said Mike, as he gently led me out into the cold night air. It was after one o'clock; we were almost the last to leave. The final dance had inevitably been Dr Hook, and Mike had gently pulled me onto the floor. Pressing himself hard against me, he held me so tightly, his mouth in my hair. I let myself sway slowly – I wasn't up to much else – and looking up from his shoulder, I saw Kate putting on her coat, helped by the man she'd been talking to most of the evening. As she walked past me, I saw her face. She wouldn't meet my eyes, but she looked – stricken. As stricken as I'd been that night, when I found out about them. I hope she regrets it for the rest of her life.

I knew Mike understood he'd escaped losing his children by a whisker. He'd peeped over the edge into the vast pool of freedom, and found it not exciting and challenging but cold and lonely. I couldn't take a perverse pleasure in his pain; I still didn't know if I could ever trust him again. It was better though, I thought as we swayed together, our bodies touching with their old intimacy, it was better that he came home. It was his home, his children, his life. He would just have to prove himself every day for the rest of our lives together. I wouldn't love him as much again.

At home we made love slowly, hesitantly, as if discovering each other for the first time. I still felt bruised, fragile, as he slid me onto the cool sheets, considerate, careful, loving, his face tense as if he feared at any moment I'd rebuff him. But I needed this – I needed to know if I could bear to be so close to him. I needed the familiarity of his body, to see if it was the same. While we made love I tried, I really tried to block out the image of them making love. But as his movements became quicker I started to cry, at first silent tears, then gradually great, racking sobs. All the emotions, all the pain of the past weeks poured out of me and Mike held me tight, his face pressed against mine. 'I'm sorry,' he said. 'I'm so sorry. I thought – I thought it wouldn't matter. I could just do it and come home, but I found I couldn't. I felt like I was going mad, I had no idea . . .' He too was really crying now, sobbing into my neck, still inside me. I eased him away and he turned to me, so we were lying face to face, our bodies pressed tight against each other, our faces inches apart, both wet with tears. He reached up and held my face in his hands, kissing my mouth, my eyes.

'Why?' I said, finally.

He looked deep into my eyes. 'Sex,' he said. 'It sounds awful but that's all it was. I don't really know *what* I was doing – I think I was half mad. You didn't want me, you were so preoccupied with the house, the baby that I felt – inadequate. Kate came on to me so strongly, I thought I could just . . . and I was drunk . . . it really felt like nothing. As soon as . . . it happened . . . I wanted her to go, to come home, but I felt so guilty. I was such a shit to you. God, I'm so sorry. I felt so bloody awful about myself I thought I had to justify what I'd done by pretending to myself our relationship was breaking down. She rang me again and again at work.'

'When,' I said carefully, 'did it start?'

'In June,' he said. 'After she came to see me. We felt so far apart – I was flattered I suppose, angry with you.'

'You were *angry* with me?' I said. 'You were *angry* with me so you slept with somebody else? That is *pathetic*. How many times?'

'Oh God, Carrie!' he said, moving slightly away from me.

'I won't ask again,' I said quickly. 'I just want to know now.'

'About four,' he said. 'I meant to finish it after our

280

holiday in France, but I couldn't. I felt so awful, so guilty – then just once afterwards. She wanted me to leave you. Oliver found out and left, but as soon as she wanted me to leave you and the children, I realized she thought it *meant* something, and I couldn't bear to see her again.'

'How chivalrous of you,' I said, coldly.

'I know,' he said, unhappily. 'But somehow I'd managed to divorce it in my mind from you and the children – yet when she mentioned me leaving you I knew it was impossible, that we were real, and that there was no way I could have both . . . so I ended it. It was all going on when we moved, it ended that week. She threatened to *kill* herself. I think she's really unstable. She kept saying she was going to ring you . . . I was terrified. It was a bloody mess. In the end she found another job, and I just wanted to forget about it, pretend it hadn't happened . . .'

'How could you?' I said. 'How could you make love to someone else? How could you threaten us?'

'It wasn't love,' he said, holding me even tighter. 'It was sex. Love is what we have.' Reassured by our love-making, he fell asleep quickly.

I lay in the darkness. Is it? I thought. Is it?

Friday 25 December
'Get that bloody dog out of here,' Mike yelled, as Turtle once again made a sly sideways grab at the chocolate decorations on the tree. The tree, hung gaudily with purple and silver tinsel, appallingly tasteless orange shiny balls and a fairy who clearly wasn't wearing any knickers, teetered perilously. Next year I really will do a designer Christmas. I will restrict myself to white and make lots of little bows and not let Rebecca choose anything. Actually having a tree in appalling taste is

great fun, as Harriet and Martin came round for a drink last night and she had to find something nice to say about it. Her house looks like a scented winter wonderland full of swags and wreaths and not a bit of fake fir in sight. She's even garlanded all the way up the stairs with natural green foliage. I had to fight hard not to strike a match.

All around us there are piles of discarded paper as the children tear into their presents, hurling Barbies, plastic ponies and cars with yellow flashing lights over their shoulders. Both children had huge pillow-cases full of presents – Mike and I each had a small pile. '*I* want a pillow case,' I'd said, as we tiptoed hysterically about the house last night carrying presents downstairs, tripping over each other, full of whisky, champagne and oysters. Mike surveyed the Christmas cake and glass of whisky sitting on the fireplace with alarm. 'You'll have to have them,' I said. 'And the carrot.' The charred remains of Rebecca's Christmas letter to Santa stirred in the grate. I mashed the remains up with the poker. It wasn't supposed to be there, it was supposed to have been read by an elf in Lapland.

'I'm not a reindeer,' he said.

'Give it to Turtle,' I said. Turtle took an exploratory bite, and then spat orange bits all over the carpet. 'Marvellous,' I said, hastily brushing the bits off the carpet so Rebecca wouldn't see.

Before putting the presents out, we had sat in the kitchen, sliding oysters into our mouths, sipping champagne, quiet in the soft light of the old kitchen. 'I *love* you,' Mike said, reaching out to take my hand across the table. 'Are you happy?'

'Better,' I said carefully, avoiding his eyes. 'Getting better.'

He knows he still has a long way to go. Even tonight,

even on this blissful, magic night, I know there is a part of me which will never be his again. It makes me feel stronger to know that I no longer need him to make me whole. How vulnerable he has become.

'But,' I added, reaching forward to pour myself another glass of champagne, 'I think I need to do some work. From home. Freelance work. I'm not cut out to be a professional mother. I don't have enough matching plates.'

'What?' said Mike.

'I need to talk to real people during the day. But I want to control my time, not some yobbo in a suit.'

'Like me,' said Mike.

'Oh, but you love all that,' I said. 'I've just – grown out of it. It doesn't matter any more.'

'Do you think you'll ever go back?' said Mike, politely restraining himself from saying 'if we need the money'.

'I might when the children are older. *If* we get desperate. But not for ages. For the first time in seven years I feel I can just *be myself*. What I want to be, not what I think I ought to be. I'm fed up with living up to everyone else's expectations. Time for *me*,' I said, swirling champagne around my glass. 'And,' I continued, reaching out to top it up, 'I want some changes.'

'Changes?' said Mike, his brow creasing slightly.

'Changes,' I said firmly, with a confidence I have never felt before. In the past I've always worried about upsetting Mike. I would do almost anything not to make him angry, or compromise what I saw as his precious free time. No matter that I was as tired as he was, that I was performing an equivalent role, somewhere, drummed into me at my mother's knee, was the belief that men need time off. Running two separate lives – home and work – was simply a woman's lot, and my

283

penance for wanting to be a working mother. I was a greedy woman who wanted it all, and I had to pay.

But now I could see, with a shining clarity, that I had been a complete mug. Working mothers don't have to kill themselves trying to be perfect. They should kick ass on a regular basis and stop apologizing for all the things they simply do not have the time to achieve. And if their partners want their money, then they have to share roles. All of them. Right down the middle. How often does that happen? Fucking never.

I was tired of being a martyr. Tired of trying to please everyone and tired of pandering to Mike's whims. It was time, quite simply, that he grew up.

'First,' I said, amazed at the strength of my voice, 'when you say you're going to be home at a certain time, you stick to it or you ring me. It's so *rude* to leave me hanging about, wondering when you're going to get home to eat a meal I've spent time preparing. My feelings matter, they matter as much as yours. If you don't get home or you don't ring then your dinner goes in the bin. Right?'

'Fine by me,' said Mike, smiling.

'Secondly,' I said, warming to my theme, 'when you are at home we share responsibilities for the children *equally*. If you want to play golf, or watch something on TV, then you ask me what my plans are *first*. I will accommodate you as long as you accommodate me. Don't automatically assume I will look after the children. I intend to spend part of the weekend doing what I want to do.'

'What are you going to do?' asked Mike. His smile was beginning to look a little thin around the edges. Tough.

'Row,' I said.

'I want to take up rowing again, like I did at university. At a women's club.'

'Really?' said Mike. 'Since when?'

'Since now. And don't make the mistake of trying to patronize me. The weekend shop,' I went on, 'is now your job. With The Children. It will give you a chance to be with them after your week at work. If you are home on time, we will share baths and stories during the week. You will not assume I will do them while you have a cold beer. Nor will I iron your shirts. I will wash them, but the ironing is your business. I hate ironing, I can't do it, and shirts are the worst. I am also going to get a cleaner two mornings a week, so I have lots of time with Tom before he starts nursery.'

'Anything else?' said Mike, leaning back in his chair, looking at me carefully to see if I was really being serious. This was a Carrie he had never seen before.

'Yup. Just because you now earn the bulk of the money does not mean you have the right to dictate to me how much money I have. We maintain a joint account, you trust me to spend what I think fit. Never,' I said, leaning forward, memories of my parents flashing through my mind, 'never think you can control me through money.'

'Carrie,' said Mike, 'I think I have about as much chance of controlling you now as Margaret Thatcher's Cabinet did. Is that all?'

'Nearly,' I said. 'The main thing I ask – and this is the most important thing of all – is your respect. No, I demand it. Don't ever think you can tell me off because you are in a position of power. You don't have the *right* to tell me off. If you speak down to me, or shout, especially in front of the children, I will leave you. Don't think I am joking,' I added, as he looked at me aghast.

'Joking?' he said. 'I wouldn't dare.'

'Is it a deal?' I said. He looked down into his glass. What chance did he have?

'Deal,' he said. 'This powerful new you is very . . .

sexy,' he continued, leaning across the table.

I reached for him first. 'I think you'll find' – sliding round the table to sit on his knee – 'that I can have the upper hand here too,' I whispered, sliding my hand downwards.

'Be gentle with me,' he pleaded.

THE END

THE RIGHT THING
Judy Astley

Funerals are strange things. Kitty hadn't really wanted to go to this one – an old school friend she hadn't seen for years – and she hadn't bargained for the way it made her think of the past. In particular, it made her think of the baby she had given birth to when she was eighteen, the baby her parents had insisted she give away for adoption. She'd called her Madeleine, and she remembered her every day, what she was like, if she was happy. But now, reminded of how cruelly short life can be, she had to see her – just to make sure she'd done the right thing.

Life had turned out pretty well for Kitty. Secure in her marriage, with her two teenage children and a house within sound and sight of the Cornish surf, she counted herself among the lucky ones. But the hole left by that first baby wasn't getting any smaller, and she decided to make the first, tentative steps towards filling it – although she, and all her family, were quite unprepared for the upheaval which followed.

0 552 99768 4

BLACK SWAN

A SELECTED LIST OF FINE WRITING
AVAILABLE FROM BLACK SWAN

99830 3	SINGLE WHITE E-MAIL	Jessica Adams	£6.99
99768 4	THE RIGHT THING	Judy Astley	£6.99
99619 X	HUMAN CROQUET	Kate Atkinson	£6.99
99687 4	THE PURVEYOR OF ENCHANTMENT	Marika Cobbold	£6.99
99755 2	WINGS OF THE MORNING	Elizabeth Falconer	£ 6.99
99770 6	TELLING LIDDY	Anne Fine	£6.99
99760 9	THE DRESS CIRCLE	Laurie Graham	£6.99
99774 9	THE CUCKOO'S PARTING CRY	Anthea Halliwell	£5.99
99681 5	A MAP OF THE WORLD	Jane Hamilton	£6.99
99778 1	A PATCH OF GREEN WATER	Karen Hayes	£6.99
99757 9	DANCE WITH A POOR MAN'S DAUGHTER	Pamela Jooste	£6.99
99736 6	KISS AND KIN	Angela Lambert	£6.99
99771 4	MALLINGFORD	Alison Love	£6.99
99812 5	THE PHILOSOPHER'S HOUSE	Joan Marysmith	£6.99
99649 1	WAITING TO EXHALE	Terry McMillan	£5.99
99696 3	THE VISITATION	Sue Reidy	£5.99
99747 1	M FOR MOTHER	Marjorie Riddell	£6.99
99733 1	MR BRIGHTLY'S EVENING OFF	Kathleen Rowntree	£6.99
99764 1	ALL THAT GLISTERS	Mary Selby	£6.99
99781 1	WRITING ON THE WATER	Jane Slavin	£6.99
99753 6	AN ACCIDENTAL LIFE	Titia Sutherland	£6.99
99788 9	OTHER PEOPLE'S CHILDREN	Joanna Trollope	£6.99
99655 6	GOLDENGROVE UNLEAVING	Jill Paton Walsh	£6.99
99723 4	PART OF THE FURNITURE	Mary Wesley	£6.99
99639 4	THE TENNIS PARTY	Madeleine Wickham	£5.99
99797 8	ARRIVING IN SNOWY WEATHER	Joyce Windsor	£6.99